"Rarely has an author painted the great American West in strokes so bold, vivid, and true."
—Ralph Compton

Ready, Aim, Bluff!

"I don't give a damn if you're a marshal," Roach spat. "A cheat's a cheat, and you got a lesson comin'."

Still calm, Buck replied, "How 'bout a marshal with a .44 aimed at you under the table?"

A mild expression of shock registered on Roach's face, and he looked for a moment as if undecided what to do. Then, inexplicably, a smirk slowly spread across his face, causing Buck to wonder. With no eyes in the back of his head, he could not see Roach's friend poised over him with a full bottle of whiskey raised to strike.

What happened next was almost over before the poker players knew what had taken place. With his left hand Casey, Buck's partner, trapped the wrist of Buck's would-be assailant, stopping the bottle while it was still over the cowhand's head. With his right he jabbed the barrel of his pistol hard into the man's side.

"All right," he ordered, "this little party is over. Buck, you still got your friend there covered?"

"I will have," Buck replied, pushing back his chair to give him room to draw the weapon from his holster.

"Damn," Casey said, exhaling.

Knowing what he meant, Buck grinned and said, "Bluffin's just part of playin' poker."

SHOOT-OUT AT BROKEN BOW

Charles G. West

A SIGNET BOOK

SIGNET
Published by New American Library, a division of
Penguin Group (USA) Inc., 375 Hudson Street,
New York, New York 10014, USA
Penguin Group (Canada), 90 Eglinton Avenue East, Suite 700, Toronto,
Ontario M4P 2Y3, Canada (a division of Pearson Penguin Canada Inc.)
Penguin Books Ltd., 80 Strand, London WC2R 0RL, England
Penguin Ireland, 25 St. Stephen's Green, Dublin 2,
Ireland (a division of Penguin Books Ltd.)
Penguin Group (Australia), 250 Camberwell Road, Camberwell, Victoria 3124,
Australia (a division of Pearson Australia Group Pty. Ltd.)
Penguin Books India Pvt. Ltd., 11 Community Centre, Panchsheel Park,
New Delhi - 110 017, India
Penguin Group (NZ), 67 Apollo Drive, Rosedale, North Shore 0632,
New Zealand (a division of Pearson New Zealand Ltd.)
Penguin Books (South Africa) (Pty.) Ltd., 24 Sturdee Avenue,
Rosebank, Johannesburg 2196, South Africa

Penguin Books Ltd., Registered Offices:
80 Strand, London WC2R 0RL, England

First published by Signet, an imprint of New American Library,
a division of Penguin Group (USA) Inc.

First Printing, August 2009
10 9 8 7 6 5 4 3 2 1

For Ronda

Chapter 1

Captain Sam Sixkiller of the Choctaw Lighthorse glanced toward the open door to see U.S. Deputy Marshal Casey Dixon leading his horse toward the small shack that served as the headquarters for the U.S. Indian police in Atoka. Just watching the man walk—like a mountain lion on the prowl, moving deceptively slow and purposely—brought a smile to Sam's face. From practical experience, Sam knew that, also like the mountain lion, Casey Dixon was quicker than lightning when danger threatened.

Sam put his coffee cup down beside his chair and got up to meet the rugged young lawman. Stepping out on the stoop, he greeted Casey. "You look like you're all ready to get started back."

"Yep," Casey replied. "I figured it was about time I got outta your way—get on back to Fort Smith."

Sam smiled. "Hell, I was fixin' to wire John Council and tell him I was gonna keep you around for a while." He was joking, but the fact of the matter was the hard-riding deputy marshal had been invaluable in rounding up a band of cattle rustlers in the Choctaw

Nation. Sam had worked with many deputies sent out from Fort Smith in the seven years he had been a captain in the Choctaw Lighthorse, but with none more determined and tireless than Casey Dixon. "When you get back, tell ol' Buck Avery I said hello. Buck used to work out this way a helluva lot, but we ain't seen him all year."

"I'll tell him if I see him," Casey promised, although he doubted he would run into him. Buck Avery was close to being a legend among deputy marshals. He was certainly the most senior of those lawmen working out of the Fort Smith court, having covered every square mile of Indian Territory years before Judge Isaac C. Parker was appointed to the district court. He was noted for working as a loner, seldom taking a partner along to help apprehend an outlaw—and never a wagon and cook, as some deputies did when being sent to some far corner of the territory. Casey favored working alone, too, although he was often called upon to work with other deputies who, like him, had less than five years' experience on the job. He was far more interested in working with lawmen like Sam Sixkiller and his Choctaw policemen. They knew the territory and they were all skilled horsemen.

As Sam walked over to shake hands with Casey, a thought occurred to him. "If you ain't in a particular hurry to get back to Fort Smith, you might circle back by way of Broken Bow. I sent one of my boys over there last week to arrest some young hell-raiser that's been shootin' up the town. Got the townfolk scared to come outta their houses, and I ain't heard nothing from my man. I'd consider it a favor if you could check on him."

"Be glad to," Casey said.

"I appreciate it. His name's Joseph Big Eagle."

They shook hands, and Casey stepped up in the saddle, saluted Sam with a single finger touched to the brim of his hat, wheeled his horse, and started out toward Broken Bow.

It could not really be called a town as yet, although a few families had settled there with high hopes for the future. A general store, a saloon that was half tent, half shack, and a blacksmith's shop were the principal businesses established to date. In contrast to what he expected, the settlement seemed peaceful enough as Casey guided his horse by the blacksmith's forge and headed for the general store. Dismounting, he looked around, surprised that he appeared to be the only soul on the short, dusty street. Looping his reins loosely over the hitching rail, he stepped up onto the stubby board stoop and opened the door to confront a double-barreled shotgun looking at him from atop a counter along the opposite wall.

Stopping abruptly, he considered the nervous middle-aged man standing behind the shotgun for a moment before speaking. "Kind of an unfriendly way to greet customers," he commented.

Showing obvious relief, the storekeeper slid his shotgun back and put it under the counter. "I'm sorry, mister, but the past few days around here has got a lot of folks kinda edgy when a stranger walks in."

"That a fact?" Casey replied. "I heard you had some trouble. Looks quiet enough now, though." He walked up to the counter. "I'm lookin' for a Choctaw policeman named Joseph Big Eagle."

"Was that his name?" the storekeeper asked. "He wasn't around long enough for anybody to know his name." He paused to give Casey a more thorough looking over. "Are you a lawman?"

Casey nodded, pulled his vest aside to reveal his badge, and said, "I'm a deputy marshal. Where did Joseph Big Eagle go?"

The storekeeper snorted contemptuously. "Oh, he

ain't gone nowhere. He's layin' beside the saloon, right where he got shot down by that drunken maniac this mornin'."

This was sobering news to Casey. "Where's the man that shot him? Is he still here somewhere?"

"Pete Drucker—he's the blacksmith—said he saw him ride out toward Eagletown. Said he was yellin' he'd be back to see us. That's why you don't see no folks walkin' around outside. The crazy son of a bitch has been ridin' up and down the town for damn near a week shootin' at everybody that sticks their nose out."

"And the Choctaw policeman, you just left him layin' out there beside the saloon?" Casey asked.

The storekeeper shrugged. "Like I said, nobody wants to take a chance on gettin' caught outside. Besides, it's just an Injun, anyway. It ain't like anybody's in a big hurry to have a funeral for him. I expect some of the boys will get him into the ground before he starts to stink. That is, if that crazy bastard don't come back before this afternoon." He shook his head as if weary of the whole situation. "It's about time they sent a marshal over here. I just hope to God you're better than that Injun."

The man's attitude did little to invoke Casey's sympathy. "Sounds to me like that *Injun* just gave his life tryin' to help you folks. I expect you and your neighbors owe him a helluva lot more than a funeral." His statement left the storekeeper short of words, and Casey abruptly moved on to the next question. "Where can I pick up the trail to Eagletown?"

Quick to reply then, the storekeeper said, "It runs east, right beside the blacksmith's." Noticeably contrite, he added, "I'll get some of the boys to dig a grave for the Choctaw policeman."

"Much obliged," Casey pronounced evenly. "What does this feller that's been shootin' up the town look like?"

"You'll know him if you run into him," the store-keeper replied at once. "Young feller, ridin' a pinto. He's wearin' a fancy Mexican-lookin' vest and totin' pearl-handled pistols."

"You ever see him in Broken Bow before?"

"Nope. And once is enough for Billy Blanton and anybody else like him."

Casey nodded thoughtfully. "Billy Blanton, huh? How do you know it's Billy Blanton?"

"Hell, he musta shouted it fifty times, ridin' up and down the street, challengin' anybody with a gun to come out and face him."

"And nobody did?"

"Nobody but your Injun policeman layin' out there by the saloon."

Billy Blanton. That was not welcome news. Billy was the youngest of four Blanton brothers who, under the leadership of their father, old Roy Blanton, had rained terror across Kansas, Texas, and Oklahoma Territory for almost ten years. It had been a while, however, since the notorious outlaw family had been seen in Oklahoma Territory, at least since Casey had signed on as a deputy marshal. Anything he knew about the notorious outlaw family had been passed along to him by deputies who had served during that time. Buck Avery had by far the most hands-on experience and was given credit for chasing the Blantons out of the nations. Now, with Billy showing up here, Casey wondered whether the rest of the family could be far away.

Before leaving the settlement, Casey went to see Joseph Big Eagle's body. He stood gazing down at the already-stiffening corpse, the expression of pain frozen on the bronze face, and the eyes staring vacantly up at the sky. Four bullet holes formed a neat pattern on his chest. *I'll try to settle up for you*, Casey promised silently before reaching down to take Joseph's badge and pistol belt. There was no weapon other than the pistol. Casey figured the killer took the policeman's rifle.

After a half day's ride from Broken Bow, it was approaching twilight when Casey saw the shacks on the other side of the Mountain Fork River. As it turned out, it was not necessary to cross the river, for he spotted a pinto like the one the storekeeper had described tied to a tent on the near side. There was a rough corral of pine poles behind the tent with one horse in it. Judging from the looks of the corral—the bark hadn't even been skinned from the poles—Casey speculated that the owner of the tent didn't figure on staying there long. The first thought that came to his mind was that the owner was most likely a prostitute or a bootlegger. With no evidence of a still, it was probably a prostitute.

Taking his time, he sat with his rifle resting across his forearm, watching the tent carefully, ready for any surprises, while his horse padded slowly up beside the pinto. Dismounting, he moved quietly up to the tent flap and, parting it just enough to peek inside, he paused to consider the scene. Lost in the middle of a lustful transaction, the lady's customer was hard at work, his bare behind reflecting the light from the lantern hanging from the tent pole. Casey glanced around the inside of the tent, noticing a decorative, hand-stitched vest on the back of a chair and a brace of pearl-handled pistols on the seat. He glanced down at his rifle, recalling the last time he had used a rifle for what he intended to do, the act of which resulted in a bent barrel. In no particular hurry, since his victim was sufficiently occupied, he glanced to either side of the tent flap. Spotting a shovel on the ground beside a shallow trench, evidently having been dug to drain water away from the tent, he propped his rifle against the tent wall and picked up the shovel.

Pulling the flap open, he stepped inside. The customer was far too invested in his quest for satisfaction to notice that someone else had joined the party. The hostess, however, was less involved in the lovemaking, and from her position on her back, smiled up at Casey, thinking him another client. Oblivious to her young lover's animal-like lunges, she winked and said, "I'll be with you in a minute."

Her comment caused her lustful stud to pause, angered by the intrusion upon his party. Turning to threaten the intruder, he was met with the full force of a swinging shovel. The shovel rang like a bell when it collided with the side of his head, knocking the unsuspecting victim off the woman and onto the floor.

Billy was game. He tried desperately to struggle to his feet and come up fighting. But his brain had been scrambled by the blow to his head, and each time he tried to get up, his knees seemed to go out from under him, causing him to stagger sideways against the bedstead and land on the floor again. Still determined, he lunged for the chair holding his pistols, but Casey pulled it out of the way before he could reach it and stepped back to watch Billy crash to the floor yet again.

Cursing like a wild man, Billy made one more attempt to counterattack. Rising to his knees, he prepared to lunge again, this time to be met with the muzzle of Casey's .44, barely inches from his right eye. "Now, you just keep it up," Casey warned, "and I'll put a bullet in your head." Billy froze for a few seconds while he thought that over. During the lull, Casey pulled his vest aside far enough to reveal his badge. "I'm arrestin' you for the murder of Joseph Big Eagle," he said. "Now get your pants on."

Glaring defiantly at the pistol pointed at him, Billy did not immediately respond, seeming indifferent to the trickle of blood now running down beside his ear. Still aware of a ringing in his head, effectively amplified by the amount of alcohol in his bloodstream, he remained on his knees, his eyes burning with anger. He was just about to get an encouraging rap on the head with Casey's pistol when he finally spoke. "Mister," he said, his speech slurred, "you don't know who you're messin' with."

"Billy Blanton is who I'm thinkin'," Casey replied with little emotion beyond a raised eyebrow. "And one sorry son of a bitch if you don't pull your pants on like I told you."

"What if I don't?" Billy snarled.

Casey shrugged indifferently. "Well, it's all the same to me, but it's a three-, maybe three-and-a-half-day ride back to Fort Smith. Your ass is gonna get mighty damn sore without your pants on, but suit yourself."

"Mister, you're a dead man. When my pa hears about this, he'll string your guts across a barbed-wire fence."

"Yeah, I've heard about your pa and your brothers, but they ain't gonna do you much good with your neck stretched about a foot or two." His patience running thin, he tired of the game of words. "Now, if you don't get up from there and get your pants on, I'm gonna save the court some trouble and shoot your worthless ass right here."

The bewildered prostitute, shocked into silence during the bizarre incident up to that point, suddenly found her voice. "I swear, Billy, I think he means it." She pulled her clothes together and sat up on the side of the bed. To Casey, she said, "Take him outside to shoot him. I just cleaned the floor this mornin'."

Billy glanced back and forth between the whore and the lawman, realizing that his life held no value to either. Settling again on Casey's stone-cold gaze, he sobered enough to agree with the prostitute's assessment of his situation. "All right, dammit, back up and give me some room."

Casey took a step back toward the bed, picked up Billy's trousers, and started to throw them to him. "Wait a minute!" the woman said. "He owes me money."

"For what?" Billy exclaimed. "We never finished the deal." Then he realized he was the one being cheated. "Why, you old whore, I paid you before we got started."

"Yeah, but you were takin' a helluva lot more time than you paid for," she protested weakly, knowing she didn't have much of an argument.

"Yeah, well, you can go to hell, too," Billy responded.

Aware that he was permitting the bickering between the two to get out of hand, Casey searched the pockets of Billy's pants. Finding a modest roll of paper money, he peeled off a few bills and threw them on the bed. "There, here's a little extra for your trouble." Then he tossed the trousers to Billy. "Get 'em on," he ordered.

"Hey!" Billy protested. "You can't give her my money."

"You won't need it," Casey said.

His face a dark scowl then, Billy dutifully began to pull on his pants. Casey watched him closely, noticing the narrowing intensity of his eyes, which warned of a desperate attempt likely coming. Casey was ready for it. When Billy buckled his belt and reached for his boots, he suddenly flung one of them at Casey and lunged at him. Casey batted aside the boot and deftly sidestepped the lunge, cracking Billy hard on the back of his skull with his pistol. The ill-advised attack ended with Billy lying stunned on the floor. "Put his boots on him," Casey ordered.

Doing as she had been told, she rolled Billy over on his back and pulled his boots on. Finished, she looked up at Casey and smiled. "My name's Lila," she said.

"When you get done with him, why don't you and I have a little go-around?"

"Thanks just the same," Casey replied, "but I've got a long ride ahead of me. I'd best get started."

"You don't know what you're missin'." She grinned mischievously.

He just smiled in reply, thinking to himself that he had a pretty fair idea.

Billy Blanton jerked his head from side to side in a frustrated attempt to shoo a curious yellow jacket away from his face. With his hands tied behind his back, he was helpless to swat it with his hat. The stoic man on the sorrel leading Billy's pinto never seemed to tire or get hungry, stopping only to rest the horses. Coming down from a hangover caused by the combination of a couple of stout taps to the head and an overindulgence in rotgut whiskey, Billy had already emptied the contents of his stomach—most of it still in evidence down the withers of his horse. Feeling as if the sides of his empty stomach were now rubbing together, he yelled, "Dammit, man, I'm dyin' from hunger. Ain't you ever gonna stop for some grub?" When Casey ignored him, he yelled again. "You know you gotta feed me. You gotta feed a prisoner. It's the law."

"What the hell do you know about the law?" Casey replied, amused that his prisoner's attitude had changed considerably from the belligerent beginning. "As a matter of fact, there ain't nothin' in the law that says I have to feed you." He paused, then added, "Especially since you gunned down a lawman." He let that sink in for a few moments before continuing. "But since you've been such a good boy, I'm gonna make camp in about a couple of hours. We oughta make Piney Creek by then, and I'll feed you."

In less than the two hours estimated, they came to Piney Creek. Casey untied the ropes that held Billy's boots in the stirrups, then steadied him while Billy threw a leg over and dismounted. "Ain't you gonna untie my hands?" Billy whined. "I can't eat unless you untie my hands."

"When I'm ready," Casey replied.

"Well, I gotta pee," Billy insisted. "I gotta have my hands untied for that." A wicked smile crept across his face. "Unless you're plannin' to help me out."

Casey gave him a long, impatient look before finally shrugging his shoulders. "All right," he said, "turn around."

When Billy dutifully turned his back to him, Casey untied the rope binding his hands together. As soon as one hand was free, Billy spun around in an attempt to strike Casey. The deputy, expecting such a move, jerked his rifle up to block the backhanded punch, catching Billy's forearm on the barrel. Billy howled in pain when the bone in his arm made solid contact with the metal barrel. "You broke my arm!" he howled, and doubled over, holding the arm.

"You just don't learn too fast, do you, Billy? You're goin' to Fort Smith to jail. The sooner you get that in that pea brain of yours, the better this trip is gonna be for you." He cocked his rifle. "Now get over there by those bushes and get your business done. And make no mistake about it—if I don't like the way you're pissin', I'll damn sure shoot you down. You'd be a whole lot less trouble goin' back over your saddle. And it really don't make that much difference to me. I get paid either way." He followed Billy over to a patch of shrubs away from the creek.

"I can't pee with you standin' there watchin' me," Billy complained. "You oughta at least turn your back."

Casey shook his head as if dealing with a child. "I swear, you must think everybody's as dumb as you. I'm tired of wastin' time with you. Piss or bust. I'm givin' you about two minutes to do somethin'."

Seeing that his thoughts of escape were out of the question, Billy began to urinate at once with no intimidation. When he was finished, Casey marched him over to a sizable cottonwood and told him to hug it. Billy complained, but knew better than to refuse. Casey grabbed the rope still tied to one of Billy's hands and tied it to the other hand again. With Billy hugging the tree, Casey was free to take care of the horses and build a fire. After he had finished his supper of bacon and coffee, he untied Billy's hands and sat holding his rifle on his prisoner while Billy ate.

"Ain't you got nothin' to eat besides bacon?" Billy complained when he had finished.

"I didn't plan on havin' a distinguished guest with me on the way back to Fort Smith," Casey said, "so we'll have to make do with what we've got."

Billy sipped the last of his coffee while he measured the somber lawman. "How much they pay you for bein' a deputy?" he asked.

"Not enough," Casey replied, "when I gotta play nursemaid to the likes of you."

"What would you say if I was to show you how to make a helluva lot more money, and right quick?"

"I'd say you'd best get up if you need to piss again before I put you away for the night," Casey replied.

Frowning, Billy persisted. "You wouldn't be the first lawman that's smart enough to take a little money on the side. My daddy's helped out more'n a few lawmen to look the other way once in a while. Daddy says it's just good business."

"Is that a fact?" Casey replied evenly. "Well, there ain't enough money to make me look the other way when a low-down bastard guns down a policeman. So you might as well get used to the idea of goin' to see Judge Parker."

Billy's face clouded up at once. "You're as good as dead, you son of a bitch!"

"Maybe," Casey said. "Now get on your feet and get your business done. I'm puttin' you to bed."

After Billy had relieved himself of some of the quantity of coffee he had consumed, he was taken back for more tree hugging. This time Casey sat him down and tied his feet as well as his hands around the tree. "A man can't sleep like this," Billy fumed, "with my hands and feet wrapped around this damn tree."

"You never know what you can do till you try," Casey said. "But I know I'll be able to sleep a helluva lot better."

The next morning, Casey found his prisoner slumped over with his chin resting on his chest, fast asleep. The routine was repeated three more times before Casey led a weary Billy Blanton to the jail under the Fort Smith courthouse and turned him over to the guards.

Chapter 2

"Well, look who's back in town. I thought maybe you'd gone over in the nations and married a little Indian girl." Charity McDonald dried her hands on her apron and came to the counter to meet him.

"Now, you know better than that," Casey said, unable to prevent the bashful grin that crept across his face. "I figured you knew I'm just waitin' around for you to get ready to marry me." He tossed it off as a friendly tease, but in his heart he wished he had the courage to confess his real feelings for her.

She responded with a coy smile. "Oh, is that a fact? Well, a girl would be foolish to marry a marshal, and I'm not a fool. Too many marshals end up with a bullet in the back and leaving some poor girl a widow." It was a regular tease between them ever since Casey had started eating routinely at the Cook's Corner. And although it was in outward appearances a tease only, Charity was well aware that the lusty young deputy likely harbored more serious thoughts toward her. It was fodder for interesting speculation, and she had to admit that she had indulged in some moments of fantasy in regard to the possibility. But she had been seeing Jared Ashton on a steady basis for almost a year, and the young attorney was justified in believing she had serious intentions toward a possible union. Her father had encouraged such a union and had applauded Jared's sense of responsibility in waiting to establish his law practice before taking on a wife. Jared was going to go places.

The two men could not have been more opposite in character and appearance. She pictured Jared, handsome and groomed in his frock-tail coat and tie, a striking figure who turned many a girl's head with his chiseled chin and dark wavy hair. In contrast, here was Casey Dixon, lean and rugged, with his mane of tawny, unruly hair, and the confident grace of a wild animal when he walked. His face appeared to have been carved from a piece of heart pine, with a smile that made her feel warm all over.

"Well, maybe I'll give up the marshalin' business if that's the only thing standin' in your way," Casey replied to her comment. "Maybe you could teach me how to cook."

She laughed and went to the stove to get the coffeepot. He always wanted coffee. She didn't wait for him to ask. He watched her as she poured. It had been a year and a half since he had first discovered the Cook's Corner and Charity McDonald. He hardly spoke a word to her for almost the entire first year, until she sat down at the table with him one slow morning. "You're one of John Council's deputies, aren't you?" she had asked. The conversation that followed was the initial spark that ignited a friendly relationship between the two.

As weeks and months had passed, the friendship became easier and easier, until Casey found his thoughts wandering back to Cook's Corner more and more when he was riding a lonesome trail in the Creek or Choctaw nations. A picture of eyes as dark as the black hair that lay soft upon her shoulders would often come to haunt his dreams as he rested beside a lonely campfire. As things stood now, he had to admit to himself that he might entertain the notion of proposing marriage if he thought he had a gnat's chance of a yes. But his reasonable mind told him that Charity probably carried on like that with most of her father's male customers. He was just one of many, and most likely not the only fool in the bunch—and yet, there was a special sweetness in her smile for him that made him think he might have a chance.

"You've been gone a few weeks this time," she commented.

"Yep, had some business to attend to over in the Choctaw Nation."

"Charity," someone called from the kitchen.

Turning to respond, she paused long enough to ask, "Are you going to eat?" When he said yes and ordered his usual breakfast, she hurried to the kitchen. Other customers claimed more of her time while he ate his breakfast, and he watched her as she moved from the kitchen to the tables, carrying food. Occasionally, he caught her eye and she would smile. Finished with his breakfast, he dallied over coffee for as long as he thought plausible before calling for her to take his money.

"We're kinda busy this morning," she said as she made his change. "Will you be in later on? Mary's gonna fix meat loaf for supper."

"Sure," he replied, "you know I can't refuse Mary's meat loaf." She gave him a genuinely warm smile, and he left, thinking how the girl always made him feel like a bumbling fool.

After leaving the Cook's Corner, he returned to the small room he rented behind the kitchen at Widow Ford's rooming house. The widow was a pleasant

middle-aged lady whose late husband had been a deputy marshal like Casey until he was shot down in a
gunfight with cattle rustlers. Knowing full well the
average income for deputies, she let Casey rent the
little former pantry so he would have a place to stay
when he was in Fort Smith.

There was no time wasted before bringing Billy
Blanton to trial. He was brought before Judge Parker
three days after being locked up and was promptly
sentenced to death by hanging. The law in Fort Smith
felt no mercy for killers of lawmen. The date of Billy's
execution was set for a week later, when he was to be
hanged with two other convicted murderers. Casey
used the time to go hunting, primarily to resupply
himself with dried jerky, a reliable staple when he was
on the move with no time to hunt.

The hanging was set for the Fourth of July, and by
many citizens of Fort Smith, welcomed as part of the
holiday celebration. Casey returned to town the day
before, and after breakfast at the Cook's Corner re-
ported to his boss, U.S. Marshal John Council. "I figure
you're goin' to the hanging," Council said. When Casey said that he was, Council said, "The day after, I
want you back here first thing in the mornin'. I'm
pickin' you for a special job, so be ready to ride."

Casey stood off to the side of the courtyard where
the gallows were, a grim structure with a shed roof
and a platform at the top of a flight of steps. The three
condemned men had already been brought up the
stairs and were seated on a bench at the back of the
gallows while their sentences were read by an officer
of the court. Looking sober and brooding, the hangman, one George Maledon, stood waiting, his mustache and long beard streaked with gray. Known to

outlaw and lawman alike, Maledon had earned the
nickname of Prince of Hangmen, for he had sent many
a condemned man to the great beyond.

The sentences read, a low hum of anticipation
floated over the crowd of spectators, for they had seen
more than a few executions since Judge Parker had
been appointed to the court. The three prisoners were
told to stand. Then they were led to the nooses awaiting them. The other two men seemed resigned to their
fate, and walked deliberately to their date with the
reaper. Billy, however, appeared to have just realized
that nothing was going to save him from his appoint-
ment with death, and his legs failed him momentarily.
After some assistance from two guards, he was finally
able to stand on his own while the hangman fit the
noose around his neck. Casey could not be certain, but
he thought he could see tears running down Billy's
cheeks when he was asked if he had any last words.
"Damn you all," was all he had to say. Moments later
the trap was sprung and the three bodies dropped, to
be instantly jerked to a sickening stop. There was a
chilling hush over the crowd for a few moments while
the bodies dangled in the wind, followed by a noisy
crescendo with even a cheer here and there. Casey
paused and reflected upon the scene for a few minutes. It was the first arrest he had made that had
ended in a sentence of death. *Helluva way for a man to
die*, he thought as he turned to leave. A bullet in the
head would have been a more humane execution—
and justified, even for a mad dog like Billy Blanton.

"Here's your man, now," John Council said as he
got up from his desk. "Come on in, Casey."

Casey walked into the marshal's office, hat in hand.
Seated to one side of Council's desk in a leather-
upholstered armchair was a man Casey at once recognized. He had never worked with Buck Avery, but he

had heard many tales about the legendary deputy marshal. Still going strong after more than twenty years in the territory, Buck looked every inch the powerful and capable man he had been when he single-handedly rounded up all five members of the Frank Dolan gang of cattle rustlers back in 1865. A big man, standing three inches over six feet, and heavy through the shoulders, Avery wore a near-benevolent look upon a face made leathery tough by the prairie sun and wind. That benign look had been the cause of more than one criminal's sorrowful decision to test the deputy's mettle. A saying commonly repeated in Indian Territory was that Buck never killed a man he didn't like.

The big deputy pulled his imposing bulk out of the comfortable chair and prepared to shake hands with the young lawman standing before John Council's desk. "Casey," Council said, "shake hands with Buck Avery. Buck, this is the man I was tellin' you about."

Avery smiled and extended his hand. "Casey," he acknowledged. "John here has been braggin' about you arrestin' Billy Blanton."

Casey shrugged. "There wasn't much to brag about." Then remembering, he said, "I worked with Sam Sixkiller over in Atoka. He said to say hello."

Buck grinned. "Sam's a good man," he said. "And any time you catch one of the Blanton boys, it's somethin' to brag about."

"It was a damn good job," Council commented, "and the reason I called you both in here today."

"I was wonderin' when you'd get around to that," Buck said.

"Have a seat, Casey," the marshal directed as he sat down again, indicating a ladder-back chair against the wall. "I'm afraid Billy was the tip of the iceberg. I got a report that the Blanton gang is back operatin' in Indian Territory again." He leaned forward to stress his next statement. "It's been three years since Buck here al-most ran the lot of 'em to ground before they slipped over the Red River into Texas. Three years they've stayed clear of Oklahoma Territory, and now I reckon things have got too hot for 'em in Texas."

His statement triggered a noticeable response in Buck's quiet composure, and the dispassionate deputy straightened slightly in his chair. Reading his reaction, Council continued. "That's right—Roy and the boys are back in our territory. They robbed the MKT train at Durant Station three days ago."

"That old son of a bitch," Buck said. "He slipped over the border to hit that train. Durant ain't more'n about twenty miles north of the Red River. I expect he hightailed it straight back to Texas and Billy musta stayed back to have a little fun."

"Well, maybe that's so," Council replied, "but wit-nesses on the train said they rode off to the north, to-ward Atoka. Billy wasn't with 'em when they robbed the train."

Casey waited patiently while the two older men thought that over. He assumed now that he had been called in to be dispatched to Durant Station, evidently working with Buck Avery, but he decided to hold his questions until Council officially assigned the case to the both of them.

"Anybody hurt?" Buck asked.

"Not bad," Council replied. "Mail clerk got pistol-whipped, but nobody got shot."

"Well, that's one good thing, I reckon." Buck paused then, waiting for Council to say what he suspected was coming. Nobody knew more about the habits of Roy Blanton than he. He had chased the Blantons all over Oklahoma Territory and nearly put an end to their robbing and murdering. But that was three years ago, and he was beginning to show signs of slowing down. He was certain that he had been given more

mundane jobs in the last couple of years—serving war-
rants, subpoenas, and summonses—because of John
Council's concern for the decline in his once-impressive
skills with a gun. Just as he figured, John laid out his
plan.

"Nobody knows the Blanton family better than you,
Buck, but I think you could use some help this time
around. When Blanton finds out about the hangin' we
had here yesterday, he's most likely gonna make some
folks pay for the death of his youngest son. Him and
his three boys have got to be rounded up as soon as
possible. That's why I'm sendin' the best young deputy I've got to help you."

"I got nothin' against Casey here," Buck said, "but
I've always worked better alone. You know that, John.
I ain't ready for the rockin' chair just yet."

"I know it, dammit," Council said, "but I also know
you ain't as fast as you used to be. Hell, Buck, your
eyes ain't as good as they used to be. I know about
those readin' glasses you use when you think nobody
can see you." He threw his hands up before him, exas-
perated. "Dammit, Casey Dixon's a good man, a helluva hand with a rifle, and from what I hear from the
other men, he don't hesitate to jump in when there's a
tough fight."

An uneasy witness to the conversation, Casey felt
that he shouldn't even be in the room while a question
of his qualifications was being discussed. His initial
reaction to the matter was that he didn't give a damn
what Buck Avery or any other deputy thought about
working with him. He preferred working alone, but he
was not flat-out opposed to partnering with Buck. He
was not confident to the point that he couldn't learn
something from someone of Avery's experience. On the
other hand, he didn't like the idea of riding with a man
who objected to his company. He listened to a few
more moments of the conversation before speaking.

"Suppose I take a walk down the hall so you two can come to some kind of agreement," he suggested. Looking at John Council, he said, "I can work with Buck, or I can do the job alone—makes no difference to me. You're the boss. Whatever you say, I can deal with." Having said his piece, he got up to leave the room.

"Hold on there, Casey," Council said. "There ain't gonna be no more discussion."

Realizing how disrespectful the bantering between himself and Council had seemed to the young deputy, Buck quickly sought to make amends. "Yeah, Casey," he said, "I didn't mean to complain about workin' with you. It didn't have nothin' to do with that at all. I've just been workin' by myself for so long, it felt kinda strange to have a partner. John's probably right. It might take two of us. I know that Blanton bunch pretty damn well, and I can tell you they ain't about to come in peaceable." He got up then to extend his hand. "I know you'll do your job, and I'll try to do mine. We'll be all right. Whaddaya say?"

Casey glanced over at Council, then back at Buck before shaking his new partner's hand. "I reckon so," he replied. So the partnership was formed, although over rather rocky ground. Two men, self-reliant, able, and confident in their abilities—neither knowing how much he could depend upon the other—agreed to the partnership.

"Stop by the Deuce of Spades about suppertime tonight, and I'll buy you a drink," Buck offered.

"Much obliged," Casey replied. "I'll do that."

Casey spent the rest of that day drawing supplies and ammunition. There was a short but noisy parade to celebrate the Fourth, so he stood in front of the hardware store to watch it. His extra shirt was in dire need of repair, so a portion of the afternoon was invested in a rather crude attempt at stitching up a long rip down the back. The result wasn't pretty, but the two torn pieces were joined. Before supper, he stopped in at the stables to make sure the sorrel was being cared for. Then he made his way through the crowded streets still filled with holiday crowds to join Buck for a drink. He was tempted to stop in at the Cook's Corner briefly to see Charity, but he couldn't think of an excuse for the visit that she wouldn't see through.

The Deuce of Spades was certainly not his choice for supper since it was primarily a saloon, but it was a regular haunt for Buck Avery whenever he was in town. It was about half past six when he pushed through the swinging doors and stood looking over the crowded room. After a few seconds, he spotted Buck sitting alone at a small table next to the kitchen door. There were a couple of glasses and a bottle of whiskey on the table, and Buck sat quietly drinking, seemingly oblivious to the din that filled the saloon.

"Howdy, partner," Buck cheerfully greeted him when he made his way through the maze of poker tables that filled most of the room. "I'm glad you showed up. Have a seat." He shoved a chair out with his foot. Casey settled himself in the chair and watched while Buck poured him a drink. "Here's to a new partnership and a good hunt," Buck said, raising his glass.

Casey downed the strong shot and grimaced with the fire it caused for a moment. "John Council said you always eat here when you're in town."

"That's a fact," Buck acknowledged with a grin. "I've got a room upstairs, so it just makes it easier to eat here, too. Friend of mine, Frenchie Petit, runs this place. Charlotte, back in the kitchen, is as handy as the cooks in the hotel. I usually just have her fry me a steak with a little potatoes and bread—pretty good eatin'."

They had another drink before Charlotte stuck her

head out the kitchen door and asked, "You ready to eat yet, Buck?"

"Yes, ma'am," he replied. "This here's my new partner, Casey Dixon. Throw another steak in the pan for him."

Charlotte cut her eyes over to give Casey the once-over. "How do you want it—same as Buck's?"

"I reckon," Casey answered. "Any way's all right, just as long as it's done on the outside."

Charlotte nodded. "I'll bring your coffee out in a minute," she said, then ducked back into the kitchen.

"I expect I'd better switch over to coffee," Casey said, "if I'm gonna be able to meet you at the stable in the mornin'."

"I admire a man that knows when it's time to stop drinkin'," Buck said as he poured himself one more drink. "Most men don't find out until they're way past their limit." He went on to relate a story about two deputies who joined the service the same year he did, and the fact that they wound up getting bushwhacked by a couple of outlaws they had been chasing, because they had celebrated a little too much the night before. Casey was to find, after riding some time with his new partner, that Buck was want to offer little parables to illustrate the right and wrong way to do almost everything.

Charlotte, a thin, mousey-looking woman with stringy gray hair, brought a couple of cups in and placed them on the table. Then she poured from a large coffeepot. In a short time, Charlotte brought two steaks, and Buck and Casey got to work on them. Casey wasn't half finished with his when the trouble at the poker table started.

Six players were sitting at the table, when their conversation suddenly stopped, and Casey heard the words repeated. "I said you're dealin' off the bottom of the deck." Casey turned toward the table in the back corner in time to hear the man accused reply. "You're a goddamn liar!" At this point, the din in the entire room went quiet. Seated with his back to the wall, Buck showed no emotion, staring deadpan at the potential altercation. Casey, never feeling comfortable with his back to a possible source of gunplay, turned his chair around so he could keep an eye on the table.

The one who had been accused, a man with black curly hair, a dark complexion, and a black frock-tailed coat, continued to deal the hand. "You're just sore 'cause you've been losing, cowboy. Maybe you ought'n be playing cards till you're better at betting."

The cowboy, already heavily invested in the poker game, as well as having drunk a fair quantity of Frenchie Petit's whiskey, was not inclined to be talked to in this manner. He pushed his chair back from the table and stood up. "I said you're a damn low-down cheat, and I'm takin' my share of that money back."

The curly-haired player put the deck of cards down and gazed calmly at his accuser. Casey guessed that gambling was his profession. It was obvious from the way he coldly measured the hot-tempered cowboy that he had faced the situation before. Fearing the likely trouble to come, Frenchie came out from behind the bar to quiet the disturbance. "You fellers need to take your problem outside," he warned.

"There ain't no problem," the gambler said. "My friend here is just having a bad night at the table." He waved a hand at the other players at the table. "Anybody else see me dealing from the bottom of the deck?" When no one spoke, he turned back to the cowboy and said, "Why don't you go on outside and cool off? And I'll buy you a drink when you come back."

Flushed with humiliation now, the cowboy felt

forced to save face. "You son of a bitch, I saw you cheat. Now, get up from there or I'm gonna drag you up."

The gambler reached down and pulled a double-barreled derringer from his boot. "If there's any dragging to do, it's gonna be me dragging your dead behind outta here."

With the situation now getting out of hand, Frenchie looked back at Buck for help, but the old deputy never blinked an eye, remaining stone-faced, as he watched the altercation taking place. Casey glanced at Buck, and seeing no response, decided it was time somebody stepped in or there was bound to be a killing. The cowboy dropped his hand to rest on his pistol, and Casey figured he was working up the nerve to pull it, even with the derringer already aimed at him.

Casey got up from his chair and quickly moved between the two men. "That'll be enough," he ordered. "I'm tryin' to eat my supper, and I can't do it with the fuss you two are makin'."

"Who the hell are you?" the cowboy demanded.

"I'm the law," Casey replied, "and if you pull that pistol, I'm gonna shove it up your ass and pull the trigger." He turned halfway around and pointed at the gambler. "Put that thing back in your boot." With things seeming to be in hand, and still pointing at the gambler, he asked Frenchie, "You know this man?" Frenchie nodded. "Does he cheat?" Frenchie shook his head. "All right, then," Casey continued. Turning to the cowboy again, he said, "It's time for you to call it a night. Get your money off the table and clear outta here. Maybe you'll have better luck tomorrow."

The cowboy continued to glare at Casey for a long moment before reluctantly breaking it off. Still burning from the humiliation he felt he had suffered, he then made a bad decision. Holding his hat under the edge of the table, he raked what money he had left into it. As he lifted the hat, he suddenly threw it at the gambler and reached for his gun. In the next instant, his hand was trapped by an iron grip before he could draw his pistol halfway out of the holster, followed by a hard right hand that flattened his nose and knocked him over the chair behind him.

Giving the stunned cowboy no time to recover, Casey snatched the pistol from him, and grabbing him by the collar, dragged him out the front door, down two steps to the street, then over to the horse trough. Yanking him up to his knees, he shoved his head into the trough, holding it underwater until the cowboy began to fight desperately for his life. Jerking the drowning man up on his knees again, he held him and waited for him to get his breath. "Dammit, I oughta shoot you for lettin' my steak get cold," he lectured. "Ain't you got any better sense than to go to prison because you lost a little money playin' cards? Now, you've got a choice. You can get on your horse and get the hell on outta here, or you can cool off in jail. What's it gonna be?"

There was no real choice to be made. He'd had all of the deputy he wanted. "I'm goin'," he muttered between coughing fits to rid his windpipe of water.

"Now you're bein' smart," Casey said. He helped him up, broke the cylinder of his pistol open, and after emptying the bullets, handed it to him. Then he stepped aside and stood watching until the cowboy climbed on his horse and rode off toward the end of the street.

Crowding on the small porch and in the doorway, a group of spectators shouldered each other aside in an effort to see the show. Standing next to his friend, Frenchie Petit asked, "Why didn't you do somethin', Buck? Hell, you just sat there like you didn't even see what was gonna happen."

Buck's frown broke into a faint grin. "I just wanted to see how he handled it."

"You mighta helped him when that jasper started to pull his gun," Frenchie insisted. He was accustomed to Buck taking charge of such incidents.

"He didn't need no help," Buck said, his smile extending slightly. The altercation had provided him with a fair notion as to the kind of partner he had. He liked what he saw.

The crowd parted when Casey walked back in the door and returned to his table, where he sat down and gazed unenthusiastically at his cold supper. Buck sat down opposite him and said, "Charlotte can throw that back in the pan." Standing in the kitchen doorway, Charlotte shook her head in disapproval of the scene just witnessed. Hearing Buck's comment, she silently picked up Casey's plate and returned to the kitchen. "You mighta just saved somebody from gettin' shot," Buck said. "That was a right nice piece of work." He favored Casey with a wide grin. "That feller was a good bit bigger'n you."

"He was a good bit drunker'n I was," Casey replied. Buck nodded, but in his mind, he doubted it would have made much difference in the outcome if the cowboy had been stone-cold sober. As for Buck's sitting out the altercation, Casey assumed that Buck would have stepped in had there been any need.

Chapter 3

A little after sunup, Casey walked into the stable to find Buck already there, looking over the horses in the corral. "Mornin'," Buck called out when he caught sight of Casey. "I figure we can get by with one pack-horse. That all right with you?" Casey said he figured one would be plenty since he traveled pretty light, anyway. "Good," Buck said, then pointed to a dingy-looking dun on the far side of the corral. "I'm thinkin' that dun over yonder will do me just fine to ride."

Casey didn't reply right away, taking a moment to look the horse over. The dun looked strong, broad chested, with legs not too long, but there were a good many horses in the corral that looked to be of better bloodline. "That blue roan over there looks like he's the studhorse of this bunch," he commented.

"I expect so," Buck replied. "But where we're goin', we don't especially want folks to know who we are. And one way to spot a marshal is if he's ridin' a fine horse."

Casey considered that for a moment, as his horse recognized him and came to the rail to greet him. The sorrel was a fine specimen of horse flesh, and Casey had paid a handsome price for him. He glanced over at Buck to find the old deputy grinning at him. "I might wanna try that gray in the middle of the bunch," Casey said, even though he wasn't sure there was anything to the idea. *We ain't been working together a day yet, and he's already teaching me things I hadn't thought of before,* he thought.

Buck cut a packhorse out of the bunch, and he and Casey loaded their camping staples and extra ammunition, saddled their new mounts, and prepared to set out for Indian Territory. Their plan was to take the San Bois Mountain trail southwest of Fort Smith. It figured to be about a three-day ride to McAlester, or Bucklucksy as some of the older residents still called it, where they would load their horses on the train and take the railroad south to Durant Station. "We might as well get on down to Durant and see if we can pick up Blanton's trail," Buck said. "I doubt we'll have much luck, though. Ol' Roy's most likely settin' back somewhere in Texas already, just countin' his money."

"What makes you think he might not ride on up in the territory, maybe figurin' to hit Atoka and McAlester?" Casey asked.

"Roy ain't been operatin' in the territory for years now. Texas is where it suits him best. I figure he just crossed the river to make one quick raid, and then hopped right back to Texas." He could read Casey's face and determined that his young partner was not so sure. "Like John Council said, I know Roy Blanton better'n anybody else. I know how he thinks, him and his boys. Junior, Buster, and Zeke are all carved outta the same piece of hickory as their pa. They're a fine passel of rattlesnakes, all right, and I expect old Roy's fit to be tied if he's found out about Billy by now. Billy was the baby, and a sure 'nough son to make a father proud—robbin', murderin' since he was high enough to put his foot in the stirrup." Buck stepped up in the saddle then and turned his horse toward the west. "Yes, sir, ol' Roy's gonna be mad as a wet hen."

Like a wizened old judge, Roy Blanton sat at a table in the back corner of Blackie Andrews' Lucky Dollar Saloon. His weathered face, testament to a lifetime of hard trails, was serene at the moment as the gruff old man slowly sipped his whiskey. He had a little money left, but the train robbery had not brought as much as he had expected. It would be necessary to pull another job before much longer. Expenses went up every year since his sons had become grown men. A lot of it was thrown away at the gaming tables as well as at the whorehouses and on whiskey. All the boys had to have their individual pocket money now. When they were younger, he carried all of the money, doling it out whenever he saw fit, but not anymore. Junior, his eldest, was still content to let his pa handle the money. But the other three threatened to break away and go their separate ways if they were not allowed an equal split. Billy was the worst and wailed the loudest if he thought he wasn't getting a full share. Thoughts of his youngest son prompted him to question Billy's brothers.

"Where the hell did Billy say he was gonna meet us?" Roy demanded.

Not really concerned, his sons concentrated on the three-hand poker game in progress. After Buster threw his hand in, he answered his father. "Hell, we told him what you said, that we'd most likely hole up at the Crossin' for a few days before hittin' the bank in Atoka."

Disgusted with his hand, Zeke threw his cards in as well. "You know Billy, Pa. He's most likely caught the scent of some little bitch in heat and probably don't even know what day of the week it is."

"Well, I ain't plannin' to sit here much longer," Roy

grumbled. "Maybe he thinks he can do better on his own and to hell with the family." The old man was ready to move on to the bank in Atoka. They had been cooling their heels at the Crossing for two days longer than he had planned, and he was getting itchy about staying in one place too long. Next to the Robbers Cave, the Crossing, named for the point where two Indian trails crossed Clear Boggy Creek, was about as safe a place as any for outlaws to hide out. It was a common occurrence to find some fugitive from the law spending most of his ill-gotten fortune with Blackie Andrews, the owner of the saloon and trading post.

Conversation halted with the sound of a horse pulling up before the dingy saloon, and the four members of the Blanton gang all dropped their hands to rest on their pistols, their gaze concentrated upon the door. From the end of the bar nearest the open door, Blackie said, "It's all right; it's Jake Townsend," and everybody relaxed again. The Blantons were not prepared for what happened next.

"Howdy, Jake," Blackie greeted the man as he burst through the door. "Where the hell have you been? I ain't seen you in a month."

"Howdy, Blackie. I've been over to Fort Smith to see my sister and her husband."

"You were kinda takin' a chance, weren't you?" Blackie replied.

"Nah, hell, it's been so long now, nobody over there would hardly recognize me. Pour me a stiff one, will you?" He paused to watch Blackie pour his drink, just then glancing at the four strangers sitting at the two tables in back. Lowering his voice, he asked, "Who are them boys?"

Blackie smiled. "Well, they didn't give their names, but I've seen 'em before. That's Roy Blanton and his sons."

His remark caused Jake to blanch noticeably. His eyes suddenly grew wide, and he nearly spilled his drink when he put it down on the bar. Almost in a whisper, he said, "They hung Billy Blanton last week!"

Blackie recoiled. "What? Are you sure?"

"Sure, I'm sure," Jake replied. "Saw it with my own eyes. Hung him and two other fellers on the Fourth of July."

Blackie cocked an eye toward his customers in the back, almost expecting them all to rise at once. Keeping his voice down, he asked again, "Are you sure it was him?"

"It was him. They read his sentence and the charges. He shot one of them Choctaw policeman over in Broken Bow."

Although he could not hear what was being said, the hushed conversation at the bar caught Roy Blanton's attention. Secretive talk aroused the suspicions of a man constantly watching for lawmen on his trail. Pushing back from the table, he stood up and walked up beside Jake. "What's all the whisperin' about?" Roy asked.

"Nothin', Mr. Blanton. I was just tellin' Blackie about somethin' I saw over in Fort Smith last week."

"Who told you my name was Blanton?" Roy demanded, looking Blackie in the eye. "My name's Jordan."

"I told him, Roy," Blackie volunteered. "Hell, I recognized you and the boys. You don't have to worry about Jake here. He's got a price on his head same as you." He paused then, but decided he might as well be the one to give Roy the news, so he blurted it out. "Judge Parker hung your boy, Billy, last week in Fort Smith." Anticipating an explosion to follow, he slid the whiskey bottle out of harm's way.

The angry frown on Roy's face froze, giving him the dark, empty gaze of a dead man. He said nothing for a long time as the shock of Blackie's statement left him without the ability to form words for the thoughts that overloaded his brain. When his voice returned, it was nothing more than a thin groan of despair at first that slowly increased in volume as the anger boiled up from his gut until it could be held back no longer. Clenching his teeth and craning his head back, he stared at the ceiling and emitted a primal roar. Once the pressure was released, he grabbed Jake by his shirt and nearly pulled him off the floor. "What are you sayin'?" he demanded. "Hang my boy! How do you know it was Billy?" His other three sons, having heard their father's eruption, rushed up to surround Jake. Roy waved them off, his attention fully on Jake. "You better tell me you're lyin'," he threatened.

"No sir, Mr. Blanton," Jake stammered, fearing for his life. "It's the truth. It was a public hangin'. I wouldn't make up nothin' like that."

"What? What is it, Pa?" Junior asked as he and his brothers crowded around Roy and Jake, not sure if the stranger still in their father's grasp required some action on their part.

Roy released Jake and turned to face his sons. "Your brother's been hung," he said with no sign of the initial rage he had exhibited. "They hung Billy." To a man, the three Blanton boys took the news with noisy protests in anger, not so much with the rage their father had felt for the loss of a son, but more so because of the insult to the Blanton name.

"Who caught him?" Roy demanded, turning to Jake again.

"I don't know," Jake said. "One of Judge Parker's deputies, I reckon." His person seemingly safe now that the angry old man had released his shirt collar, Jake felt free to talk. "From what I heard from other folks watchin' the hangin', your son killed a Choctaw policeman down in Broken Bow, and maybe shot up the place a little. One of Judge Parker's deputies brought him in and they strung him up two or three days later."

"By God, somebody's gonna pay for this," Roy swore, "if I have to ride into Fort Smith and shoot that judge down right in his damn courtroom."

Junior and Buster exchanged nervous glances upon hearing their father's vow. It was Zeke who spoke up, however. "I figure somebody's gotta pay for Billy's hangin', Pa, but I don't rightly see how smart it would be for us to go ridin' into Fort Smith." His father glared at him for a long moment, then without a word, stormed out of the saloon.

His sons followed him outside, where they found him standing beside his horse and staring out across the creek, one hand on the saddle horn. After a few moments, he turned to address them, his voice calm once more. "Zeke's right. We can't go to Fort Smith, but we can make 'em pay for what they done to Billy. I know I promised to stay clear of this part of the country, but this makes things different, and things is a little too hot for us in Texas right now, anyway." He looked away again. "Yes, sir. I'll make 'em pay, Billy."

Walter Lassiter left his horse and buggy at the livery stable, as he did every morning except Sunday, and walked up the street to the hotel. Entering the kitchen through the back door, he said good morning to the cook as he passed through to the dining room. "Good morning, Mr. Lassiter," Millie greeted him as he sat down at his usual table by the window.

"Good morning, Millie," he returned. "I'll have my usual."

At this early hour, there were as yet only a few patrons in the dining room: one of the hotel guests at a table next to his, and four men eating breakfast at a table near the door. Lassiter nodded to the hotel guest, but the men at the other table gave no indication of noticing him.

Millie brought his coffee right away, and before he had finished his first cup, she came back with a plate of eggs, bacon, and potatoes. Lassiter did not linger long over his breakfast, cleaning his plate with no dallying. He liked to get to his desk at the bank a good thirty minutes before his two tellers arrived for work, and an hour before opening for business. Pushing his chair back, he stood up while he fished in his wallet for a couple of bills to leave on the table. Leaving via the front door, he didn't notice the four strangers getting to their feet behind him.

In front of the hotel, Roy Blanton and his sons waited a minute or two while the banker walked briskly toward the bank. Then they climbed on their horses and followed along behind him at a slow walk. Pulling up behind him just as he was fitting his key in the lock, they dismounted, and Roy told Zeke to stay with the horses.

Hearing them come up behind him, Lassiter turned to inform them. "The bank won't be opening for an hour yet, gentlemen."

"It's openin' early today, pilgrim," Buster said as he whipped his pistol out and poked Lassiter in the stomach with the barrel. "Now, turn around and unlock that door. Hurry up!" he prodded when Lassiter's nervous fingers proved rebellious under the pressure.

"You men are making a big mistake," the banker stammered, trembling as he finally got the door unlocked. "We have law in this town now, and he's right down the street."

Roy, standing on the bank porch and keeping a watchful eye on both ends of the street, grew impatient with the banker's fumbling. In a fit of anger, he whirled around and stuck his pistol against the side of

Lassiter's head. "I'm gonna make a wind whistle outta your skull if you don't open that damn door right now!" The banker turned the key and burst into the room. Roy turned to Zeke. "Zeke, take them horses around back and keep your eyes peeled." Then he followed Junior and Buster into the bank and locked the door behind him. "All right, mister, you got about half a minute to get that damn safe open. Buster, get him at it. If he don't move fast enough to suit you, shoot him. We'll use dynamite to open the damn thing."

"Pa," Buster replied, "we ain't got no more dynamite. We used all we had on that train."

"Get at it!" Roy bellowed, losing his patience again. His grizzled face glowed red with anger beneath the gray stubble that covered most of it, giving him a demonic look that shook Lassiter to his core. The frightened man opened the safe wide and immediately stepped out of the way while Junior and Buster dived in. Seemingly uninterested in the money at that point, Roy continued to glare at Lassiter. "What time does the sheriff stop by?" he asked, guessing that it might be routine, as it was in a lot of towns.

Convinced that the robbers must have complete knowledge of the security practices, Lassiter was too scared to lie. "Any minute now," he answered meekly.

"What kinda signal do you use to tell him everythin's all right?" Roy demanded.

"No signal," Lassiter squeaked timidly. "There's no signal."

"God damn you!" Roy roared, and stuck the barrel of his pistol against the side of Lassiter's jaw. "I'll blow you to hell right now!"

"The shades!" Lassiter screamed. "If the shades aren't up, he stops in!"

"I thought so," Blanton said.

Junior dropped the sack he had filled with cash and started toward the windows to put the shades up.

"Leave 'em be," his pa said, thinking about his promise to his youngest son. Prodding the banker again, he
asked, "Sheriff? Deputy? Who?"

"Choctaw Lighthorse," Lassiter answered fearfully.

"Haw!" Roy exclaimed. "Injun police. Well, we owe
Billy one, don't we, boys? Take ol' Mr. Banker there
back of the cage and sit on him." He walked over to
the door and pulled the shade aside far enough to take
a look up the street. Seeing no one, he unlocked the
door and joined his sons behind the counter. "We'll
just sit here and wait for the Injun," he said. "Junior,
gimme your shotgun."

Sam Sixkiller glanced at the clock on the wall over
his desk. It was about time for the tellers to go to work
at the bank. He got up, strapped on his handgun, and
prepared to take a walk down the length of the street,
a routine he had agreed upon with Walter Lassiter.
The bank had never been robbed, probably because
the Choctaw Lighthorse was originally headquartered
in Atoka until three years ago when the Union Agency
for all the Five Civilized Tribes was moved to Musko-
gee. Since then, Sam and one policeman, who had just
been killed in Broken Bow, were the only Choctaw
policemen working out of Atoka, with Sam serving
more as a local sheriff for the town. The citizens of the
town paid for a modest supplement to his regular sal-
ary for that service.

Comfortable with the town's low incidence of crime
in recent years, he was now concerned with the appearance of the Blanton gang at Durant Station. It had
been three years since the Blantons had been run out
of the nations, most of the credit for that going to Buck
Avery, but the loss of Joseph Big Eagle by the hand of
Billy Blanton was enough to put all lawmen in the territory on alert.

He said good morning to Henry Jenkins as he

walked past the dry goods store, and continued on along the dusty thoroughfare. Approaching the bank, he noticed that the window shades in the two front windows were still down. It didn't cause him to be overly alarmed. There were no horses tied in front of the building, and it wouldn't be the first time Lassiter had forgotten to raise the shades. Sam grunted in amusement at the thought, for he sometimes suspected that Lassiter left them down on purpose to test his *alarm* system.

"Good morning, Sam." Sixkiller heard the greeting as he neared the porch. Turning toward the sound, he saw Ed Tuttle, one of Lassiter's tellers, crossing over from the hotel.

"Mornin', Mr. Tuttle," Sam replied. "Better let me go in first. The shades are down." Tuttle, as unconcerned as Sam, smiled and stopped to lean against the porch corner post while the lawman entered the bank.

The door was unlocked, again nothing unusual since it was time for the tellers to arrive. Without concern enough to draw his revolver from the holster, Sam opened the door. At first, there appeared to be no one in the bank. He was about to call out for Lassiter, when Roy Blanton popped up from behind the teller's cage. Sam Sixkiller's last mortal image was of Blanton's vengeful grin as a blast of buckshot slammed into his chest and knocked him out the open door to land on the porch floor.

Shocked out of his wits, Ed Tuttle backed off the porch, almost bumping into the other teller just arriving for work. "What . . . ?" was all Jason Burke could manage when he saw Sam's body on the porch. In the next moment his astonishment turned to cold terror when the menacing image of Roy Blanton appeared in the doorway. Fright robbed Ed Tuttle of any thought but escape. He turned and ran. With blind panic, Burke followed suit, stumbled off the porch, and ran around the corner of the building, only to meet Zeke Blanton head-on. The sound of the shotgun blast brought Zeke running with the horses. With no idea what the shooting was about, he shot down Burke as he sprinted away. Rounding the building then, he saw his father standing over the fallen lawman. "You all right, Pa?"

"Yeah," Roy replied, "I'm just dandy, but this Injun sheriff ain't feelin' so good." He drew his pistol then and put a bullet in the dying man's brain. "I expect we're about done here," he said. "We'd best get along."

"By God, I reckon that's one less lawman to worry about," Buster whooped when he joined his father on the porch.

"That's a fact," Roy agreed. Then he reached over and jerked Buster's hat from his head and proceeded to whip his son violently about his head and neck with it. "That's for bein' so damn dumb," he said when he tired of flailing his clueless son. "We ain't got no more dynamite, Pa," Roy mocked. "You ain't got the brains of a blue jay. I didn't want him to know that."

"Oh," his simpleminded son responded, still confused.

Roy then turned back to call through the open doorway. "Junior, find somethin' to tie that feller up, and do it quick. We got to get outta here."

Out in the street, the four bandits climbed on their horses with guns drawn to discourage any heroic thoughts of the local citizens. A few curious souls had emerged, drawn by the sound of gunfire, but upon seeing the four mounted outlaws, quickly sought safety behind closed doors. Smugly satisfied, Roy Blanton led his sons out the south end of town at a gallop. Intent upon leaving the scene as quickly as possible, he nevertheless pulled up when he espied an obscure shack displaying a simple sign over the door that proclaimed POLICE. On angry impulse, he emptied his pistol, firing at the shack. Needing no reason to follow suit other than their father's example, his three sons did likewise. When there was no return fire, Roy dismounted and kicked the door open. Looking around the empty room, he saw a lantern on the desk. Smashing it on the top of the desk, he struck a match and set it ablaze. He stood in the doorway watching the flames gather strength while the boys crowded in behind him. Feeling as if another blow had been struck in retaliation for Billy's execution, he turned and ordered his three sons back in the saddle. "Let's get the hell outta this damn town," he roared as he stepped up in the saddle. Wheeling his horse around a couple of times, he glared back down the street defiantly, daring anyone to challenge him. No one dared. Whipping his horse into a gallop again, he led his sons as they raced out of the unfortunate little town, leaving a cloud of dust to combine with the dingy gray smoke billowing from the police shack. With no prior planned destination, they headed back to the Crossing to count their money and celebrate.

Chapter 4

After two days in the saddle, following a trail that led through the San Bois Mountains, Casey and Buck rode through a rugged stretch of sandstone hills and cliffs, some rising as high as fifteen hundred feet. The sides and tops of the hills were heavily forested with pine and oak and dotted with boulders.

"I trailed a train robber through this stretch of hills about five years ago," Buck said. "I lost him for almost half a day until I found his horse at the bottom of a cliff. It was in a natural corral, formed by rocks. Well, I climbed through a bunch of rocks and trees and found him holed up in a cave. I worked my way up to the mouth of that cave, halfway expectin' to get a belly full of lead, but nothin' happened. I figured he was waitin' for me to come in after him. I was a sittin' duck, I'll tell ya. I finally said to hell with it, I'm goin' in. Come to find out he had slipped out through a hole in the top. I'd been chasin' that son of a bitch for four days, and he got away while I was sittin' there waitin' behind a rock. I crawled out, too; found myself on the top of a cliff. I looked over the edge and there he was, layin' on the rocks below, deader'n hell. I don't know if he jumped or fell. The boys over in McAlester told me I had found Robbers Cave. Most of the outlaws in Texas and the nations knew about it—hid out there when they was on the run."

"Reckon you could find it again?" Casey asked, mildly curious.

"Maybe, if I had a reason to," Buck replied with a shrug of his shoulders, "but there ain't gonna be nobody we're lookin' for in there, so I wouldn't waste our time lookin' for it."

Casey couldn't help but wonder how Buck could be so sure. If it was a regular hideout for fugitives, it couldn't hurt to take a look just to be certain.

Buck didn't wait for discussion. "Come on," he said. "I know a good spot to camp if we get a move on." He nudged the dun into a comfortable lope and started out again.

With only a half hour or so of daylight left, they came upon a small spring. "This suit you?" Buck asked as he guided the dun to the other side.

"Suits me," Casey said, so they went about making camp for the night. "I expect we'll strike McAlester early enough tomorrow to catch the afternoon train to Durant Station."

After taking care of the horses, they gathered enough wood to build a fire to boil some coffee and roast some of the dried venison Casey had prepared while awaiting Billy Blanton's hanging. "This eats right good," Buck declared. "You done a good job on it." He gave Casey a wink. "Somebody taught you how to dry jerky. You ain't been layin' up with an Injun woman, have you?"

Casey chuckled. "No, I guess I just watched my ma fix it enough when I was a kid." The thought brought to mind a picture of his mother cutting strips of venison to dry on the racks his father had built for the purpose. A small woman, married to a tall man,

Pauline Dixon had worked hard to scratch out an existence in the Ozark Mountains of Arkansas. Left to raise their only son after Casey's father went off to fight for the Confederacy, she learned to live off what the forests and rivers offered. Most of the food was provided by her young son's skill with an old single-shot rifle. She was a strong woman, but when word came that his father was not coming back from the war, it broke her spirit. A year later, she died. The doctor couldn't say why. *She was just tired*, was all he offered.

"It's been a while since I've et any wild meat," Buck said. "Maybe when we get done with this job, I'll do some huntin' myself. I'm gettin' tired of huntin' men." He paused to reflect. "I wouldn't admit it to John Council, but I'm gettin' a little long in the tooth for this business." He went to his saddlebags and fished around in one of the pockets, finally pulling out a scratched-up briar pipe and a pouch of tobacco.

Casey studied the old deputy for a few moments while he loaded the pipe, tamped the load, and lit up. He wondered if he was looking at himself in about fifteen or twenty years. He realized that he had spent no time really thinking about his future and what he would have to fall back on when he reached Buck's age. It was something that normally never occurred to him, but looking at Buck sitting on the other side of the fire with a ring of tobacco smoke floating around his head brought the reality of the inevitable to his thinking. He thought about the money he had earned in the year just passed. Living from day to day, he had never kept close count on his earnings: two dollars for making an arrest, six cents per mile for traveling to the place of arrest, ten cents per mile for bringing the prisoner back to Fort Smith, fifty cents for every time he served a subpoena. And John Council as his boss took twenty-five percent off the top before he got paid.

When all was said and done, he seriously doubted if he made much more than five hundred dollars for the year. It left nothing to put away for the time when he was too old to do the job. It also wasn't a helluva lot to offer a wife if he was so inclined. Telling himself he was straying into dangerous thoughts, he brought his mind back before he started thinking about Fred McDonald's dark-haired daughter again.

"What the hell are you gonna do if you quit?" Casey asked. Buck, like him and all deputies, was paid under the same fee system.

Buck responded with a tight-lipped smile as if reluctant to answer the question. Finally, he put his coffee cup down beside him and thought a moment before replying. "I reckon I've been pinchin' my pennies to try to save up a little somethin' to fall back on. I've got a little cabin over on the Kiamichi don't nobody know about. I reckon I'll just hunt and fish till I turn my toes up." That was all he was willing to offer. He didn't think it wise to share the fact that he was a silent partner with Frenchie Petit in the Deuce of Spades.

Casey nodded his head thoughtfully. It was a subject he didn't care to dwell on at his young age, so he decided he had spent enough thought on the matter for now. "Well," he said, getting to his feet, "maybe we'll be shot down by some outlaw before we have to face the problem." He walked over to check on his horse.

"Might be I should be a little more particular when I pick a horse," he said to Buck as he took a look at the gray's left-front hoof. This one's got an ornery streak in him. I guess I just got too used to ridin' my sorrel." Maybe Buck had been right when he suggested they'd be spotted for lawmen if they rode finer-looking horses, but he wished now that he had ridden his horse. Blanton's gang would know they were deputies anyway. Unlike this hardheaded gray, his sorrel tried to anticipate his boss' intentions and responded immediately to his bidding. *And now the hardhead is trying to get a sore foot*, he told himself, thinking of the gray again.

It was early afternoon when the two lawmen rode into the odd collection of structures that made up the settlement of McAlester, close by the tracks of the MKT, or *the Katy* as it was called locally. They went immediately to the railroad depot to check on the arrival of the afternoon train to Durant. "Won't be for an hour yet," they were told by the stationmaster. "Are you Buck Avery?" he asked. When Buck said that he was, the stationmaster handed him a telegram. "This came in last night."

"Damn," Buck exhaled slowly, then handed the telegram to Casey. "The Blantons robbed the bank in Atoka yesterday. They killed Sam Sixkiller."

This was sorrowful news to Casey. As he read the telegram, he thought of his recent participation with Sam and some policemen from the Creek Nation. Sam was a good man, a dedicated lawman. He would be hard to replace. Casey found it hard to believe Sam had been bushwhacked when he walked into the bank. He seemed the kind of man who would be around forever, like Buck. He was not careless, and Casey wondered how he could blindly walk into an ambush. He looked up at Buck, who shook his head sadly, having been a friend of Sam's for many years longer than Casey had.

"I guess we'll be gettin' off the train at Atoka," Casey said.

Buck nodded his silent agreement. He had been wrong in insisting that the Blantons would hop back across the river to Texas after hitting Durant. It troubled him because he had been certain he knew Roy

Blanton's mind and could predict what the notorious outlaw would do. His gaze lingered on the young deputy for a moment longer. Confident and fearless, Casey was, ready to stand toe to toe with the Blantons even though outnumbered two to one; Buck remembered that he, too, was that way once. Now he feared that this next confrontation with his old nemesis might be the most deadly.

The train pulled in pretty close to the scheduled time. There was no livestock car attached, but there was a half-empty boxcar with enough space for three horses. The conductor was reluctant to permit it, but when Buck insisted it was official business of the Federal Court for the Western District of Arkansas, he conceded. The horses were crowded into the car, and Buck and Casey stayed with them for the forty-mile ride to Atoka.

"Goddamn!" Buck exclaimed, and screwed his face up in disgust. "You was right when you said you shoulda been more careful pickin' a horse." His remark was inspired by the tear-producing acrid aroma of freshly laid horse dung, courtesy of Casey's gray gelding. Hardly an experienced train traveler, the gray was not comfortable with the strange sensation of the gently rocking boxcar, the result of which caused a rush to the exit in his bowels. The boxcar was well made to the point where there was little wind that blew through it. That quality worked just as well to contain odors manufactured from within. Consequently, thirty-five miles of the forty-mile trip were passed with the door open and the two lawmen standing by it with their nostrils in the wind.

When the train began slowing down as they were approaching Atoka, Casey ventured away from the open door long enough to remove the packs from the packhorse. The load might prove to be too awkward for the horse to disembark without injury. As soon as they rolled to a stop, Casey and Buck jumped the horses off the train. The conductor and the engineer walked back to the car as Casey was loading the pack-horse again.

Anxious to see that no damage had been done to the freight loaded in half of the car, the conductor climbed inside. He was immediately met with the pungent odor and confronted with the origin. Rushing back to the open door just as the two deputies were climbing up in the saddle, he yelled, "Hey, what about this mess you left?"

Replying with a straight face, Buck said, "There's an official procedure for that. You can put it in a sack and ship it back to Fort Smith, or you can keep it in the depot and wait for Fort Smith to send somebody to come get it. Much obliged for the ride." He wheeled his horse and followed after Casey, who had not both-ered to wait.

Riding up the street, they stopped briefly to look at the burnt-out ruins of the late Sam Sixkiller's office. "I reckon ol' Roy was lettin' folks know what he thought of them hangin' Billy," Buck remarked.

"And what he thinks of the law hereabouts," Casey added.

"I reckon," Buck agreed. "Let's go on down to the bank to see what we can find out."

Walking the horses slowly, they noticed the guarded stares sent their way from the stores and shops by people turned cautious since the last strangers visited their town. It seemed to Casey that the bank robbery had killed the town's spirit.

Walter Lassiter looked up to see the two riders pull up before the bank and dismount. Making no move to get up from his desk to greet them, he continued to watch them as they stepped to the door. He didn't know what they wanted, and didn't care, for that mat-ter. His bank had been wiped out by the robbery. At this particular point, there was not much he could do for any potential customers. From the rough appearance of the two men now walking in the door, it occurred to him that they might even be thinking of robbery. If they were, they were going to be sadly disappointed. The thought almost caused a bitter smile to play upon his lips. He finally rose from his chair and went to the front of the cage. "Can I help you gentlemen?"

Buck spoke up. "I'm U.S. Deputy Marshal Buck Avery, and this is Deputy Casey Dixon. We're here to see what we can do about the folks that robbed your bank, Mr. . . ."

"Lassiter," the banker filled in the blank. Then he walked over to the cage door to meet them. He had never met any of the deputies out of Fort Smith, but he had heard of Buck Avery. Everybody in the territory had.

"Yes, sir, Mr. Lassiter," Buck continued while Casey stood silently listening. "We're hopin' to catch up with the men who did this, and maybe get some of your money back. What can you tell us about what happened?"

"Well," Lassiter said, "there were four of them. Three came into the bank and the other one held the horses outside. The one that seemed to be the boss was an older man. The others were all young men. Horace Ramsey, he's the blacksmith, says he thinks it was Roy Blanton and his sons, the same bunch that robbed the train down at Durant. I wouldn't know one way or the other, but one of the robbers called the old man Pa. Anyway, they shot Jason Burke, one of my tellers— been with me ever since I first opened the bank—shot him down for no reason at all. He was just trying to get out of the way. They cleaned out my safe, and then they just stood around in here and waited for Sam Sixkiller to come in the door. They didn't even try to get away when they could have. I think they had in mind to kill him all along. They shot him down when he walked in. Then they left. That's about all I can tell you."

"Well, I'm right sorry to hear about Sam and your teller," Buck said. "We'll sure do our best to catch up with 'em. Much obliged for your help."

Casey, waiting for Buck to continue questioning the banker, was somewhat surprised when the old deputy turned toward the door, so he spoke up then. "Which way did they go after they burnt Sam Sixkiller's shack?"

"Horace said they took the south road outta town," Lassiter said. "I couldn't say. They left me tied up behind the cage." He shrugged his shoulders, evidently thinking about something further, then said, "Some of the men talked about forming a posse, but there weren't enough volunteers, so nothing ever came of it."

"Headed south, huh? That's what I thought," Buck said. "They might be halfway back to Texas by now."

"Maybe," Casey said, "but they might not be in a hurry to get back. Accordin' to what Mr. Lassiter said, they don't seem to think there's any reason to hurry. They might be plannin' to do a little celebratin' first. If we can pick up their trail, they might not be that far ahead of us."

"You might be right, partner," Buck replied. "It's gonna be tough to track 'em, though. Their tracks are already a couple of days old, and pickin' 'em out of a bunch of other tracks in the road ain't gonna be easy."

"You're right about that," Casey agreed. "Let's go talk to that blacksmith. If he saw which way they left, he might be able to help us figure out which tracks are theirs."

Horace Ramsey laid his hammer aside and walked

out of his shed to meet the two men approaching on horseback. "Marshals?" he asked when Casey and Buck stepped down.

"That's right," Buck answered.

"I thought so. I saw you was over at the bank talking to Walter—figured you was sent here about the bank robbery."

Buck introduced Casey and himself before questioning the blacksmith. "Mr. Lassiter over at the bank said you saw the gang leavin' town."

"That's a fact," Horace replied. "Went right by my forge, headed for the trail to Boggy Creek."

"What's out that way?" Buck asked, not recalling a town of any size in that direction. "Where does it go?"

"Boggy Creek," Horace replied as if wondering if the deputy was hard of hearing.

"Is that all? Ain't no settlement or nothin'?"

"Nothin', unless you wanna count the Crossin', which ain't no more'n a tradin' post," Horace replied.

"I know the place," Buck said, turning to inform Casey. "More saloon than anything else, it's about half a day's ride from here. Feller named Blackie Andrews owns it—got a little tradin' post attached to it that used to be run by a Mexican named Garcia. Half his customers are outlaws on the run."

"That's the place, all right," Horace said, "and last I heard, the Mexican still takes care of the tradin' post, but it's the saloon that carries the load."

"Sounds like a place we oughta be checkin' out," Casey said.

"I oughta tell you," Horace said, "the Crossin' ain't right on the trail. You have to turn off on an old Injun game trail before you get to the fork where Muddy Boggy joins Clear Boggy. It ain't easy to find if you ain't ever been there before."

"Much obliged," Buck said. "I've been to Blackie's place, but I ain't never gone there from this side of it."

He turned back to Casey again. "Say, partner, you might wanna let the smithy here take a look at the hoof on that gray. It wouldn't do to let him go lame on us."

"I suppose you're right," Casey replied. Although he was reluctant to lose any more time, it made sense to let Horace look at the hoof.

At Casey's direction, Horace walked over and lifted the gray's left-front hoof. It didn't take him long to spot the problem. "Hell, I can see right off what's wrong," he said. "Has he been walkin' kinda ginger on it?" When Casey allowed that he had, Horace said, "Whoever put his shoes on didn't get 'em straight; at least he didn't get this one on straight. So one of the nails is cuttin' into the sensitive part of his hoof. He's feelin' it every time he puts his weight on it."

"Well, we're in a hurry. Can you fix it?"

"Maybe we oughta not be in too big a hurry," Buck interrupted. "The afternoon's already gettin' along on us. If we start out now, we'll likely get to the Crossin' in the middle of the night sometime, and that's providin' we can find that cutoff trail in the dark."

"I reckon you're right," Casey reluctantly agreed. "Can you fix him up?" he asked Horace.

"Sure. I got time to shoe all four feet if you're gonna be stayin' overnight. Or if you just want that one fixed, I can use the same shoe—just take it off and straighten it."

"Just fix the one, and we can at least ride till dark," Casey said.

"Damn, partner," Buck complained, "you sure are in an all-fired hurry. It ain't gonna amount to more than an hour or more head start on that trail. It ain't worth it when we could stay in the hotel here and have us a drink or two tonight. Whaddaya say? We can get an early start in the mornin'."

Casey gazed at his older partner for a long moment,

deciding. If he had been alone, he would have started out to Boggy Creek without a thought otherwise. Looking at the pleading eyes of the most famous deputy marshal in Oklahoma Territory, he gave in. "All right, we'll start out first thing in the mornin'." He had the feeling that Buck thought the whole chase was a useless endeavor. Maybe he was right. Maybe Blanton had hightailed it back to Texas.

"Now, that was a fine supper," Buck declared when Millie came around again with the coffeepot. He gave her a wink, and she rewarded him with a coy smile in deference to his age. When she returned to the kitchen, Buck said, "Now all I need is a couple of drinks of whiskey. Whaddaya say, partner?"

"You go ahead," Casey said. "I wanna go see about my horse. I'll catch up with you at the saloon."

The two deputies walked out of the dining room together. Then Buck headed toward the saloon while Casey returned to the blacksmith shop. "I was just fixin' to get to your horse," Horace said when Casey walked in. "I figured you wouldn't need him till mornin'."

"Well, I'd like to take him over to the stable with the other two horses," Casey said.

"How's this horse ride?" Horace asked. "You pretty satisfied with him?"

Horace's interest in the gray surprised Casey. The horse certainly wasn't much to look at. "Tell you the truth, he ain't my regular horse. He's goin' back to the corral when we get back to Fort Smith."

"You have trouble holdin' him to a steady gait? Does he want to trot a lot?"

Mildly astonished, Casey answered, "As a matter of fact, he does, but I figured he's just lazy—trottin's easier."

Horace stroked his chin thoughtfully. "Might be,"

he said, "but I was lookin' him over while you was at supper. I ain't sure the last feller that shoed him knew his business. If it was my horse, I'd fit him to lower his hind-feet angles. The shoes he's wearin' has got 'em too high. That'll make a horse tend to trot instead of gaitin'."

"And you can fix that, right?" Casey asked with a knowing smile.

"I sure can."

Casey had to think it over for a minute before deciding he should do it for the gray's sake. "Mister, you're a slick salesman. Go ahead and do it, but I'll play hell tryin' to get my money back from John Council."

"Yes, sir," Horace said, "and if you'll pay me now, I'll take him over to the stable for you tonight."

He got to the saloon later than he had planned, but it was obvious by the state of intoxication that Buck had already accomplished that his partner had not waited for him. At a back table there was a six-hand poker game in progress, and Buck was in the middle of it. Casey walked to the bar, ordered a glass of beer, and stood there sipping it slowly.

"You one of the marshals in town?" the bartender, a thin, bald man with a handlebar mustache, asked. When Casey replied that he was, the bartender went on to tell him that Buck was doing all right for himself in the game. "I swear it looks like he's winnin' every other hand. And maybe it'd be a good idea to let you know that a couple of those boys don't take kindly to losing. They're cowhands from the Lucky K ranch, 'bout five miles north of here, and they can get a little ornery when they're liquored up good. Last month, Roach, he's the big one wearin' the Rebel cap, damn near carved up some feller from McAlester with a bowie knife. I sent for Sam Sixkiller, and he rode him and his friends outta town." He glanced over at the table for a second. "It didn't take long for word to get around that Sam's dead."

"I expect Buck will keep things under control," Casey said.

"I hope so," the bartender replied. "Last time it cost me a couple of chairs and a cracked tabletop."

Casey got another beer and walked over to watch the card game. "You want in, partner?" Buck asked when he saw him.

"Nope," Casey answered. "Looks like you're doin' pretty good. I might change your luck."

"Seems to me he's too damn lucky," Roach, the cowhand wearing the Rebel cap said, "luckier than anybody oughta be." There was no smile on his face when he said it.

Buck chuckled delightedly. "That's right, boys, Lady Luck always rides with the pure of heart." He threw his hand in. "But I'm gonna let you boys have this hand."

"It's about time," one of the others remarked. "I'll call."

Casey watched a few more hands before becoming bored with it and going back to the bar for another beer. By that time, Buck's luck seemed to have returned. *He's having a hell of a good time tonight*, Casey thought, *but he's going to have one awfully big head in the morning.* He was inclined to turn in for the night, but judging by the sour expressions on the faces around the table, and the free-flowing whiskey, he thought it best to stick around for a while to make sure Buck got up to bed all right.

He didn't have to wait long before the inevitable happened. When his last raise was called, Buck showed his hand and crowed, "Aces and tens, boys." Roach and one other player who had remained in to call threw their cards in, disgusted. One of the other

cowhands, equally disgusted, got up and went to the
bar for another full bottle of whiskey.

Finally Roach had reached his boiling point. "That
last ace come off the bottom of the deck," he said,
looking Buck straight in the eye.

"That's right," the player sitting next to him said. "I
saw it." A stony silence descended upon the table.

Buck shook his head sadly and sighed. "I'm disappointed in you boys," he said calmly. "Here we was,
havin' a nice friendly game, and you have to go sayin'
somethin' like that." He looked around at the glaring
eyes centered on him. "I'm just gonna forget you said
that, and we'll get on with the game."

"You ain't too bright, are you?" Roach said. "We
don't tolerate card slicks around here. If you wanna
walk outta here on your own two feet, you can leave
the money on the table and get up outta that chair and
head for the door." He drew a large skinning knife and
stuck it in the table before him.

Sitting at a table near the front of the room, Casey
watched the developing storm with more than a little
interest. Remembering the card game at the Deuce of
Spades when Buck sat it out and let him handle the
trouble, he decided to wait to see if Buck could take
care of his problem by himself.

"Well, I reckon it is gettin' around to my bedtime,"
Buck said. "And it looks like this game's over, don't it?
I'm sorry you fellers turned out to be sore losers, but I
won the money and I'll be takin' it with me."

"The hell you are!" Roach snarled, jerked his knife
up, and stabbed an ace of diamonds perilously close to
Buck's hand.

Chairs scraped back from the table, and all eyes
were on Buck, who still remained unperturbed as he
spoke. "Are you sure you wanna threaten a U.S. deputy marshal with that knife?"

"I don't give a damn if you're a marshal," Roach spat. "A cheat's a cheat, and you got a lesson comin'."

Still calm, Buck replied, "How 'bout a marshal with a .44 aimed at you under the table?"

A mild expression of shock registered on Roach's face, and he looked for a moment as if undecided what to do. Then, inexplicably, a smirk slowly spread across his face, causing Buck to wonder. With no eyes in the back of his head, he could not see Roach's friend poised over him with a full bottle of whiskey raised to strike.

What happened next was almost over before the poker players knew what had taken place. With his left hand Casey trapped the wrist of Buck's would-be assailant, stopping the bottle while it was still over the cowhand's head. With his right he jabbed the barrel of his pistol hard into the man's side. "All right," he ordered, "this little party is over. Buck, you still got your friend there covered?"

"I will have," Buck replied, pushing back his chair to give him room to draw the weapon from his holster.

"Damn," said Casey, exhaling.

Knowing what he meant, Buck grinned and said, "Bluffin's just part of playin' poker."

"You fellers," Casey ordered, indicating the two players who were obviously not with the cowhands, "get on out of here." Signaling the three ranch hands, he said, "You three are under arrest. Get your hands palm down on that table. Buck, take their guns."

While Buck was relieving the three disgruntled ranch hands of their sidearms, the bartender moved up beside Casey and whispered, "There ain't no jail. The Blantons burnt it down."

Casey paused to consider that for a moment. He could turn them loose, but he didn't want to worry about getting jumped by them later on if they decided to try to get their money back from Buck. "What time

do you open up in the mornin'?" he asked the bartender.

"Usually 'bout nine thirty, ten o'clock," he replied.

"You got a storeroom or some place where we can
lock 'em up overnight?"

"You can't lock those three up in my storeroom,"
the bartender replied, concerned. "They'd tear that
room apart."

"All right," he decided, "I'll take 'em to jail. You
ready, Buck?" When Buck replied that he was, Casey
said, "We're takin' you boys to jail for the night. You
can get your firearms from the bartender here when he
opens up in the mornin'." He gave the bartender a
glance and a nod to make sure he understood. "Let's
go. Start walkin'." He prodded the man in the back
who had held the bottle. Buck herded the other two
behind him.

Once in the street, they had to walk their prisoners
about fifty yards down to the ruins of the police station. "Buck, you think we oughta shoot 'em in the legs
like we usually do, so they can't try to run?"

"I reckon," Buck replied, knowing Casey was bluff-
ing.

"Now, hold on, dammit," Roach exclaimed. "We
ain't gonna run!"

"Whaddaya think, Buck?"

"I reckon they've learned their lesson," Buck said.
"But if this one runs, I'm shootin' to kill. This son of a
bitch accused me of cheatin'."

"All right, then, let's get movin'." He took a coil of
rope from one of his prisoners' horses. Leaving the
horses tied to the hitching post, he followed Buck and
the cowhands down the street.

"Hey, wait a damn minute," one of the prisoners
complained upon seeing the pile of blackened timbers
that was all that remained of the police station. "You

can't leave us tied up here. We've got cattle to work in the mornin'."

"Yeah," Roach added, "we'll get fired if we don't show up in the mornin'."

"I expect you shoulda thought about that before you decided to carve up an officer of the law," Buck said.

Finding one long section of iron bars that had been the front of two cells, Buck tied Roach and one other, hand and foot to the heavy metal. The third member of the party was tied to a large partially burnt heavy timber that had served as the building's ridgepole.

Satisfied that their prisoners were secured, they left them with one final thought from Buck. "You boys are lucky it's a warm night. You can stay here and think about your evil ways and remember that crime don't pay." Turning to Casey as they walked away, he said, "How 'bout a little drink before we go to bed? I can afford to buy."

"I expect you've already had enough to kill an ordinary man," Casey replied. "Me, I'm goin' to bed. We got a long ride in the mornin'."

It was a sad and sick deputy marshal who was awakened before daybreak the next morning. "Get up, Buck," Casey said, shaking his partner by the shoulder. "We've got to get goin'. Roy Blanton ain't likely to wait around for us to come get him."

"Who?" Buck mumbled, the sound of his own voice threatening to shatter his fragile head.

"Blanton," Casey said.

"Oh." He thought about that as his throbbing brain began to work its way back from the whirlpool of alcohol. "Yeah," he finally said, "I'm up."

"Good," Casey said. "You get yourself together while I go over to the stable and get the horses."

He left the old deputy to try to shake off the prior night's drunk, half expecting him to be passed out again when he returned. He saddled his and Buck's horses and loaded the packhorse. Still it was not close to daylight when he returned to the hotel to find Buck out front waiting for him. "Well, I see you made it," Casey said.

"Oh, hell yeah," Buck replied with a weak show of enthusiasm. "It's a workin' day. I'm ready to go." He made a sour face when he evidently tasted a bit of last night's celebration. "I wish to hell the kitchen was open, though. I could sure use some coffee."

"Yeah, me too," Casey said. "But we don't have time to wait around for a couple of hours for the kitchen to open. We'll stop after a few miles and make some coffee. We're gonna need daylight, anyway, to find that cutoff trail."

In the saddle, they started toward the south end of the street. When they reached Sam Sixkiller's burnt-out shack, Casey pulled up and dismounted, leaving Buck in the saddle. Stiff, chilled, and sick, his three prisoners said nothing when they saw the deputy approach in the dark. "I'm gonna turn you loose now," Casey said. "You got a choice. You can get on your horses and make it back to save your jobs, or you can wait till the saloon opens to get your guns."

"Just turn us loose," Roach said.

"All right," Casey said. "I'll untie your hands, and you can untie your friends."

Back in the saddle, he wheeled the gray, and they started out for the Crossing. He set a brisk pace for the better part of two hours, following a trail barely discernible until the sun rose over the hills to the east. It was a silent ride. Casey knew Buck felt like hell, but he would burst before admitting it. They drove on until coming to a good spot to rest the horses. By this time, Casey was as desperate for a cup of coffee as Buck probably was, so he didn't waste any time getting a small fire started. The fire felt good in the chilly morning air, even though the first rays of the morning sun promised another hot July afternoon. Soon they were drinking coffee and finally felt like talking.

"What a night," Buck exclaimed. "I tell you, partner, I can't do that like I used to when I was your age."

Casey laughed. "At least you had a good run of the cards. You did all right." He shook his head, thinking about the scene in the saloon. "That feller wearing the Confederate army cap was sure you were dealin' off the bottom."

Buck chuckled. "Hell, I was. I was surprised he was sober enough to see it, though."

Chapter 5

Roy Blanton sat on a bench on the porch of Blackie Andrews' Lucky Dollar Saloon, taking in the afternoon sun. He took off his hat to reveal a thick shock of dirty gray hair that still held the shape of the hat molded into the heavy strands. There was a bottle of rye whiskey beside him and a glass half full in his hand. The bank job in Atoka had been more profitable than he had anticipated. And since they had been disappointed in the take from the train robbery in Durant, he figured his sons deserved a little time to celebrate before moving on. Now he was getting itchy to leave. Blackie would no doubt be sorry to see them go. He was making a good profit from their two-day stay, both in his saloon and the trading post attached.

He downed the whiskey in the glass and methodically filled it again, his thoughts drawn to his sons, who had disappeared into the trading post, no doubt to bargain with Garcia. He had done well by his boys. Life had been good, hard at times, but good for the most part. He had taught them that everything was there for the taking, and it belonged to those strong enough to take it. One day in the not-too-distant future, he could see that the time would come when he was not up to living in the saddle. He had been think-ing about that lately, and he couldn't deny a certain feeling of melancholy that came with it. But he felt confident that his boys would take care of him when he got too old to ride. Junior, especially, would see that his pa was provided for, and he expected that he, be-ing the eldest, would see that his brothers didn't forget how much they owed him.

Of his three living sons, Junior was naturally his obvious successor to inherit the mantle as head of the family. Buster, fearless and sometimes reckless, was often slow in the head, a condition that Roy believed may have come from a kick in the head by a horse when the boy was twelve years old. He needed some-one to tell him what to do; then he would do his best to please. Zeke was the one most likely to want to split off from the family and go his own way. He was wild, as wild as Billy had been. The two of them would of-ten compete to see who could do the most outrageous stunts, or take the biggest chances. They were all good boys. He was proud of them. Their mother may not be especially proud of the path of life the boys followed. He was aware of that, even though she never ex-pressed her disappointment that her sons had all cho-sen to follow their father's lawless style. She knew better than to speak out against it. Her favorite had been Billy, the baby, and he had to chuckle when he thought about it. Billy had turned out to be the wildest of the bunch. *More like his old man*, Roy thought. His reverie was interrupted by the sounds of an argument at the door of the trading post. Only mildly interested since the boys were always arguing about something, he turned a casual attention to the matter.

It turned out to be a confrontation between Zeke and Juan Garcia; his other two sons were merely amused spectators. Roy was trying to decide whether it was worth the bother to get up from his seat to find out what the fuss was about, when the dispute spilled out into the packed clay yard of the store. Blackie's Mexican store clerk was nose to nose with Zeke, both men yelling at each other. "Junior!" Roy Blanton called, summoning his eldest.

Sporting a wide grin, Junior walked over to the porch. "It ain't nothin', Pa," he said. "Zeke just offered ol' Garcia ten dollars for a go with his wife, and the Mexican didn't like it too much." Still grinning, he looked back to check the progress of the argument.

"Huh," Roy snorted, not really concerned. "That woman's old enough to be Zeke's mother."

Junior laughed. "You know Zeke. It don't matter that much to him. Young or old, pretty or ugly, skinny or fat, he says he's like Jesus Christ—he loves 'em all."

"Watch your mouth, son," Roy cautioned. He had very few inhibitions, but he was strict about taking the Lord's name in vain.

"Hell, it ain't me that said it," Junior was quick to explain. "I'm just tellin' you what Zeke said."

Roy watched the argument still in progress until Zeke suddenly pulled his gun and stuck it in Garcia's face. "I wondered how long it was gonna be," Roy said with a weary sigh, put his hat on, and stood up. "Zeke, put that damn gun away," he commanded as he stepped off the porch. Walking over to the pair of antagonists, he grabbed Zeke by the shoulder and pulled him out of Garcia's face. "Dammit, boy, this is where we do business! If you got the itch for a woman that bad, go round behind the house and tend to yourself." Then he directed Garcia to go back inside and forget about it.

It was not that easy to dismiss for the Mexican. "This man has insulted my wife," he protested. "He spoke to her like a common prostitute and tried to lay his hands on her." The longer he complained, the greater his indignation grew. "He has insulted my honor when he offered me money to let him have his way with her."

Roy Blanton was not a patient man once he had issued his orders. "Dammit, man, I said to forget it. A man workin' for Blackie Andrews can't have much honor to give a shit about, anyway. Now, that's the end of it. Don't push your luck with me."

The dark, squinting eyes beneath the heavy lowered brow promised Garcia that there would be hell to pay if the belligerent outlaw was pushed too far. Garcia, being a man of reasonable intellect, got the message. He was no longer dealing with a wild young scoundrel. "As you wish," he said. "We will forget the incident ever happened." He turned and went immediately back inside.

Junior and Buster beamed wide in their amusement until their father gave them a stern look of reproach. "Dammit, we do business here," he repeated. "Nobody but a damn fool shits where he sleeps." Of the three sons, Zeke was the only one who saw no humor in the incident, and it wasn't over as far as he was concerned. He glared back in anger at his brothers' grins when their father turned to go back to his bench on the porch.

Anna Garcia thought about the trouble that had taken place earlier in the store as she threw the supper dishwater out the kitchen door. It had been a terrifying moment when the young outlaw grabbed her by the arm. Still, she was ashamed to secretly admit that there was a wicked satisfaction in the thought that at age forty-one she was attractive to a man of his young age. There was also a certain amount of gratification in the way Juan had responded to defend her honor. It had been some time since her husband had shown any excitement in regard to her. Glancing through the doorway to the other room of their living quarters, she saw Juan sitting before the fireplace, smoking his pipe, his belly full. She placed the dishpan down on the table, wiped her hands on her apron, and went out the kitchen door again to take the path to the outhouse.

It was not yet dark, so she held the door of the outhouse open long enough to peer down through the round hole in an effort to see if there were any snakes or other demons lurking in the eerie darkness below the seat. She always had a fear that something would suddenly attack her while she was relieving herself. When she could see nothing threatening, she closed and latched the door and proceeded to perform her ritual. Finished, she cleaned herself with a cloth hanging there for that purpose and opened the door to find young Zeke Blanton leaning on one arm against the door frame.

"Good evenin', Miz Garcia," he said, a lecherous grin spread across his homely features.

Stunned speechless for a moment, Anna could only respond with, "You want to use the outhouse? I am finished."

Zeke laughed at the woman's frightened comment. "Nah," he drawled, "I ain't gotta use the outhouse. I just came to help you use it." He grabbed her by the arm when she tried to duck under it. "Hey, what's your hurry? I saw how you was lookin' at me this afternoon in the store."

Terrified at this point, Anna stumbled over her words. "Please . . . my husband . . . ," she pleaded desperately. "Your father, he said to leave me alone!"

"Come on, you know you want it. Hell, I'll still pay you, give you twice as much, twenty dollars. Whaddaya say to that? Me and you'll go round behind this outhouse and won't nobody know about it but us. No harm done. Whaddaya say?"

Trembling in his grasp, she pleaded, "Please, sir, let

me go. I am a married woman. I don't do things like that."

He shook his head as if addressing a naughty child. "You might as well make this easy, 'cause it's damn sure gonna happen." She opened her mouth to scream, but he clamped a rough hand tightly over it before she could make a sound. She fought him with everything she could manage, but was subdued by a blow to her head with the barrel of his pistol. When she fell limp in his arms, he dragged her around behind the shack.

She did not remember the first part of her ghastly experience, becoming aware only after he was on top of her. Horrified, she screamed, a loud piercing scream. He tried to stifle it, but could not in time. "Damn you!" he cursed, knowing everyone around was bound to have heard her. Though she struggled desperately, he fought her, intent upon completing his evil business. He was interrupted by the sound of someone running from the back of the trading post. "Damn you!" he spat at her again, and rolled off her.

Fearing what he knew was happening, Juan grabbed a shotgun and ran out the kitchen door when he heard Anna scream. He never had a chance. As soon as he charged around the outhouse, he was met with three slugs in his chest from the waiting gunman. Anna began to scream continuously until Zeke smashed her across the face with his gun barrel to silence her. It was only a matter of seconds before everyone rushed to the scene of the murder, brought by the screams and gunfire.

The last to arrive was Roy Blanton. With eyes blazing sparks of anger, he took in the scene, scanning from Anna Garcia, bleeding and crying on the ground by her dead husband, to Zeke standing by, stuffing his shirttail in, a look of indifference displayed upon his face. The look on Blackie Andrews' face was one of utter disbelief as he stared down at his late employee. Junior and Buster stood to one side, watching Blackie in case he felt the urge to retaliate for the murder of his store clerk. After taking it all in, Roy finally took action.

Walking up to Zeke, he struck him hard across the face with the back of his hand. "I told you," he growled. "We do business with these people!" His son staggered backward a few steps and automatically reached for his pistol. "You pull that damn gun," Roy roared, "and I'll send you to hell right now!"

Zeke quickly removed his hand from the gun handle. "I'm sorry, Pa. It wasn't my fault. She's been shinin' up to me all day, and when she cornered me back here, well, hell, I wasn't gonna turn it down." With his father's eyes boring into his, he hastened to build on his story. "And then that crazy Mexican come running at me with a shotgun. I didn't have no choice." He looked from his father to his brothers, searching for understanding.

His brothers, knowing him all too well, simply grinned in response. His father was still in the process of making up his mind. It was an unlikely story, but it made it a lot easier to deal with if what Zeke said was true. "You boys get the horses saddled and get ready to ride."

"Hell, Pa," Buster started, "it's most 'bout dark."

Roy jerked his head around sharply. "Do what I tell you," he barked. He waited for them to leave for the corral before addressing Blackie, who had held his tongue out of fear for his safety. "Looks like you lost your man," Roy said. "I'm sorry about that, but he ain't the first man shot because of a loose woman. Sorry it had to happen, though. I reckon it won't be hard to find another clerk for your store. I'll leave you a hundred dollars to help you out while you're lookin' for another'n."

Blackie continued looking down at the sobbing widow. He knew Anna well enough to doubt Zeke's version of the story, but he was helpless to do anything about it. Juan Garcia was a good man. He was going to be hard to replace. But Blackie was afraid to attempt retaliation for his death, or his wife's honor. Finally he spoke. "Mae!" he yelled, turning his head toward the saloon. "Mae!" he yelled again, calling his Choctaw wife. In only a few seconds, a lantern appeared at the corner of the saloon. "Come get Anna and take her back inside," Blackie said.

The two men stood watching in silence as Blackie's wife hurried over to Anna's side and helped the devastated woman to her feet. When they had disappeared inside the kitchen, Blackie simply said, "Juan was a good man."

"It's a sad thing when you lose a good man," Roy replied, confident now that Blackie harbored no thoughts of revenge. "Well, I expect me and my boys will be gettin' along." He turned and walked away, leaving Blackie to take care of the body.

In the corral on the other side of the saloon, the Blanton boys were saddling the horses and preparing to break camp. "Yes, sir," Buster said, japing his brother, "ol' Zeke sure has got a way with the women."

"Don't he, though?" Junior responded. "She just wouldn't leave him alone, would she? Followin' him around like a dog in heat."

Buster laughed, enjoying the banter. "You know, Zeke, she's a widow woman now. You and her might wanna get married, since she's so sweet on you."

"You go to hell," Zeke replied, "both of you."

Joking aside for a moment, Buster lamented, "I'd sure rather stay here tonight instead of movin' on."

"What difference does it make?" Junior asked. "Camp here or camp down the road a piece, it's all the same."

"This camp is closer to the whiskey," Buster said, then added with a grin, "And Zeke's gal."

Tired of his brothers' fun at his expense, Zeke said, "Shut your damn mouth or I'm gonna shut it for you."

"Uh-oh," Junior said, "you're gonna rile him in a minute."

Buster sneered his reply. "Shit, he's all talk, just like when he was tellin' Pa how that woman chased after him." It was enough to ignite his brother's fuse.

Zeke charged into Buster, flailing his fists left and right. Caught by surprise, Buster backed away, laughing while trying to ward off his brother's onslaught. When one of Zeke's wild punches landed on Buster's mouth, splitting his lip, it was not funny anymore. Wading into Zeke, winging punches as fast as he could throw them, he halted his brother's advance. At a standoff then, they stood toe to toe, swapping punches, much to Junior's entertainment. They kept at it, with no one gaining the advantage, until a cyclone of wrath in the form of Roy Blanton suddenly descended upon them. Raising welts with each blow of his quirt, Roy flogged his two sons relentlessly until they both cowered at his feet, trying to cover their heads to avoid the stinging leather that snapped and popped across their backs.

Ceasing only when his arm became tired, he cursed them and commanded, "Finish packin' up them horses like I told you!" He shifted his menacing glare to focus on Junior.

"I'm near 'bout ready, Pa," Junior quickly blurted, and backed away in case his father had in mind giving him a taste of the quirt.

As Zeke and Buster limped off like two whipped dogs, Roy turned to his eldest. "I've tried to raise you boys proper, and that means no fightin' brother agin brother. You shoulda stopped 'em, you bein' the oldest."

"Yes, sir, I know that now. I shoulda stopped 'em. Next time I will."

"There better not be no next time," Roy replied. "Now, dammit, I aim to get goin', and I mean right now."

"Yes, sir," Junior responded, then felt compelled to ask a question. "Why are we in such a hurry to get away from here? Why don't we just head out in the mornin'?"

Sufficiently calm to talk to his son now, Roy explained. "I don't know Blackie Andrews that good. He ain't said much about Zeke shootin' that Mexican, but he might just have a burr up his ass about it. Him and that Injun woman that lives with him, I don't trust 'em when my back's turned. And with us camped right up beside the corral, there's too many ways to sneak up on us. It'll be best to ride away from this place and camp where we can see who's comin' and goin'."

"Why don't we just shoot the lot of 'em?" Junior asked.

The thought had occurred to his father, but he had rejected the idea. He explained, "We may need Blackie sometime again. There's a lot of outlaws hidin' out in the nations, and a lot of 'em are Blackie's friends. You never know who might be lookin' to shoot you in the back."

Chapter 6

Coming from the store, where he had been trying to teach Anna to tend the counter until he found a man to take over Juan's job, Blackie Andrews shook his head in frustration. Juan's widow was a bright enough woman, but trading with trappers, hunters, and ordinary saddle tramps was not in her nature. It was out of the question for her to estimate the value of a pelt from any animal. Blackie would have to do that, at least until he could find someone who was as good at it as Juan had been. *Poor Juan*, he thought. He had put him in the ground two days ago. Just the thought of it was enough to make Blackie seethe with anger. *Roy Blanton*, he thought, *ought to keep closer reins on those half-crazy sons of his. Where the hell am I going to find somebody to replace my man?* Anna wanted to. She was trying hard to learn how to trade, but Blackie knew he couldn't depend on a woman. It was a man's job.

About to step inside the saloon, he caught movement in the corner of his eye, and stopped to peer off toward the creek. Two riders, they didn't look familiar at once. Staring hard at the visitors, he began to think that one of them looked familiar. As the riders drew closer, he realized who it was. It had been some time since he had seen him, but there was only one man he knew who rode so nonchalantly in the saddle. He turned to meet them, his feet spread wide, hands on hips, a smug grin on his face.

"By God, I thought you was dead," Blackie called out as soon as they were in hearing distance.

"Howdy, Blackie," Buck returned. "I thought one of your customers would have cut your throat by now."

Both riders were carefully checking for signs of anyone else around. Noticing, Blackie said, "There ain't nobody here. I reckon you're lookin' for somebody." He had an idea who that somebody might be. Thinking of Garcia again, he hoped to hell that Buck would catch Blanton.

Pulling the horses up in front of the saloon, Buck and Casey dismounted. "Blackie, say hello to Casey Dixon," Buck said. "Casey, meet a by-God miracle." When both men looked at him for explanation, he said, "It's a damn miracle he ain't in jail."

"How do, Casey," Blackie said, smiling wide enough to expose the chew of tobacco clamped in his back teeth. Turning again to Buck, he said, "Them's mighty harsh words to use on an honest merchant. I thought we was friends." He turned his head aside to spit, then stepped back to take a longer look at the old lawman. "I swear, Buck, there's a helluva lot of gray in them whiskers. You sure you ain't too old to be runnin' all over this territory? Ain't it about time they put you out to pasture?"

"Huh," Buck snorted with contempt for the remark. "I reckon there's a few more winters in this old hide yet." Never comfortable when someone joked about his age, even though it was said in good humor, he abruptly ended the japing and got down to business. "We're lookin' for Roy Blanton, and I'm thinkin' he musta come this way."

The comment turned Blackie's smile off, and he paused before responding. One rule he had always lived by ever since opening his business at the Crossing was to give no information to lawmen regarding the comings and goings of his customers. This time, however, it was different. Blanton had it coming. He turned his head aside and spat emphatically in the dust. "He was here, him and three of his boys."

A little surprised by Blackie's voluntary admittance, Buck asked, "How long ago?"

"He left here two nights ago."

"Did he say where he was headin'?"

"Nope, and I didn't ask him."

"Did you see which way he headed when he left here?" This came from Casey.

"Yeah, I watched him leave. He started out to the north, following Boggy Creek." His tone flat and serious, he looked the young marshal in the eye when he answered him.

As good as any at judging a man's attitude, Buck found it interesting that Blackie answered every question quickly and forthrightly, as if trying to help the deputies—a practice that was not common to men of his stripe. "I got a feelin' you ain't partial to ol' Roy," he commented. "Did the old son of a bitch cheat you outta some money or somethin'?"

"One of those crazy sons of his shot my store clerk," Blackie replied. "You remember Juan Garcia. He was a better man than all them Blantons put together."

"Sorry to hear about that," Buck said. "He was a good'un."

"Yeah, well, water under the bridge," Blackie said with a sigh. "You fellers gonna stay for a while? I'll have Mae fix you some supper."

Buck cocked an eye in Casey's direction. It was plain to see that the sound of a cooked meal appealed to him, but there was still an hour or two of daylight left. "Probably be easier to pick up their trail in the mornin'," Casey said, bringing an instant grin to Buck's face.

"Good idea, partner," Buck said. Turning quickly to face Blackie, he added, "But we'll be outta here early in the mornin'." Back to Casey again, he said, "It's bad for Blackie's business for a couple of lawmen to hang around too long."

"Buck's right," Blackie said with a chuckle. "It could ruin my business if word got out that I associated with the likes of you two. But I reckon it won't hurt for just one night. There ain't nobody hidin' out in the bushes waitin' for you to leave."

The evening passed quietly, somewhat of a rare occasion when Buck and whiskey were in close proximity, as Casey had discovered in their brief partnership. Blackie's Choctaw wife cooked supper for them, and they had a few drinks while Buck and Blackie talked about earlier times in the nations. They retired to their bedrolls at a reasonable hour with Buck still relatively sober. Casey lay by a campfire built on the ashes of one used by Roy Blanton and his sons two nights before. He was still awake when he heard Buck's snoring signaling his retreat. Casey smiled at the sound, thinking that he might not be able to get to sleep himself with the noise. Lying on his back, looking up at the pinpoints of starlight in a moonless sky, he thought about Charity McDonald. Why? He couldn't say. He turned over on his side, and in seconds, was fast asleep.

Mae fixed breakfast for them in the morning, rising to start her kitchen fire before they rolled out of their blankets. Blackie refused to take their money for the breakfast, saying they had paid for everything the night before. They thanked him for his hospitality and took their leave of the Crossing.

The tracks of four horses leading off to the northeast confirmed the direction Blackie had indicated when asked which way Blanton had headed. "I ain't never knowed Blackie to be so free with information about one of his customers," Buck commented as they paused momentarily to study the tracks. "He's wantin' us to catch up with Roy."

The trail held to the northeast, generally heading toward the Kiamichi Mountains, causing both lawmen to wonder about Blanton's destination. When they struck the Kiamichi River, the tracks followed the river, still in a direction leading northeast. "I can't figure where the hell they're goin'," Buck said when they stopped to rest the horses. "There ain't nothin' I know of out this way but a few scattered farms."

"Looks to me like they're bound to break off one way or the other," Casey said. "If they're thinkin' about hightailin' it back to Texas, like you figured, it don't make a lot of sense to keep goin' in this direction. They oughta be cuttin' away from the river pretty soon and headin' back south. If they're not thinkin' about striking out for Texas, then my guess is they're plannin' to hit McAlester. If that's what's on their minds, then they'll most likely follow the river farther up and head out to the northwest."

Buck nodded as he thought it over. "I reckon we'll just find out, won't we?"

They continued to ride along the river through the hill country, following tracks that told them Blanton had no idea he was being followed, until coming upon a campsite. Roy and his sons had stopped there on the bank of the river overnight. From there, the trail left the river and started out to the northwest, a direction that would lead to McAlester.

"Looks like we're comin' full circle," Buck commented as they departed the riverbank, "back to McAlester." He grunted, amused. "If we'da knowed Roy was gonna cut back to McAlester, we coulda waited right there for him, instead of chasin' all over these hills. For all the good we done in Atoka, it wouldn't made much difference."

"They hit the bank in Atoka," Casey thought aloud. "I reckon they're thinkin' on robbin' the new bank in McAlester."

"I expect so," Buck said. "What about the Choctaw Lighthorse? Are there any stationed there? Do you know?"

"There were," Casey replied, "but not anymore."

"Then that bank's settin' there, just plump and waitin'," Buck said.

"Well, look at this," Roy Blanton exclaimed as the four rode into town just as the dying rays of the sun settled down for the evening. "First time I rode through here, there wasn't much more'n J. J. McAlester's general store. Now look at it, stores and a bank." He paused to give his sons a grin. "And a hotel and saloon for folks like us that has a lotta money." He received an enthusiastic response from all three boys. "We'll get the horses took care of first," Roy went on. "Then we'll get ourselves a room in the hotel, and you boys can buy you some supper and wet your whistles if you want. I'm gonna take a little walk around before it gets hard dark, see what that bank looks like."

With the horses stabled and fed, the Blantons walked up the street to the hotel, each with saddlebags over one shoulder and a rifle in the opposite hand. Already feeling as if he owned the town, Roy threw the door open wide and strode up to the desk to confront Wilbur Morris, the clerk. "We're gonna need two rooms for the night," he announced.

Already staring wide-eyed the moment the door was flung open, Wilbur blinked a couple of times while he looked the four strangers over. Men who looked as rough as these did not as a rule rent rooms in the hotel. They usually slept with their horses. He responded courteously, as he had been trained. "Yes, sir, Mr. . . ." He waited for the name.

"Jordan," Roy replied without hesitation.

"Yes sir, Mr. Jordan, we have a couple of rooms near the kitchen I can let you and your party have for two dollars per person per night." He smiled at Roy patiently. "That would be in advance, of course."

A slow grin began to spread across Blanton's rough features, and he cast a cold eye on the face of the clerk. "Maybe you didn't hear me good, sonny. I want two rooms upstairs, the best you got." He pulled a roll of bills from his vest pocket and counted out fifty dollars. "I'll be wantin' some other things, too, so when this runs out, you let me know."

"Yes sir, Mr. Jordan," Wilbur replied, his attitude changed considerably. He spun the guest register around for Roy to sign.

Roy spun it back and said, "You just write John Jordan and company on it, and give me the keys." He turned to wink at his boys, who were all grinning broadly.

"Yes, sir," Wilbur said, and filled in the name. He turned and pulled two keys from a keyboard with no keys missing. "Rooms twenty and twenty-one," he said. "They're facing the front of the hotel, so you can see everything in the street from your window."

"I want me one of them bathtubs," Roy said. It was a luxury he had experienced only once before.

"I'll have someone bring one up to your room," Wilbur said.

"With plenty of hot water," Roy said. He glanced at Junior, whose expression was questioning his father's sanity. "I got a hankerin' for one of them tub baths. You want one?"

"I reckon not," Junior answered, and glanced at his

brothers, who both backed away before the invitation was extended to them.

Roy looked back at the clerk. "I think I'll take a little walk right now, soon as I put my stuff in the room. Have 'em heat me up some water in about an hour."

"What the hell's got into him?" Buster whispered in Junior's ear, lagging behind so as not to be overheard by his father.

"I don't know," Junior whispered back as they went up the stairs. "I think it's got somethin' to do with gettin' old. Folks do funny things when they start gettin' old. Their mind goes on 'em." It had really never occurred to Junior before that his pa would ever show signs of aging. As he thought about it now, he really had no idea how old Roy was. In fact, he wasn't real sure how old *he* was, but he was confident he was either twenty-seven or twenty-eight. It didn't matter which, but he had to surmise that his pa was getting close to sixty, if he hadn't already reached it. He decided he'd better keep an eye on the old man in case he started doing other crazy things.

The boys wasted no time before heading for the saloon after Roy doled out some additional pocket money. Their father went for his walk down the street, looking over the town. When he had time, he liked to get a feel for the whole section of town he was planning to work in—what types of stores and shops; which ones would likely offer a place for a man with a rifle to wait in ambush in the event he had to run for it after the holdup. He was especially interested to see if there was any evidence of a Choctaw police presence. So far, there was not.

Crossing over the street to the bank, he noticed the bars on the windows. As he walked by, he peered in. Although it was past closing time, there were still people inside, all employees, so he paused to take a look at the short counter and the door that led to another room. Through the doorway, he could see part of a massive safe. *One of them new ones,* he thought. *That might be a problem if we can't get somebody to open it.* He could count no more than two people. That part was good. Satisfied, he reversed his steps and walked back up the street, glancing again at the buildings on each side. *Another plum,* he thought, *ripe for the picking.*

Roy stopped by the saloon on his way back and found his sons well into a bottle of whiskey. They were seated at a table in the middle of the room. There were not many patrons in the saloon, probably because the evening was young. What few were drinking an early supper had situated themselves at the outermost tables, giving the three loud-talking young ruffians plenty of space. Roy couldn't help but chuckle.

"Set yourself down, Pa," Buster sang out in a lusty greeting when he saw Roy walk in. "We got an extra glass for ya. Better jump in while there's still somethin' in the bottle."

Roy pulled up a chair and joined his sons. He held his tongue while Buster poured him a drink. Then he asked, "Did you eat anythin' before you started fillin' your gut with this poison?"

Both Buster and Zeke looked to Junior to answer. "No, sir," he said. "We just thought we'd have a little drink before we et. We was fixin' to go back to the hotel, when you came in." He could tell by the look in his father's eye that Roy didn't believe him.

Feeling in a celebratory mood because of the apparent ease of robbing the bank in the morning, Roy did not take the opportunity to scold them. "Drink too much of that stuff on an empty stomach and you'll be sicker'n dogs all night and not worth a cuss to me tomorrow. We'll have one more and then we'll go get some supper. We've got work to do tomorrow."

"Uh-oh, Pa," Junior said, and nudged Roy's elbow.

They turned as one to look toward the door and the Indian policeman who had just walked in.

"Just hold still and don't do nothin' unless I shoot first," Roy warned. "Just go right on with your drinkin'."

While they watched, the policeman walked over to the bar and talked to the bartender, occasionally glancing around the room, but focusing mainly on the four strangers at the middle table. After a few minutes, he ambled over to the table. The barroom fell quiet as he stopped behind Zeke's chair. "Evenin'," he said. "You fellows are new in town."

"That's right," Roy answered. "Probably won't be around your little town more'n two or three days." He graced the lawman with a wide smile. "You the sheriff here?"

"No. There's no sheriff here now. I was sent down here from Tuskahoma." He said nothing more for a long second, looking around at the surly faces.

"You're kinda out of your territory down here, ain'tcha?" Roy replied.

"We go where we're needed. The bank in Atoka was robbed a few days ago by a man named Blanton, and he killed one of our policemen." He let that sink in before adding, "He had three sons with him." He paused again, then asked, "Are these men your sons?"

Roy threw back his head and laughed. "These three? Nah, they ain't my sons. I ain't got no sons . . . daughters either. My name's Jordan. These fellers and me work together. We just came down from Oklahoma City. We're in the coal minin' business—heard there was talk of new coal deposits around here." He looked over at his sons, all with grim faces. "How 'bout it, boys? We must look like a bunch of outlaws." Finally catching the cue from their father, they laughed.

Roy's act was good enough for the policeman to have doubts. "People around here are pretty nervous about any strangers right now," he explained. "We don't want the same thing to happen here that happened in Atoka. I have to question any strangers."

"Sure you do," Roy bellowed. "I don't blame you or the other folks around here."

"Enjoy your evening," the policeman said, and moved back to the bar. After a few more minutes, he left the saloon.

"Damn, Pa," Buster said, "you had me believin' you was a coal miner."

His brothers laughed, but Roy growled low. "Maybe he bought that story and maybe he didn't. But I hope the bastard shows up tomorrow. I'll make another payment on Billy's grave." He stood up. "Let's go get some food in us. Then I've got a little plan up my sleeve for this town." They filed out after him, oblivious to the hard stare from the bartender.

John Redwing stepped off the low stoop of the saloon and went directly across the dusty street to the dry goods store where Floyd Ramsey was just in the process of closing for the day. Recognizing the Choctaw policeman, Floyd put his broom aside and came to meet him. "I was gettin' ready to close up," he said. "Is there somethin' you need?"

"No, sir," Redwing replied. "I don't need to buy anything. Do you keep a weapon here in the store?"

Not sure why the question, Floyd said, "I got a rifle in the back room. Why?"

"You might wanna keep it handy tomorrow," Redwing replied solemnly. "I'm not sure, but I think the Blanton gang, the ones that held up the bank in Atoka, might be planning to rob the bank here tomorrow."

"Jesus . . . ," Floyd slowly exhaled. "How do you know that?"

"Like I said, I'm not sure, but there's four strangers

in town that don't look just right to me, and they fit the description of Roy Blanton and his three sons."

"Well, what do you expect me to do about it?" Floyd asked.

"Nothing, unless it actually happens. But if it does, and they do get away, I want everybody to be ready for them. I'll talk to all the other business owners, either tonight or when they open in the morning, and we can make it hot for anybody riding down the street."

"Damn, I hope you're wrong about those fellows," Floyd said. When he detected a look of doubt on the Indian's face, he quickly assured him. "I'll do my part if they come riding this way."

"Good," Redwing said, "if everybody helps, maybe we can stop the Blantons from robbing this town."

"Damn right," Floyd responded, now finding a spirit of bravado. "We need to teach all that wild scum that think there's no law in the nations that we'll stand up to them." Then another thought occurred to him. "Why don't you just go ahead and arrest them tonight if you're sure they're the Blanton gang?"

"I'm not sure. The older man says his name is Jordan and the others are not his sons. He may be looking to start a new business in McAlester like he says. I just think it pays to be cautious." He turned to leave. As a final word, he said, "If they are outlaws, and they come charging down this street, you'll know they got by me. It will be up to you and the others to stop them."

John Redwing duplicated his visit to the dry goods store and any other merchants he found still open that night. The others were told early the following morning. By midmorning, the whole town was alert to the possibility of an attempt to rob the bank. As a rule, the bank opened later in the morning, so when Fred Barnett arrived to unlock the door, he was surprised to find a stranger sitting inside the small entrance waiting for him. "I'm afraid you'll have to wait until the bank opens in about half an hour," Barnett said.

The stranger got to his feet, and showing his badge, identified himself as a member of the Choctaw Lighthorse. He then explained why he was there and told Barnett of his suspicions of the four strangers who had arrived in town the day before. As expected, Barnett was duly alarmed. He had heard about the robbery in Atoka, and the two men killed. "Mother of God," he exclaimed, "what are you going to do?"

The policeman explained that he couldn't do anything unless they made a move, even though they were dead ringers for the Blanton gang. "Maybe they ain't even plannin' on robbin' your bank, but I wouldn't bet on it."

"Hell," Barnett said, "I'll just close for the day. I've got a new safe and nobody knows the combination but me. I'll just close up and go home."

The policeman thought about that idea for a moment. "I don't know about that," he said. "Some of these outlaws are usin' dynamite on these safes, and gettin' 'em open, anyway. How much you got in that safe right now? Very much?"

"Hell yes," Barnett exclaimed, "over six thousand dollars, most of it railroad money."

"All right," the policeman continued. "Take all but a little bit of change for the tellers out of the safe and hide it somewhere. Then if the robbery does happen, don't put up no fuss. Tell 'em there ain't no money. Open the safe for 'em, so they can see for theirselves. When they see there ain't nothin' to steal, they'll just hightail it outta town. That way nobody gets shot, and no money gets stole."

"I don't like to have that much money hid someplace unprotected," Barnett said, obviously apprehensive.

"It won't be for that long. I'll guard it for you if you're afraid somebody might find it."

A timid man by nature, and already feeling his breakfast churning in his stomach, Fred Barnett was faced with his worst nightmare. As he stood fretting over the decision he had to make, his teller came in the front door. Surprised to find Barnett standing with a stranger near the door where the safe was located, he paused. Barnett quickly told him the man was a Choctaw policeman. Deciding then, Barnett said, "Stanley, go on and get ready to open." Turning back to the policeman, he asked, "Where are you gonna be if they come in?"

"I'll be right outside, waitin' for 'em."

Still not certain he was doing the right thing, Barnett asked, "What if they get mad when they find no money in the safe? They might kill me."

"They're after the money. They'd be more apt to shoot you if you wouldn't open the safe. Besides, like I said, I'll be outside waitin' for 'em."

"All right," Barnett said, too frightened to know what was best, "we'd better hurry. Wait here."

He went into the next room and frantically began dialing the combination on the massive safe. It took two attempts before he correctly spun the combination. As soon as it was open, he hurriedly stuffed bundles of currency into two large canvas bags. "I'll put them in the back room in the supply closet," he said when he came out, dragging the bags.

"Here, lemme give you a hand," the policeman said, taking one of the bags. They took them to the back of the building. Stopping just short of the back door, he said, "Unlock this door."

"Why?" Barnett asked.

"So I can go out that way."

Barnett hesitated. "We don't ever unlock that door," he said.

"We're gonna unlock it today," the policeman said as he pulled his pistol and aimed it at Barnett's stomach.

The banker's eyes opened wide, astonished by the lawman's sudden impatience. Still confused, he nevertheless did as he was told. As soon as the key turned in the lock, the door was pushed open from the outside, and Roy Blanton stormed into the room, followed by Zeke. Buster remained outside, holding the horses.

"Mornin'," Roy greeted the dumbfounded banker, a wicked grin beaming on the outlaw's face. Turning to Junior, he asked, "Is this all of it?"

"All but a little change locked up in that big ol' safe in there," Junior replied. "There's another feller up front."

"Go get him, Zeke," Roy ordered. Then he called through the open door, "Buster, throw some rope in here." Back to Junior again, he complimented his eldest on a job well done. "You done a helluva good job, son—saved us a lot of hassle."

"Thanks, Pa," Junior said, basking in his accomplishment. He took the badge from his vest and threw it on the floor. "Don't reckon I'll be needin' that anymore," he said, grinning at the speechless banker.

When Zeke herded a frightened teller to the back, he and Junior tied the two bankers up and left them in the back room. When they had loaded the two sacks of money on the horses, they departed the town, riding behind the buildings, since Roy had noticed that there seemed to be a rifle propped close to the front of every store on the street. Once clear of the town, they swung back to the southeast on the same trail that brought them to McAlester.

As for the armed camp that McAlester had been transformed into, the wary merchants braced for the shootout until long after noontime. When nothing had occurred that would suggest the bank had been robbed, some of the more curious went to the bank to question Fred Barnett. The CLOSED sign on the door stopped them for a while until Gabe Denton discovered John Redwing's body behind his shed, and came running to spread the news. It was after that when the rear door to the bank was discovered open, and the two bankers were freed.

After hearing Barnett's story regarding the morning's events, Floyd Ramsey could not help but comment, "Fred, I can't believe you'd be so damn stupid that you'd take that money out of the safe." Devastated, the duped banker could say nothing in defense of his actions. It was difficult to admit, even to himself, but he had been too frightened to think.

Chapter 7

Loping along at an easy pace, Casey decided it had been money well spent to let Horace Ramsey, back in Atoka, change the angle on the gray's rear hooves. It was a lot smoother ride without the annoying habit the horse had of breaking into a trot for no apparent reason. Still following a trail left by the Blantons through a land of tree-covered hills, he figured they could be no farther than a day's ride from McAlester. The sun was rapidly sinking behind them, and Buck had already suggested that they make camp at the first likely spot. With Buck behind him, leading the packhorse, he guided the gray toward a narrow notch in the hills ahead, then suddenly pulled back on the reins.

Waiting until Buck came up beside him, he asked, "You smell that?"

Buck took a couple of deep sniffs. "Yep, smoke."

Both men looked above them at the breeze rustling the leaves atop the trees. "Yonder way," Buck said, pointing toward a wooded hill on their left, "on the other side of that hill, either a campfire or a house."

"I don't reckon we could be lucky enough for it to

be the Blantons," Casey speculated, "but we can damn sure find out."

Buck considered the possibility for a few seconds before replying. "Could be," he allowed. "We need to be careful about this, though." He studied the hill between them and the source of the smoke a minute more. "Maybe it would be best if we split up and come in from both sides." Casey nodded his agreement. "One of us can ride up through that notch, and the other one go around and climb up on top, so we could have a rifle above the camp. The only trouble is it looks pretty steep on the back side of that hill. Might be a tough climb. Might have to leave your horse and climb up on foot."

"I can go climb up on top," Casey quickly volunteered.

"I was hopin' you'd say that," Buck said with his customary grin. "You're a helluva lot younger than me. It might take me half the night to climb that hill."

"Let's go then," Casey said, ready to act.

"Hold your horses. I know you're young and strong, but don't be in too much of a hurry to get up there. Give me time to get in position in case it's who we think it is."

"Right," Casey replied, and nudged the gray forward. Halfway around the hill, he found that Buck had been right in guessing the back side to be steep. It was almost a cliff, in fact. "Hell," he mumbled to the horse, "it might take *me* half the night." He tied the gray and the packhorse to a tree branch, drew his rifle, and began the rugged climb.

On the opposite side of the hill, Buck pushed his horse hard in a hurry to reach the campfire before Casey got in position on top. As he had assumed, the notch took him to the other side in short order. Within minutes, he saw the source of the smoke and four figures seated around it. There was little doubt in his

mind that it was Roy Blanton and his three boys. Instead of taking cover and waiting for Casey to get into
position on the hilltop above, he rode straight toward
the fire. In the gathering darkness, he walked his horse
slowly into the clearing, almost right on top of them,
before he called out, "Hello the camp. I'm comin' in."

Four guns cocked simultaneously as the four automatically rolled away from the fire. After a moment,
Roy Blanton cautioned in a low voice, "Hold your fire
till we can see who it is. Don't look like but one rider."
Then in a louder voice, he called back, "Come on,
then."

With his pistol trained on their visitor, he watched
the rider approach the fire and stop a few paces short.
"Damn," Roy exclaimed. "Buck Avery . . . Hello, Buck."

"Roy Blanton," Buck acknowledged, "and the boys."
He nodded. "I thought it was you; smelled your
smoke."

"What the hell are you doin' on my tail?" Roy
asked. "Wasn't that money I gave you three years ago
enough? Hell, it was enough to set you up for life."

"What the hell are you doin' raidin' back here in the
territory?" Buck came back. "We made a deal. I kept
my end of the bargain."

"Hell, that was three years ago. You oughta been retired by now, you old fart," Roy replied, eyeing the old
deputy with suspicion. "So you found us. What are
you aimin' to do about it, seein' as how it's your gun
agin our four?"

"Well, that's just it, dammit. If you'd gone to hell
back to Texas after you robbed that train at Durant
Station, it wouldn't have caused no problem. Now I
ain't by myself. I expect in about ten or fifteen minutes
there's gonna be somebody on that hill above us that
ain't lookin' for no payoff." His statement caused all
four Blantons to react, straining to look up toward the

hilltop. "I've tried to stall him for a week, hopin' you'd have sense enough to get the hell outta this territory, but he's like a damn bloodhound."

"Get ready to ride, boys," Roy ordered his sons. His gun still drawn, he turned back to Buck. "It pleasures me to know that you're lookin' out for us." He paused to give Buck a sinister smile while his sons scrambled to get their horses. "Or are you aimin' to try to stop us?"

"Well now, that don't sound very likely, does it? With you holdin' a gun on me already, and there being four of you. No, I don't cotton to the idea of havin' you get caught, either, and shootin' your mouth off about how much you paid me to let you jump over to Texas. I'm just tellin' you now, you'd best get outta here right now before my partner gets to the top of that hill."

Roy grinned. "Fair enough. All right, boys, let's get the hell outta here." He waited a moment while Junior led his horse up and handed him the reins. "You mean there ain't but one man up there?" he asked Buck.

"That's right, but he's as good as four, and he can pick you off one by one before you can say jackrabbit," Buck said. "Now, dammit, Roy, get goin'! Get on back across the Red."

Roy chuckled. "Just like old times, ain't it, Buck? Tell you what I'm gonna do." He reached into his saddlebag and pulled out a bundle of paper money. "Here's a little somethin' for the warnin'."

Buck hesitated for only a second before taking the money and quickly jamming it down in his saddlebag. "One more thing," he said. "You'd better nick me in the shoulder, so I have some kinda reason I let you get away."

"Why, I'd be happy to, Buck," Roy said, and drew his pistol again.

"Now, take good aim, dammit. Just crease me. I don't wanna go around with my arm in a sling for a week or two."

Without a word of warning, Roy shot, striking Buck high on the shoulder. Yelping with pain, Buck sank down to sit on the ground, holding the wounded shoulder. "Git, dammit!"

The four outlaws started out at a gallop through the notch Buck had used to approach the camp. They had gone only a few dozen yards when Zeke pulled even with his father. "There ain't but one man back there on that hill," he shouted. "I'm goin' back and get him." He wheeled his horse and charged back toward the camp.

"Zeke!" Roy yelled after his son, but Zeke was already out of range of his voice. He hesitated for a moment, trying to decide if he should go back, but Junior and Buster were already halfway through the notch. *Zeke'll have to take care of himself*, he thought, and kicked his horse into a gallop after Buster and Junior.

Still sitting on the ground, waiting for Casey to appear, Buck was astonished to see Zeke suddenly come charging back through the camp. "You damn fool!" he shouted. "What the hell are you doin'?" Zeke didn't have a chance to answer.

Casey had just gained the top of the steep hill when he heard the gunshot that nicked Buck. Threading his way recklessly through the oaks and boulders on the hilltop, he arrived at the crest in time to see Buck on the ground and Zeke pulling his horse to a stop. It was a hurried shot in the darkness below him, but he didn't have time to wait. He could see that Buck was already down, and was in danger of getting shot again. He caught Zeke in the shoulder, firing as soon as he came out of the saddle. Zeke went down immediately, sprawling several feet from Buck, his collarbone broken by the .44 slug.

Seeing his man down, Casey came crashing down through the brush, weaving in and out of the dark oaks. Below him, Zeke rolled over, grimacing with the pain. "The son of a bitch," he moaned as he struggled to his feet, then sank back on the ground.

"Zeke!" Buck yelled when it appeared the injured man was unable to get back on his horse. Zeke turned to face him, a look of surprise frozen on his face when he saw the .44 pointed at him. Three shots from the revolver finished Roy Blanton's son. Two more put Zeke's horse down. "Sorry," Buck murmured, "but I couldn't take a chance on you shootin' off your mouth." He sat back then and waited for Casey.

"Buck!" Casey shouted as he ran to his partner's side. "You all right?"

"I'm shot," Buck said. "I'm sorry, Casey. I guess I'm gettin' slow in my old age. I wasn't sure it was them, and I let 'em get the jump on me. I tried to stop 'em, but they got away."

"How bad are you hurt?" Casey asked, anxious to get after the other three.

"I don't know. It's painin' me somethin' awful. I don't know if I can ride or not."

Casey looked over at Zeke Blanton's corpse. "What about him?" He knew he had hit him with his shot.

Buck hesitated while he made a show of being in pain. "You knocked him down, all right, and I told him he was under arrest. He pulled his gun and didn't give me no choice but to shoot first. I reckon I was firin' a little wild. I didn't mean to shoot the horse."

The situation presented a definite dilemma for Casey. They had wasted an opportunity to apprehend the Blanton gang. He found it surprising that Buck had allowed them to get the jump on him when they had been sitting around a campfire. His first concern at the moment, however, was to make sure Buck was all right, even though the Blantons were getting away in the dark. As far as giving chase right away, his horse was on the far side of the hill. He didn't like the idea of leaving Buck without a horse or he would have taken his. He could have used the outlaw's horse. It was too bad the horse got in the way of a couple of stray shots.

"Well, I reckon they got away from us this time," Casey finally said as he laid his rifle aside and knelt down to determine the extent of the old deputy's wound. "We'll have to track 'em in the mornin'."

"That's what I get for bein' so all-fired in a hurry to catch 'em," Buck lamented. "I shoulda waited for you to get your rifle on 'em before I made a move. Dammit, I'm gettin' too old for this business."

"We'll get after 'em when it gets light," Casey said, trying to bolster Buck's spirits. "Can you get up?" When Buck said he thought he could, Casey said, "Come on, I'll help you. Let's get over by the fire so I can take a look at that wound."

After a brief examination of Buck's shoulder, Casey had to report, "Looks to me like your shirt's hurt more than your shoulder." He looked at his partner, doing his best to hide the astonishment he felt over Buck's apparent incapacitation after nothing more than a flesh wound. Maybe he was simply suffering from the shock of having been shot at close range. *Maybe he's right*, Casey thought. *Maybe he is getting too old for this*.

Guessing what Casey must be thinking, Buck pulled his bandana from his neck and stuffed it inside his shirt, covering his shoulder. "Hell, it ain't nothin' but a scratch," he said. "I was more winded from runnin' up that damn slope than anythin' else." Without help from Casey, he got to his feet. "I expect we'd best leave this place in case they get some ideas about comin' back to jump us later on tonight." He started kicking dirt over the fire. "We'll get on my horse and go get yours—make camp on the other side of this hill."

Casey gave the idea a moment's consideration before expressing his opinion. "Seems to me it would be better to go get the horses, then come back here—put the horses outta sight and wait here in case they *do* come back." He shook his head thoughtfully. "I mean, if he gives a damn about his son, he might come back to get him." He paused to look at Buck. "Don't that make sense to you?"

Buck didn't answer right away. After a moment, his familiar slow smile appeared and he said, "Well, I guess it does at that."

After fetching Casey's gray and the packhorse, they returned to Blanton's campsite. Casey led all three horses back in the trees where they wouldn't be seen by anyone approaching the camp. He and Buck split up then to take positions on two sides of the clearing. With some more of Casey's jerky for supper, they lay in wait, watching for visitors.

Through the long night hours, Buck's mind was laden with guilty thoughts of a decision he had made more than three years before, and the dread that his chickens had come home to roost. Why, he wondered, did he think that a thief and murderer like Roy Blanton could be taken for his word. *Times were hard,* Buck told himself, *I'd been too many years as a deputy marshal, and I didn't have a pot to piss in, or a window to throw it out of. Folks would say that ain't enough reason to turn your back on your oath. But them folks ain't ever had to face the talking end of a rifle for pennies a day.*

He shifted his position to ease the gentle throbbing he felt in his shoulder, hoping as he scanned the clearing where the fire had been, that Roy would not return for Zeke's body. He would not be as worried if he could be sure they could shoot all three of them down.

But the odds were too long that one or all of the Blantons might be captured, and Casey would take them prisoner if at all possible. Buck couldn't afford to take that chance. *Damn the luck!* he swore to himself.

As he lay there in the dark, he could not prevent his mind from wandering back to that day near the Little River. He had dogged Roy Blanton and his four sons for two weeks, finally able to strike their trail a few miles east of Idabel. He had been certain that Roy had a favorite hideout in that part of the territory somewhere north of the Red River and the Texas border, but he had never had any success in finding it. This time, Roy and his boys led him right to it. Around ten miles from Broken Bow, not far from where the Little River joined the Mountain Fork River, Roy had built a cabin back up in the hills. It was his retreat where he rested up between the raids he and his sons conducted on banks, railroads, ranchers, and any other victims in their disregard for the law.

Buck closed his eyes for a second, wincing with the thought of that day. Just like the present night, he had sneaked up on them while they were all sitting around a fire, roasting a beef they had stolen that afternoon. Before they knew he was there, he caught them with no chance to react. *The Blanton gang!* He had them cold, his Winchester daring any one of them to make a move. The boys were younger then. Billy, the youngest, was no more than fourteen or fifteen. Buck remembered Roy's eyes blazing with anger to have been caught helpless like that. "You aimin' to take us all back to Fort Smith?" he had asked. When Buck told him that was the general idea, Roy said, "Fort Smith's a long ride from here, and you got five of us to watch. That ain't gonna be easy for one man to go without sleep, watchin' to see that nobody gets loose."

He wasn't telling Buck anything the deputy had not already been considering. If only to make his job a bit easier, he had wished one of them had tried to go for a gun, so he could have reduced his number of prisoners by one or more.

"There's a way all of us can come out ahead," Roy had continued. "We was fixin' to slip over the Red in the mornin', and get on back to Texas, get outta Oklahoma for good. You and the Injun police have been makin' it kinda hot for us here in the nations. I've got money from three bank jobs and one mail car holdup hid near here; a little more than fifteen thousand dollars. It's worth my freedom to turn that money over to you, and you can do whatever the hell you want with it. Just let me and my boys slip over the Red, and you won't see us in Injun Territory no more."

Looking back now, Buck realized that he should have never hesitated, but he did, and Roy read the hesitation in his eyes. That much money would insure his old age, which was not that far in coming.

"What are you gonna get for takin' us in?" Roy insisted. "The glory of catchin' Roy Blanton? How much does that pay? How much is that gonna help you when they put you out to pasture? Not a damn cent is how much. I'm givin' you a chance to look out for yourself. The damn U.S. Marshal's office sure as hell ain't gonna take care of you when you get too old to do the job. You're ridin' on one side of the law, and I'm ridin' on the other, but it all comes out the same. Ain't nobody gonna look out for you, but you. What's it gonna be? Glory or money?"

"I could just take you in and take the damn money, too," Buck had said.

Blanton had smiled at that. "Well, now, that's a thought, ain't it? There's too many things that'll keep that from happenin', though. Number one, you don't know where the money's hid. Number two, you still gotta worry about keepin' an eye on all of us all the way to Fort Smith. Number three, if you try to shoot us, you can't kill us all before one of us will get you. Nobody wins but whoever's left holdin' the money. My way, everybody wins."

"How do I know you won't shoot me if I let you go?" Buck remembered asking. It had been enough to let Roy know he had caused a crack in Buck's moral wall.

"Wouldn't make no sense to shoot you," Blanton replied. "Killin' a U.S. marshal would just stir up too much fuss. Instead of havin' one of you lawmen after us, I'd have the whole damn bunch of you. This is just a business deal between me and you. Let us go, and you'll be settin' pretty with enough money to tide you over, and we'll clear outta Oklahoma Territory. No sense in anybody gettin' killed or goin' to jail over this."

"All right," Buck had finally said. Even now, he could still remember the dry feeling in his mouth. It was the first and only time he had betrayed his badge. The final moments of that fateful day were now a jumble in his mind. But he remembered that there was no trust on the part of either party until the deal was completed. Roy and three of his sons had packed up and gone to retrieve the money from its hiding spot while Buck held Billy Blanton as hostage until they returned with his share. As promised, Roy dropped a sack with fifteen thousand dollars at Buck's feet. Then with guns drawn by everyone, the Blantons withdrew cautiously until safely able to wheel their horses and depart, heading for the Red River.

It had taken a while, but Buck came to justify the event in his mind to the point where he considered he had it coming for all the years of service he had given to the U.S. Marshal's office. Blanton had kept his end of the bargain for three years, but now he was back, bringing Buck's troubles with him.

Thirty-five yards away, lying close beside the trunk

of a large oak tree, Casey Dixon watched the clearing where Zeke's body lay. Like Buck, Casey was sorting through some serious thoughts of his own. He was still puzzled over Buck getting himself shot, and the old deputy's reaction to a minor wound. He knew for a fact that Buck had been shot several times before, enough to regard the scratch he picked up tonight as nothing at all. The apparent lack of urgency on Buck's part was another thing that Casey couldn't understand. Maybe he was partially to blame. He should have taken Buck's horse and chased after Blanton while he could see to follow them. *Things just happen the way they do*, he finally told himself. *Buck will be all right in the morning*. The only thing that didn't add up was the fact that Zeke Blanton's gun was still in his holster.

When first light came, Buck did indeed seem to be back to his usual easygoing self. Once it was light enough, he signaled Casey to crawl up a little closer to the clearing. Nodding, Casey moved away from the tree and picked out a better spot behind a rock a few paces ahead. Blanton might not show, but the odds were good that he would.

Chapter 8

"Yonder, Pa!" Buster Blanton exclaimed, pointing to the corpse lying a few yards from the ashes of the fire. "It's Zeke!"

"Keep your voice down," Roy commanded. "They'll hear you." It was his son's body, all right, and the sight of it twisted his guts inside him till he wanted to explode. But his sense of survival told him to hold back until he was sure of the situation.

"There ain't nobody here," Buster insisted. "They're gone."

"They're here," Roy said. "Buck Avery knows I'll come back to get my boy. I'll get Zeke, and by God, I'll have my revenge."

"You want me to go get him, Pa?" Junior asked.

"No, dammit, you stay put. You wanna get yourself shot? They're still here, I told you. Now, stay down till I tell you to move."

All remained quiet in the clearing as the first rays of light probed the narrow gulch between the two steep, tree-covered hills. Shortly after, the misty gray of the predawn minutes began to fade and colors began their gradual return to the trees and sky. The little valley was quiet as a tomb as desperate men waited. Abruptly the sun peeked over the eastern side of the gulch and seemed to focus on the corpse near the middle of the clearing. Nothing moved, with the exception of one lonely buzzard circling high above the hills. There was going to be a battle; the hills, the trees, and the boulders knew it. And somehow both sides knew the enemy was present, even though there had been no visual evidence to confirm it. Suddenly a sharp sound shattered the silence like the crack of a rifle.

Roy Blanton jerked his head around to cast an angry glance at Buster who had absentmindedly cocked his rifle. "Damn you!" he hissed. "You've given us away!" He immediately backed away from the boulder and signaled his two sons to do the same. "We've got to find a better place. They know we're here now."

"I'm sorry, Pa, I . . . ," Buster started to apologize.

"Shut up!" Roy interrupted. "Follow me." He crouched low, running below the crown of the clearing, working his way back to another cluster of rocks closer to the spot where they had left the horses.

On the far side of the clearing, Casey signaled Buck and pointed in the general vicinity from which the metallic sound had come. Buck nodded and shifted over to the other side of the tree giving him cover. Casey signaled again, trying to tell Buck that he was going to drop back farther in the trees and circle around behind. Buck nodded his understanding.

Moving rapidly in an effort to get around behind Blanton, Casey darted from tree to tree, almost out of sight of the clearing. Pausing to catch his breath and scout the forest before him, he started to move again, when a rustling of leaves about forty yards away caused him to freeze. In a few moments, a solitary figure appeared, pushing his way through a thick stand of laurel. It was one of the sons, no doubt intent upon doing the same as Casey, trying to locate the two law-men.

Casey dropped slowly to one knee, holding close to the tree trunk. Free of the laurels, the outlaw started toward a large boulder some twenty yards in front of him. "Hold it right there!" Casey ordered. "You're under arrest!"

Startled, Buster stopped dead still for a few seconds, looking around him frantically, trying to locate the source of the command. "Drop your gun," Casey called out. "You're under arrest." Whirling toward the sound, Buster opened fire, shooting wildly in Casey's general direction with no sighting of his target. Casey remained patient, firing only when Buster had emptied his gun and decided to run. Aiming low, Casey put a bullet in Buster's leg, causing the outlaw to trip and fall.

Surprised and confused by the sudden shots from Buster's gun, Roy looked around him to find him missing. "Buster?" he questioned, staring wide-eyed at Junior.

"He said he was gonna circle around," Junior replied.

"I told him ...," Roy started angrily, then said, "Come on!" He left the cover of the boulder and started making his way as fast as he could through the trees while still trying to exercise caution.

Separated from the notorious outlaw and his eldest son by only fifty yards of thick forest, Casey had sprung to his feet as soon as he saw Buster go down with a bullet in his leg. Wasting no time, he ran after the wounded outlaw and caught him still on his hands and knees. He planted a solid boot in Buster's ribs, knocking him over on his back before the unfortunate man could recover. Buster managed to raise his pistol and pull the trigger, forgetting that he had emptied it seconds before. With Casey's .44 stuck in his face, he gave up.

Now, from the other side of the clearing, Casey heard Buck's rifle, telling him that his partner must have caught sight of the other two Blantons. "Get up," he told Buster.

"I can't, you son of a bitch," Buster said. "You shot me in the leg."

"Which one are you?" Casey asked. When the young outlaw spat defiantly that he was Buster, Casey said, "You ain't hurt that bad. Get on your damn feet or I'm gonna shoot you in the other leg."

Buster reluctantly struggled to his feet. With his gun cocked and still aimed at his prisoner's head, Casey ordered him to drop his gun belt. After his holster dropped to the ground, Casey ordered him to unbuckle the belt holding up his trousers. Then he backed his prisoner up to a small tree, and with his belt, tied Buster's hands behind his back and around the trunk. "You just make yourself comfortable," he said. "I'll be back to get you in a minute." He then plunged into the laurel thicket Buster had just come from.

As Casey stepped carefully through the brush underneath the trees, his cautious eyes scanned the forest before him. Up ahead, he could hear the constant exchange of rifle fire as Buck and the other two Blantons engaged in a gun battle. Some ten or fifteen yards short of the clearing, he stopped when he saw the branches of a large pine move just as a rifle fired. *There they are*, he thought. A moment later, he saw bark fly from the tree as Buck sought a lucky shot. The trunk of the pine stood between him and the outlaws, giving him no clear shot. With his rifle aimed at the tree, he waited, hoping to get a target.

After a fifteen-minute standoff with Buck peppering the pine with rifle shot, there seemed to be no advantage for either side. Thinking it his duty, Casey made an effort to stop the shooting. Calling out to

Blanton, he said, "Throw down your guns, Blanton. No need for another one of your sons to get killed. We've already got Buster."

Roy looked around frantically, searching for Buster, hoping it was a bluff. "They got him, Pa," Junior wailed, even though he had not seen Buster get hit. With rifle slugs from Buck's Winchester whistling through the branches, sending bark flying, he knew that there had been no return fire from his brother.

In answer to the call to throw down his weapons, Roy rose up slightly to yell back his response. "You can go to hell! You ain't got no upper hand in this fight." He leveled his rifle and fired at Buck. In the process he gave Casey a target.

Still waiting patiently for a clear shot, Casey took it, although it wasn't much of a target. No more than Roy's left forearm was exposed when he aimed his rifle. Knowing he wasn't likely to get any more of a target, Casey squeezed off one shot that struck Roy's forearm and shattered the wrist bone. Roy screamed in pain and dropped the rifle.

Horrified, Junior froze for a moment. He had never seen his father shot before, had never heard a scream of pain from the old man. In fact, he had never ever considered the possibility that his pa *could* be hurt. "Come on out, Blanton," he heard Casey shout. "It's over." He stared with wide-open eyes at his father, bent over now, holding his shattered wrist, writhing in pain with blood already spattered in splotches of red on the ground. At first, he waited for Roy to tell him what to do, but his father was in too much pain at that moment. Then it hit him that he, as the eldest son, had the responsibility of saving his father. Once he was sure, he was swift to act. Pulling Roy to his feet, Junior lifted the old man to his shoulder and retreated toward the horses. Hefting him into the saddle, he asked breathlessly, "Can you ride, Pa?"

"I can ride," Roy replied painfully, his anger and lust for revenge subservient now to the need to survive. "You'd best get me to Doc Garvey."

Several minutes passed before they knew that Roy and Junior had retreated. When Casey realized they had withdrawn, he ran toward the big pine where he had last seen them, calling to Buck as he ran, "Buck! They're runnin' for it!"

Buck emerged from the rocks on the other side of the clearing and yelled, "What was the shootin' back down in the trees?" He had heard the short exchange of gunfire between Casey and Buster.

"Buster!" Casey called back as he sprinted across the clearing after Roy. "He's tied to a tree back there!"

About to run after Casey, Buck stopped when he heard the reply, his mind racing. "I'll pick him up," he shouted, and ran immediately toward the group of trees Casey had just vacated. With no time to argue the point, Casey plunged ahead, fighting vines and low-growing brush in an effort to catch up to the Blantons before they could get to their horses. He was too late. The two outlaws were racing down through the notch by the time he reached the spot where their horses had been tied. In frustration, he fired a parting shot after them, but the range was already too great.

Feeling helpless at that point, he stood staring at the trees long after they had disappeared. With his horse tied in the trees beyond the far side of the clearing, there was little chance of overtaking Blanton. He and Buck would have to go back to tracking. At least they were thinning out Blanton's gang and had one prisoner to bring to justice. His thoughts were distracted at that point by the sound of a single gunshot behind him. Thinking Buck might be in trouble, he quickly retraced his steps.

It had taken Buck a few minutes to find Buster tied to a tree in a small thicket of pines. "Well, Buster,"

Buck said, shaking his head as if scolding a child, "what a fine mess you got yourself into. Why the hell didn't you keep runnin' like I told you to?"

"Get me loose," Buster demanded, "and hurry up."

"Hell, boy, I can't do that. You shouldn'ta got yourself caught."

"Dammit," Buster swore, "you've been paid to do it."

Buck's face took on a serious expression. "Yep, I reckon that was the biggest mistake I ever made." His thoughts seemed to turn inward for a few seconds while he contemplated his dilemma. "Well, I reckon there ain't nothin' I can do about that now, so I'm gonna set you free."

"Well, hurry up, dammit." Buster's scowl was followed by a look of shocked surprise when Buck drew his pistol and, without hesitation, put a bullet into his brain.

"You're free," Buck commented dryly. "Say howdy to ol' Satan. Tell him I'll be along directly." Buster slumped to the ground, his body sagging to one side, held by his hands bound to the tree. Buck watched him for a moment to make sure he was dead. "I'm in too deep to take a chance," he murmured to the corpse. After taking a quick look around him to make sure Casey was not approaching, he hurried to untie Buster's belt and dragged him a few feet away from the tree. Then he picked up the dead man's revolver and laid it on the ground beside his hand. It was only moments later when he heard Casey calling him.

"I'm back here," Buck called out, and waited until Casey found him.

"What the hell . . . ," Casey started when he saw the body.

"Looks like he got that belt undone somehow," Buck said. "He jumped me when I came through that thicket there. I didn't have no time to think about it.

There wasn't no choice." Eager to divert the conversation, he asked, "What about Roy and Junior?"

"They got away, dammit," Casey replied. He reached down and picked up Buster's pistol, opened the cylinder, and spun it. "Empty," he said. "You'da thought he mighta remembered his gun was empty." He turned and smiled at Buck. "I guess Lady Luck was shinin' on you today."

"Well, you know Buster wasn't never very bright."

"Reckon not," Casey replied. "I guess we'd best get on their trail. We're not showing much in the way of takin' anybody in for trial, are we?" That was as much as he said on the matter, but it registered in his thoughts that it was strange that Buck had managed to hit Buster in the back of his head after he'd been jumped.

"No," Buck replied to his comment, "but we are gettin' the job done of stoppin' the Blanton gang. Three down and two to go, and you think you wounded Roy?"

"I only got one shot—hit him in the arm, couldn't have been very serious," Casey replied. Then, thinking they had wasted enough time talking, he said, "I'll get the horses."

"We're gonna have to do somethin' with these bodies," Buck said, causing Casey to pause. "And we need to round up their horses."

Inclined to worry about those details later, Casey said, "To hell with the bodies. We can catch their horses, but, hell, let the buzzards take care of the bodies." He was puzzled by Buck's lack of a sense of urgency, with Roy and Junior gaining ground on them by the minute. "We sure as hell can't take 'em back to McAlester. And we've got the old man and his son on the run. The old man is wounded. They're gonna be tryin' to get someplace to take care of him."

"We'll track 'em," Buck assured him, "but we need

to at least put these two in the ground. Accordin'
to regulations, that's what we're supposed to do—
accordin' to the book."

Casey shook his head, amazed. "When did you
start goin' by the book?" He turned and began trotting
toward the other side of the clearing. "I'll get the
horses. We can dump the bodies between those rocks
over there and pile some more on top of 'em. We're
wastin' time."

Working as quickly as he could, Casey caught the
two outlaws' horses while Buck disposed of the bodies,
stripped of their weapons and anything else of value,
in the rocks at the side of the clearing. Casey loaded the
personal items on their horses, wishing he and Buck
didn't have to be burdened with them, but knowing
they couldn't leave them to wander. By the time they
were ready to ride, they had lost almost an hour.

Clear of the notch between the two hills, they
stopped to examine the trail that had led them from
McAlester the day before. "This don't make no sense,"
Buck complained as he looked closely at the fresh
tracks. "They're headin' back toward McAlester."

Casey dismounted to see for himself. After searching the trail closely, he had to agree with Buck. Not
satisfied, he searched through the trees lining the trail,
in case they tried to cover their tracks by doubling
back toward the east. In a short time, he gave it up.
"Looks like that's the way they're headed," he agreed.
In the saddle again, they started back to McAlester.

The tracks were fresh, and there had been no attempt to hide them as the two outlaws galloped west.
Making good time, Casey and Buck were able to push
the horses hard for a few miles, then changed over to
the captured horses to give theirs a rest. They hoped to
make up some of the distance this way. Coming to a
wide creek, they splashed across to discover no tracks
on the other side. Both riders pulled up short.

"They've been runnin' flat out up to here," Buck said, "but ol' Roy musta took over right here. 'Cause now, they're thinkin' 'bout hidin' their trail. I knew all the time they weren't headin' back to McAlester."

"I'll go this way. You go that way," Casey said, and started walking the horses along the creek bank, looking for the place where Roy and Junior came out of the water. After scouting the west bank for almost a half mile with no sign, Casey crossed back over to the east side and searched along that bank until returning to the spot from which he had started. He glanced up to see Buck returning on the same side of the creek.

"Nothin'," Buck answered before Casey asked the question.

"Me neither," Casey replied. "I followed the creek till I got to a little waterfall. They woulda had to come out of the water to get around it."

"Dammit, they had to come out somewhere," Buck insisted. "They sure as hell didn't ride the creek all the way. Roy's pretty damn slick, but he can't fly."

A thought struck Casey then. He dismounted to examine the trail they had followed until reaching the creek. After a moment, he said, "They rode into the creek and turned around, and came out the same way they rode in." Pointing out tracks going the opposite way, he said, "We were riding so fast, we didn't even notice the tracks coming outta the creek. And they were smart enough to go into the water to turn around, so we wouldn't likely notice."

"Well, it worked, didn't it?" Buck replied. "Roy Blanton is a pretty sly ol' fox. That's the reason he ain't been caught all these years."

They turned around and started backtracking, moving at a more careful pace, watching for the point where the Blantons left the trail. In about a quarter of a mile, where the trail led through a series of small hills, covered with pines and oaks, the reversed tracks ended. Looking up at the thick-forested hillsides, Casey said, "They picked a good place to leave the trail."

It took a little time, but Casey finally found a hoofprint pointing up the slope on the south side of the trail. Farther up, he found another and a footprint, telling him that one or both of the men had led the horses up the hill. By now, it was getting along in the afternoon and they had already spent considerable time trying to track the two fugitives. Casey had a nagging feeling that they were rapidly losing ground. There was no answer to the problem other than pushing as hard as they could, and hoping the outlaws would have to stop soon to tend to Roy's wounds or rest the horses.

The trail was picked up again south of the hills and seemed to be headed toward a small range of mountains the local folk called the Jack Fork Mountains. "It's a half day's ride from here to the Jack Forks," Buck said, "and we ain't got a half day's daylight left. We got maybe two or three hours before we'd best take the first water hole we can find and make camp. We've got a lot of stock to take care of."

Casey couldn't argue the point, so they stayed with it until coming to a small stream just before dark. They made camp beside the stream, and pulled the saddles off all four horses, since they had been ridden hard all day. The next morning, they continued on, following a trail that led them up into the mountains and down the other side. After another day, the trail ended again at the banks of the Kiamichi River.

"We can cross over tonight or cross over in the mornin'," Buck commented. "Whatever suits you best—don't make no difference to me. I got a feelin' we ain't gonna find no tracks on the other bank, anyway."

Although he didn't express it, Casey was of the same opinion. The slow-moving river was the next logical place for Roy to try to disguise his trail again.

Casey looked around him, then gazed at the other side, already dim in the evening light. "This looks about as good as any," he said. "If we wait till mornin', we'll be able to see better."

"Suits the hell outta me," Buck announced. "I ain't thinkin' about much but a cup of hot coffee right now." Without waiting for more discussion on the subject, he dismounted and led his horse and the packhorse over to a small glade near the water's edge. Casey followed, leading the two saddled horses. Rummaging through the packs, Buck said, "We're runnin' low on supplies. There ain't more'n a couple handfuls of coffee beans left, and we're gonna have to hunt somethin' to eat when this bacon is gone, and that ain't gonna be long. I can kill somethin' to take the place of bacon, but there ain't nothin' that'll take the place of coffee."

Casey listened to Buck talk while he tended to the horses and Buck went about building a fire. He figured that was one thing that made them a good partnership; Buck liked to talk, and he didn't.

"We ain't gonna find no tracks on the other side of the river in the mornin'," Buck went on, "because it looks like Roy's hightailin' it back to Texas. Our job is gonna be to find where he came outta the water downstream." Casey shrugged without comment. It made sense.

Just as they expected, the following morning there were no exit tracks on the other side of the river. Once again, the search was begun, scouting the riverbanks on both sides, this time to no avail. There was no sign that the two fugitives ever came out of the river. They rode down the river until it made no sense to go farther. Although it didn't figure to go along with a desperate run for Texas, they had no other option but to scout the banks upstream from the point where the tracks ended. The result at the end of the day was the same. Roy and his son had disappeared, gone up in smoke, as if they had suddenly taken wing. It was irritating to the point of frustration for Casey. Buck seemed downright philosophical about it, saying, "Sometimes the fox gets the rabbit. Sometimes the rabbit gets away."

His complacency didn't help Casey's mood. "We'll just have to try it again tomorrow," he decided. "We missed it somewhere. There were several places where, if a man was real careful, he might be able to lead his horse outta the river and not leave any tracks. We've just got to look closer."

"Yep," Buck said, his tone patronizing, "we'll look closer tomorrow."

As if verifying their failure to apprehend the two remaining members of the Blanton gang, they were awakened the next morning by a light rain. When the rain had not stopped by noon, they feared that any tracks there had been might be washed away. It was not until twilight that Casey agreed to give up the search, admitting that they had been beaten. He wasn't comfortable with the idea, even though Buck tried to put it in the perspective that nobody came out on top every time. "There ain't no doubt in my mind that Roy Blanton is headed back to Texas just as fast as he can run. We didn't catch him, but we damn sure hurt him bad and run him outta our territory. That's as good as an arrest."

"The hell it is," Casey grumbled. There was really nothing more they could do at this point, so they figured they might as well go on back to Fort Smith and report what he considered to be their failure. But he knew that, as far as he was concerned, the job wasn't finished.

Chapter 9

"I swear," Junior Blanton marveled, "I never saw Pa drink that much whiskey before."

"He's about ready to go," Doc Garvey said. "It takes a lot more when a man knows what's comin'." He filled the tin cup about half full again and helped Roy hold it up to his mouth. Roy dutifully sipped the burning liquid as fast as he could, his head already rolling from side to side so much that Junior had to help hold it straight. Dull, lifeless eyes stared drunkenly from under eyelids at half mast as the old man took shot after shot with a good portion of the whiskey running down his chin. "You keep your eye on him," Roy slurred drunkenly to Junior. Hearing the warning, Garvey grinned at Junior.

Pretty soon, Roy began to make a gurgling sound and then abruptly he passed out. "He's ready," Doc said. "Let's make this quick. I don't know how long he'll be out. Hold that arm still. Don't let it move."

With Junior holding his father's arm flat against the table, Doc picked up his ax and poured the rest of the cup of whiskey over the blade. Doc Garvey was not a doctor. He learned what he knew while an orderly in a

Confederate army hospital. He had helped on many amputations of arms and legs while in the army, but this was his first since he had become the next-best thing to a physician for outlaws and highwaymen. Most of his patients came to him with gunshot wounds or knife slashes. The amputations he had been a part of in the military were performed with saws, but in this case, he decided an ax would get the job done quicker. His concern was to stop the massive bleeding that would occur when the hand came off, and he figured with the job done with one clean blow, he'd have more time to control the bleeding. Roy had already lost a great deal of blood before Junior brought him there.

"You ready?" Doc asked. Junior nodded and clamped down tight. Doc spat in his hand and rubbed his palms together, then picked up the ax again. Fascinated, Junior watched wide-eyed as Doc raised the ax above his head, let it hover for a brief moment, then struck downward in one swift motion. The hand, just above the wrist, flew up like a wood chip and fell to the floor. Roy sat straight up and screamed, then fainted dead away.

"Don't let go of that arm!" Doc exclaimed as blood spewed out of the stump of Roy's arm. He stuffed a cloth against it to try to slow down the bleeding. "Hold that on there," he said to Junior. "I've got to tie off them arteries." Working at a frantic pace, he pushed a loop of twine over the flowing vessels and pulled it tight. He then grabbed another rag and pulled a poker, which had been heated to a cherry red, from the coals in the fireplace, and working as fast as he could, closed up the veins and arteries. For a long moment, it appeared that he was not going to success-fully stop the bleeding, but finally he released a sigh of relief when the major stream slowed and then stopped. He stepped back and wiped the sweat from his face. "Damn, it was *Katie bar the door* there for a minute," he allowed, pleased with his work. "Now I'll put on the pad. Then we'll bandage it up."

Taking a circle of pork with the skin still on, he covered the bloody stump, giving a continuous commentary as he worked. "Pork's best for this. It'll soften that stump and protect the bone." He took needle and gut twine and stitched the pad to Roy's arm. "A patch of meat right below the hog's head is the best for this. You're lucky you got here right after I killed a hog. Your pa is gonna be sick as a dog when he wakes up again, and he's gonna hurt like hell for a while, but it'll heal." He glanced up at Junior, who was looking a little pale. "Why don't you go on outside and get some fresh air while I bandage him up?" Grateful for the chance, Junior went out the door and lost the contents of his stomach behind the house.

Roy Blanton woke up to a throbbing hell. The pain in his left arm seemed unbearable as each beat of his pulse sent a burning spear of flame down his arm to singe his hand, a hand that was no longer there. He tried to sit up, but, weakened by the severe loss of blood, could not. Hearing his agonized moans, Doc and Junior got up from the table in the kitchen and went in to see the patient.

"Damn you, Garvey," Roy moaned feebly, "you've damn near kilt me."

Doc shrugged, unconcerned. "I told you it was gonna be rough. It's gonna pain you like hell for a spell, but it'll heal. I've seen a lot of boys recover all right; saw it all the time durin' the war. You just need to give it a little time." He glanced at Junior as if to explain to him. "That there hand had to come off. Gangrene was already settin' in. If I hadn'ta took it off, it woulda spread all the way up his arm, and you'da had to take it off at the shoulder—and that's a helluva lot riskier. He'da died for sure."

Grimacing with the pain, Roy demanded, "Where's my hand?"

"In a bucket by the door," Doc answered. "I was fixin' to throw it to the dogs."

"Goddamn you," Roy spat between clenched teeth. "I want my hand! Junior, you make sure he don't throw my hand away, or I'll shoot both of you."

"Whaddaya want your hand for?" Junior asked, unable to understand why anyone would want to save such a grisly souvenir.

"You just do like I told you," Roy answered, his voice strained by the effort. He was not willing to confide in his son, or anyone else, but he feared going to his everlasting fate without all his parts.

"All right, Pa," Junior said. He turned to look at Doc, who answered his gaze with one of amused astonishment.

"Whatever you say," Doc said with an indifferent shrug of his shoulders. "You're the payin' customer." He watched his patient for a moment more before saying, "I'm gonna give you a little more medicine right now, maybe take away some of that pain." He got a bottle of whiskey from a shelf near the bed and held it before Roy. "Here, take a pull outta this bottle."

Roy eagerly took the bottle, and with Doc helping him hold it steady, gulped down a large swallow, almost choking in the process. Serving as painkiller and anesthesia, whiskey was the only medicine available to Doc Garvey. It had no painkilling properties beyond rendering the patient drunk to the point where he was unaware that he had pain. But it seemed to help Roy once he had drunk half the bottle, because he lapsed into a fretful sleep once again, his voice trailing off with, "I want my hand. . . ."

"He's doin' fine," Doc assured Junior. "I'll see what I can do with the hand." He stood over the bucket, staring at the purple-gray appendage while he tried to decide what to do with it. After a moment, he went into the back room, emerging a few minutes later with a piece of oilskin. "Maybe this'll do the job," he said, and wrapped the hand in it. He held it out to Junior, but Junior backed away from it as if it were a living thing. Doc shrugged. "I'll put it in the shed out back for now. Then your pa can have it when he wants it." He started toward the door. "I don't know about you, but I could use a little grub. I'll put some more coffee on when I come back." Coffee sounded agreeable to Junior, but he had no appetite after dealing with his father's severed hand.

Seated at the kitchen table again, Junior drank his coffee while watching Doc devour chunks of meat sliced from a smoked ham hanging by a hemp cord in a corner of the kitchen. Just making conversation, Doc questioned Roy's son on the happenstance of coming to him for help. "So you say you had ol' Buck Avery hisself on your tail?" Junior nodded. Doc gave that some thought. "Don't too many outlaws shake ol' Buck, once he picks up the scent."

"We ain't like most outlaws," Junior said with a trace of pride.

"You're sure you didn't lead him here? Buck don't know about my place here. He might know about me, but he don't know about this place." It was the first question Doc had asked when Roy and Junior had showed up at his cabin near the Kiamichi, but he now sought a little more reassurance.

"Well, he ain't showed up, has he?" Junior replied. "Him and that other deputy weren't that far behind us. If we hadn'ta lost them, they'd be here by now."

Satisfied, Doc pushed his empty plate aside and sat back in his chair. "You sure you ain't hungry?" When

Junior shook his head, Doc went on. "Yes, sir, it ain't easy to shake ol' Buck. How'd you lose him?"

"Pa knows how Buck figures," Junior said, again with a touch of pride. "We didn't lose him till we got to the river. Pa said Buck would be sure we would head straight for Texas, so we swum the horses upstream instead of downstream till we come to a creek that was wide enough to lead the horses up it. We went up that creek for about three or four hundred yards before we got outta the water. Then we laid up in the woods and waited for them to show up. We figured if they did, they were gonna meet up with a shower of lead. They never showed. After a while, with Pa gettin' worse and worse, we went back down the creek and came on upriver to your place."

"Well, you came to the right place. I expect your pa mighta died if he'd gone much longer with that rotten hand." He poured more coffee in Junior's cup. "You're more'n welcome here for as long as it takes to get Roy back on his feet." Doc was well aware of the recent bank robberies in Atoka and McAlester, so he figured there was plenty of money in those saddlebags that Junior kept such a close eye on. And the longer the two of them stayed, the more he could charge for his services.

Things didn't go so well for the recovering patient during the following three days. Roy developed a fever and seemed to go in and out of his conscious mind for long periods of time, and for a while, it looked like he was more likely to die than pull out of it. A worried Junior begged Doc to save his pa, telling him that he would be well paid for the job. The fever broke on the fourth day, and Roy, weak and drained, woke up to find Doc and Junior standing over his bed. He startled them when he opened his eyes and muttered, "My hand?"

"Safe and sound," Doc answered cheerfully. "You had me and Junior worried there for a spell, but I believe you've by-God whipped it. You feel like eatin' now?"

"No," Roy replied, and grimaced as if just then reminded of the painful stump beside him. "Get me some coffee," he said. While Doc was getting the coffee, Roy looked his son in the eye with some of the old angry spark returning. "That son of a bitch," he growled. "I'm gonna kill him for takin' my hand."

Confused, Junior thought he was referring to Garvey. "Pa, I thought you understood that was what he was gonna do. You'da died if he didn't."

"Buck Avery, dammit," Roy snarled. "He'll pay for my hand, and that damn other deputy, too. He's the one that shot it off."

"Casey Dixon," Doc volunteered as he came through the door with the coffee and overheard Roy's vow. "He's the deputy ridin' with Avery. Young feller, he's the one that arrested your boy Billy over near Broken Bow. I've been hearin' about him a lot here in the nations. From what they say, he's a regular stud horse."

That bit of information was enough to bring Roy's blood to a boil. The old man sat up in bed, and might have gotten up if Junior had not been there to restrain him. "Take it easy, Pa," he pleaded.

"Lemme go, dammit!" Roy bellowed so aggressively that Junior, out of force of habit, immediately obeyed and released his hold on his father's arm. Roy threw his blanket aside and got to his feet, only to discover he was too weak to stand, which infuriated him further. He sat back on the bed, his face a rough mosaic of fury, framed by a mass of unkempt dirty gray hair; he was a menacing sight in spite of his fragile health. Junior, acquainted with his father's frequent storms of rage, stood silently by, waiting for the calm vindictiveness to return. Doc, however, had never witnessed Roy's unbridled rage. He stood speechless, still holding the cup of hot coffee.

After a few silent moments passed, Doc set the cup down on the table beside the bed and quickly stepped back in case another thundercloud was building. "Casey Dixon," Roy repeated calmly, inserting the name into his permanent memory, as he stared at the stump of his left arm. "Where's my hand?"

"I put it in the shed out back, where nothin' can get to it," Doc quickly responded.

"Well, bring it in here," Roy ordered.

"I'll get it," Doc replied, and abruptly left the room.

Roy sank back on the pillow then, having exhausted himself in the process of venting his anger. Fully realizing now how feeble he was, he begrudgingly accepted the fact that he would need time to recover from his amputation and regain his strength. "We're goin' home," he told Junior, "till I can get on my feet again. And then I'm goin' huntin' for two deputy marshals."

Luella Blanton paused to lean on her hoe while she gazed at two moving objects on the far side of the open field on the other side of the creek. Visitors were seldom seen in this remote area of White Oak Creek, and strangers never. The few families that knew who lived in the two cabins close by the bank of the muddy creek never talked about it for fear of deadly reprisal.

Luella continued to stare at the two riders, unable to make out their identity at that distance, until they turned into the field and appeared to be heading her way. She dropped her hoe and ran from the garden, back toward the cabins. "Ma!" she shouted when she was a few yards away. "Riders comin'!"

Almost instantly, a thin, frail woman appeared in the open doorway of the larger of the two cabins, her yellowed gray hair swept away from her face and held by a bandana tied around her head. Though she seemed puny at first glance, a closer observation of the woman revealed a lean strength in sinew and bone, tempered by long years of hard work and hard times. Cora Blanton looked beyond her fourteen-year-old daughter toward the two riders approaching. When Luella crossed the footbridge across the creek, Cora said, "Get in the house and stay there." Then she went to the corner of the stone fireplace to fetch the rifle propped there.

Unemotional over the prospect of strangers calling on her, she stood waiting just inside the door, rifle in hand. She felt no sense of alarm. The years had left her far too tired to be fearful about much of anything. With the two riders almost to the garden now, a small spark in her nearly exhausted reserve of emotion caused her to prop her rifle against the door frame as she recognized her husband and eldest son. Weary relief instead of a sense of joy descended upon her, followed by a sudden feeling of concern for the three sons who were missing. She walked to the edge of the porch and waited while Roy and Junior guided their horses a few dozen yards upstream to the shallow forge.

"Howdy, Ma," Junior said as he dismounted in front of the porch.

"I didn't look for you to be back this soon," Cora responded. "Where's your brothers?" It was only then that she spied the bloody bandage on the stump of her husband's arm. "Oh, my Lord in Heaven . . . ," she gasped, almost in a whisper.

"Pa! What happened?" Luella cried out when she ran from the cabin and saw her brother steadying her father as he climbed down from his horse.

"I'm gonna need some healin'," was all Roy offered at the moment as he stepped up on the porch and went directly inside.

"Where's my boys?" Cora demanded as he walked past her. Receiving no response, she turned back to Junior, holding the horses' reins. "Where's your brothers?"

"They're dead, Ma," Junior answered, lowering his head as if taking responsibility. "All three shot down by marshals."

Although the shock registered in her weathered features, she did not cry out nor shed a tear. She had learned that oral lament brought no results, and her tears had dried up many years before. This was a day that she had known would come—had been bound to come, considering her husband's violent occupation. And now she realized that the day was here. She stood silent for a moment longer before saying, "Put the horses away and come in the house. I'll fix you somethin' to eat." Then she turned and followed her husband into the cabin, walking past her grief-stricken daughter.

"I'm hungry," Roy said to his wife when she followed him in the door. Pointing toward a large gray metal coffeepot on the edge of the stove, he asked, "Any coffee in that pot?"

"Some," she answered. "Been settin' there since breakfast." She poured a cup and set it on the table before him. "What happened to my boys?" She fixed him with an accusing eye.

"Don't go lookin' at me with that evil eye," he admonished. "Buck Avery and Casey Dixon, that's what happened to 'em. Put your damn evil eye on them. They're dead men, soon as I get my strength back and my arm heals up."

Cora lowered her gaze, thinking about her sons, Buster, Zeke, and Billy. She would grieve for them alone when she was in her bed tonight. She paused to look at the blood-soaked cloths wrapped around the stump where his hand used to be. "I'll need to put on some fresh bandages." She didn't ask how it happened. "Luella, slice some of that side meat and put it on the stove," she said when her daughter walked in. "And stop that blubberin'. It ain't gonna bring your brothers back."

Roy took a sip of the strong black coffee and made a face. "This stuff is rank. Luella, put on some decent coffee."

"I told you it had been on the stove since breakfast," Cora commented patiently.

"Breakfast today or yesterday?" Roy snarled. Accustomed to his ill humor and complaints, she ignored the remark. "Anybody been pokin' around since we been gone?" he asked.

"Nary a soul," she replied as she cut up some potatoes to put in the skillet with the bacon.

He acknowledged her reply with a satisfied grunt. He and his boys had been a concentrated project for the Texas Rangers during the past two years. But so far they had not discovered this place on White Oak Creek, half a mile from where it flowed into the Sulphur River. There was an open field on the other side of the creek, where at times a few odd head of cattle grazed, and a garden on the near side. But the cabins were not easily spotted in the dense growth of white oaks and cottonwoods that formed a canopy over the murky water of the creek. Roy considered it home because that's where his wife and daughter were. The main cabin was not as big as the house he used near Broken Bow, Indian Territory, and that was the reason he had built a smaller cabin next to it. The smaller cabin was nothing more than a bunkhouse for his sons.

"I smell somethin' cookin'," Junior said as he entered the cabin and dropped the saddlebags by the door. "I could eat the south end out of a northbound mule right now." He went to the cupboard for a cup.

"Give it a minute," his mother said when he started to reach for the coffeepot. "It ain't hardly finished boilin' yet." Turning to Luella, she said, "Take them saddlebags in the other room."

Luella took the bags into the bedroom and hung them over the footboard of the bed. When she returned, she said, "That meat, or whatever it is in your saddlebags, smells like it's turnin' rank."

Junior gave his father a quick look. Roy immediately ordered, "Don't bother anythin' in them bags." Junior gave Luella a quick glance that told her not to pursue the issue.

The old man sat at the table long after he had finished his meal, lost in his gnawing hatred for the two deputy marshals who had been responsible for his agony. So deep was he immersed in his vengeful thoughts that he was no longer aware of anyone else in the room. It was a face of the man even Cora had never witnessed. More than half an hour passed before he spoke again, and then it was only to announce that he was going to bed.

Sweeping aside a stray gray strand that had escaped from the bandana around her head, Cora watched him slowly shuffle into the bedroom and close the door. Misery had come home. She sighed and picked up his empty coffee cup. She would get the details of her sons' demise from Junior later.

Chapter 10

Charity McDonald pulled a chair away from the long table by the window so she could sweep a little pile of dried mud left by one of her supper customers. There had been an unusually large crowd for a Wednesday night, and she was feeling a bit weary. It was still a good two hours until dark, the time when her father usually closed for the day. A few hungry strays might come in looking for something to eat, but she would routinely serve them at the counter so that she could go ahead and set the tables for breakfast.

With little more than halfhearted effort, she pushed the chair back under the table, then paused to glance out the window when someone in the street caught her eye. She quickly scolded herself for the slight skip in her heartbeat when she recognized the rugged form of Casey Dixon riding beside the imposing bulk of Buck Avery. The two deputy marshals walked their horses up the middle of the street. Behind them, three horses trailed; one with packs and two saddled but no riders.

Confident that she could not be seen at the edge of the window, she watched as they passed by the Cook's Corner, waiting to see if Casey looked her way. Glancing neither right nor left, he rode easily in the saddle, his focus evidently on the stables near the courthouse. *Damn you*, she thought, *you just keep looking straight ahead. You're going to look this way. I know you are.* The two lawmen were even with the door when Casey suddenly looked at the entrance for a long moment before turning away again. *Aha*, she thought, and smiled to herself. Suddenly she was not weary anymore. She glanced at the clock on the wall behind the counter. *Two good hours till dark*, she thought.

Her smile was still in place when she turned around to find her father standing there, his arms folded across his chest, his face wearing a stern reprimand. "Honey, I hope for your sake you're not thinking any romantic thoughts about that deputy. He's a nice enough young fellow, I don't deny that, but a man like that doesn't have much of a future. One day he'd leave you widowed and crying, maybe with two or three young'uns to look after. It would be a hard life, I'm afraid. For goodness' sake, Charity, be smart. Think about your possibility for a good life with someone like Jared Ashton. Your life hasn't been as easy as most girls' since your mother died, and you having to help me in the diner. With a man like Jared, you won't have to work like a hired hand all your life. You owe it to yourself not to make a foolish decision now."

Embarrassed, for she realized that some of her thoughts may have been more apparent than she had imagined, she flushed scarlet. Her father had hinted a few times lately, but this was the first time he had made an earnest appeal to her senses. "Casey and I are just friends, Daddy," she said, although not so convincingly. "You worry too much about me." She gave him a reassuring hug and declared, "I'm not planning to marry anybody anytime soon."

"Jared offers you a future," her father said. "I'm sure Casey Dixon is a fine young man, and it ain't

right to let him think he's got a chance when you
know he hasn't."

By the time Buck and Casey had unsaddled the
horses, turned them loose in the corral, and turned in
Zeke's and Buster's personal effects, it was getting
along toward dark. John Council had already gone
home, so they would have to wait until morning to
make their reports. "Might as well call it a night ourselves," Buck said. "Come on over to the Deuce of
Spades with me and I'll buy your supper."

"Thanks just the same," Casey replied, "but I
wanna see if they've been takin' care of my horse
while we were gone. Then I reckon I'll just go on back
to my room."

"Well, if you change your mind, you know where
I'll be."

"I'll see you in the mornin' at John Council's office,"
Casey said. He was truthful when he had said he
wanted to check on his horse. Although the gray he
had chosen for the job had turned out to be depend-
able, and a comfortable ride once his rear shoes were
fixed, Casey missed the sorrel. The horse had been his
partner for almost four years, and a man gets used to a
horse, just as he does a wife. That thought led him to
think about the main reason he had turned down
Buck's invitation—Charity McDonald. It would be a
little while yet before the diner usually closed, and he
preferred to stop by when there were only a few customers left and Charity had more time to visit. When
he and Buck rode by, he almost thought he got a
glimpse out of the corner of his eye of someone standing by one of the windows. *Maybe it was her*, he
thought as he threw his saddlebags over his shoulder,
picked up his rifle, and went to the corral to say hello
to the sorrel.

*   *   *

At the same time Casey was patting the sorrel gelding's neck, Charity McDonald was surprised by the unexpected appearance of Jared Ashton driving a horse and buggy. He pulled up in front of the diner and walked in the door, holding a bouquet of wild flowers and beaming a wide smile. "I thought I'd stop by and give you a ride home," he announced.

Astonished, Charity looked from Jared to her father, who was beaming as wide as the dashing attorney. "Well, that's mighty grand of you," she replied, blushing, "but I'll be a little while yet. We haven't closed."

"Oh, go on," her father insisted. "Mary and I can close up."

"Well, I guess I can go then." She took the flowers he held out to her. "I'll just take these home and put them in some water." She took off her apron and handed it to Mary, the Choctaw girl who worked in the kitchen. Turning back to Jared, she thought, *God, he is so devilishly handsome*, and her instincts told her he had something on his mind in addition to a ride home. She was sure he had been getting around to it for the past two weeks.

Casey stepped inside the Cook's Corner, dropped his saddlebags by the door, and propped his rifle against the wall while looking around the empty dining room for Charity. Fred McDonald glanced up from behind the counter when he heard the door open. Recognizing Casey, he said nothing for a few moments while trying to make up his mind. Finally, he shrugged and called out, "Can I help you?"

Seeing Charity's father then, Casey replied, "Am I too late to get somethin' to eat?"

McDonald paused, still deciding. "No, you can get something if you'll settle for some bacon and eggs, or something we can fix real quick. We're getting ready to close."

"Bacon and eggs sounds good," Casey said. "I don't wanna put you out any. I got in kinda late, or I woulda been here earlier."

Fred McDonald took a long look at the young deputy. Lean-muscled, tousled hair, with a week's growth of whiskers, he looked tired and hungry. McDonald's heart softened a little. "Sit down here at the counter. We haven't emptied the coffeepot yet. I'll get you a cup while Mary scrambles some eggs for you."

"Much obliged," Casey said. "I'd be lookin' at a couple of strips of jerky for supper if I was too late to eat here."

While he waited for his supper, he glanced around the room several times, hoping to find that Charity was there after all. McDonald watched him from the kitchen. There was an honest strength about the young man that outshined his humble manner, he had to admit. McDonald decided he could genuinely like the man if he wasn't certain he had an interest in his daughter. When the eggs and bacon were done, he took the plate from Mary and placed it on the counter before Casey. Then he poured himself a cup of coffee and sat down on the stool next to him.

"You just missed Charity by a little bit," McDonald said. "Jared Ashton picked her up in his buggy." He watched closely for some reaction to that news. There was no outward sign of any kind from Casey, although the comment registered deep within. McDonald continued. "She'll be sorry she missed you. She says she likes to talk to you." He took a long sip of coffee. "Charity likes to talk to a lot of people. That's just Charity's way."

Casey continued eating. "Yes, sir," he said, "your daughter's a nice lady. I enjoy talkin' to her, too." He was not slow in picking up the intent of McDonald's casual conversation. He admitted to himself that if the roles were reversed, he might seek to discourage a dirt-poor lawman from taking a serious interest in his daughter. He didn't linger over his coffee. As soon as he cleaned his plate of the eggs and bacon, he got up and asked, "How much?" When McDonald took his money, he said, "Much obliged," and left.

He didn't notice the person sitting in the dark corner of the rooming house porch until he heard her voice as he climbed the front steps. "Back in town, are you?" He looked then to find Ethel Ford sitting on the swing, holding a cup of coffee.

"Evenin', Miz Ford," Casey replied. "Yes, ma'am, I just got back a little while ago. I didn't see you sittin' out here in the dark."

"I like to sit out here and have some coffee in the evenings. It gets so stuffy in the house this time of year. You want some coffee?"

"No thank you, ma'am. I just came from supper."

Even in the darkness, she could sense his weary mood, and from her many years of marriage to a deputy marshal, she understood the strain of endless lonesome and often-dangerous trails. "Why don't you sit down and visit awhile," she invited, "keep an old lady company for a bit."

He laughed and pulled a rocking chair over closer to the swing. "Why, thank you, ma'am. That would be nice."

Ethel Ford was a sensitive woman, and clever in her intuition when it came to recognizing troubled young men. A few minutes' conversation told her that the rigors of the job were not the thing weighing heavily upon his mind. That being the case, she felt confident that the problem was most likely female related. "You know, you're a fine-looking young man, and from what I can see, a hardworking man. I'd say it's about time you thought about finding a young lady and maybe starting a family." The probe proved to be successful.

"To tell you the truth," he volunteered, "I've been thinkin' about that very thing."

"Good for you," she replied, "and I'll bet you've already got someone in mind."

"Well, I reckon I have, but I'm not sure she's thinkin' about the same thing I am," he said.

"There's only one way to find out for sure," Ethel said. She laughed then. "I didn't even know I wanted to get married until Edgar Ford popped the question out of the blue one day. We got married two weeks later." She laughed again as she recalled it.

"I don't know," Casey hesitated. "I don't know if I've got enough sand to come right out and ask. I ain't sure how she feels, but I'm pretty sure her pa ain't too crazy about the idea."

"You must have some kind of notion, otherwise you wouldn't have even thought about her. Who is she?" When Casey hesitated to answer, she continued to prod him. "Oh, for pity sakes, what's her name? I'm not going to tell anybody."

He felt like a schoolboy being teased by his mother. He wished now that he had never confessed what was on his mind. "Charity McDonald," he reluctantly mumbled.

"I shoulda guessed," Ethel said. "She's a handsome woman, all right, and a nicer girl I've never met. You two would make a fine couple." She seemed genuinely pleased with the notion. "Have you told her how you feel about her?"

"No, ma'am," he stammered.

"Well, what are you waiting for?" Caught up in the fairy tale now, she took over the quest. "You get yourself cleaned up in the morning, shave that scrub off your face, and put on some clean clothes. Do you have any clean clothes?" He nodded. "Well, put 'em on. And you go see her first thing. She's probably wondering if you're ever gonna get up your nerve."

"I've gotta report in first thing in the mornin'," Casey said.

"Well, go after that," Ethel said. "If you come home tomorrow night without telling Charity what's in your heart, I swear I'll break a broom over your back, and then I'll go tell her myself."

Casey was overcome by a feeling of complete alarm. He couldn't think of an answer for Ethel, so he simply got to his feet and said, "I expect I'd best go to bed now."

"You remember what I said," she called after him as he headed for the door.

"Yes, ma'am," he uttered meekly. It was not a question of whether or not he gave it more thought as he lay on the straw tick that served as his mattress. To the contrary, he could think of nothing else. His anguish kept him awake until the wee hours when exhaustion finally took over and let him sleep the remainder of the night.

He was in the washroom before anyone else got up the next morning, feeling none too refreshed after his near-sleepless night. He bathed, he shaved, and he put on his clean shirt, all the while arguing with himself about the wisdom of exposing his deepest thoughts to the world. He had halfway convinced himself that the best thing to do was, as the Widow Ford had advised, to get it over with, to let Charity know his thoughts. By the time he left the washroom, however, he had changed his mind once again.

Waiting for him on the back porch that connected the washroom to the kitchen was Ethel Ford, hands on hips, fixing him with an accusing gaze. "Do you remember what I said last night?" Blushing, he nodded.

"I meant it," she said, and stood aside to let him pass. "I'll tell her myself," she threatened.

It was a thoroughly chastised young deputy who walked into John Council's office that morning. Buck was already there, seated in the overstuffed chair, just as he had been on that first day. Before Casey could speak, Buck let out a long, low whistle. "Damn, John, look at that!" he said to his boss. "You didn't tell me we was supposed to get all gussied up this mornin'."

"I was about due," Casey replied with a sheepish grin.

"Maybe that oughta be the standard for deputies around here," John Council joked.

His comment caused Buck to chuckle. "I reckon that would sure as hell mean my retirement."

With the japing of the freshly scrubbed deputy over, Council got down to business. "I was hopin' you boys would be lucky enough to bring old man Blanton in, but I reckon you did the best you could. I telegraphed the Texas Rangers that you had managed to cut the Blanton gang down to the old man and one son, and they were most likely headed back down that way."

"I'm pretty sure they're back in Texas," Buck was quick to agree. "We made it plenty hot for 'em here, even if we didn't get all of 'em. Roy's wounded. We ain't sure how bad, but Casey shot him, and they was hightailin' it straight to the Red River."

"Well, we'll let Texas worry about him for a while," Council said. "I want you both to write your report on the job. Then I expect you could use a little time off. I don't have anythin' that can't wait, so go fishin' or somethin'."

"You're the boss," Buck said, and grinned at Casey. Casey nodded his agreement, thinking that he might have plans of a personal nature that could take advantage of a little off time.

With nothing more to discuss, the two deputies got up and went to a long table in the outer office to write their reports. It took a while, since Council demanded details when it came to substantiating requests for reimbursement of expenses. It was still fairly early when the reports were completed, however, and Casey had not yet eaten breakfast. His intention was to take care of that next, so he turned down Buck's invitation to join him at the Deuce of Spades for a morning drink. Suspicious, Buck took a step back, cocked his head to one side, and squinted hard at Casey. "You've got a woman on your mind," he accused, his grin becoming wider by the second. "You always like to eat at Fred McDonald's place. Have you been sparkin' that McDonald gal?" He didn't wait for an answer, and Casey didn't offer one. "That's the reason you got all duded up this mornin'. I shoulda known you was up to somethin'." He slapped himself on the thigh and laughed. "The whole time we was ridin' together, you never let on you had somebody you was thinkin' about back here in Fort Smith."

Getting up to leave, Casey simply said, "It wasn't anybody's business."

His response delighted Buck. He threw back his head and roared with laughter. "You're right about that. I'll see you later on. If you need any help with that little gal, I'll be hangin' around the Deuce of Spades most of the time. Good huntin', partner."

Fred McDonald glanced up from behind the counter when Casey walked in the door. He could not help but notice the change in the young deputy's appearance from that of the night before. It didn't take much thought to guess why. "Good morning," he said, making an effort to sound cordial. "What can we do for you? It's a little early yet for dinner."

"Mornin'," Casey returned. "I ain't had breakfast yet. Reckon I could get some more of those eggs and bacon?"

"Yes, sir," McDonald replied. "You sure can. Have a seat." With a wave of his hand, he indicated any of the vacant tables.

Casey couldn't help but notice an overly cordial welcome from Charity's father this morning. It served to create a spark of confidence for the mission he had set for himself. He chose a table near the window and sat down while McDonald disappeared into the kitchen. In a few minutes, Charity came from the kitchen with a steaming cup of coffee. Smiling brightly, she glided over to his table and placed the cup down before him. "As soon as Daddy told me you were out here, I knew you'd want this."

Matching her warm smile, he said, "Yep, this is the best coffee in town." He wanted to tell her why he had really come, that he had something he had to tell her that was burning his insides wanting to get out. But he could not bring himself to speak of his feelings for her just yet.

She pulled a chair back from the table and sat down. "You've been gone quite a while," she said. "Daddy told me you stopped in last night. I left early. I'm sorry I missed you."

"I'm sorry I missed you, too," he said, then wondered if he was being too bold. When she continued to smile at him, he decided that he might as well empty his magazine and get it all out on the table. "There was somethin' I wanted to tell you," he stammered. He had no sooner uttered it when he felt a cold hand clamp down on his insides, for when she crossed her hands on the table, he noticed the ring on her finger. While she waited for him to continue, he paused and hesitated. "Is that a new ring there?" he asked. "I never noticed it before."

"Yes," she replied, holding it out for him to admire. "This is the reason I left early. Jared Ashton asked me to marry him last night, and I said yes. He's been beating around the bush for six months, and last night he popped the question. We haven't set the date yet, but it'll be sometime soon. Maybe you can come to the wedding."

Beyond being stunned, he felt as if he had just been gutted. He wondered later if she had not been puzzled by the look of shock that must surely have been in his eyes. Barely able to find words that made any sense, he managed to utter, "I think I'm gonna be out of town for a long spell."

"Oh," she responded. "Well, what was it you wanted to tell me?"

"I musta forgot it," he said. While she gazed quizzically at his sudden awkwardness, he tried to hide the devastation he felt in his heart. "It wasn't anythin' important." He was saved for the moment when Mary brought his breakfast, allowing him to try to recover his composure. As he looked down at the plate, his mind was trapped in a whirlpool of disillusionment, so intense that the eggs and bacon were no more than a blur. "What?" he heard himself say when she asked a question.

"I said you're not going to be able to eat those eggs if you keep pouring salt on them," she responded. The realization of the cause of his abrupt change suddenly dawned on her. The news of her engagement had seriously affected him.

"I'm not really hungry, anyway," he said. "Coffee's all I wanted. I've got to get goin'. How much do I owe you for the eggs?"

Many times she had been convinced that the soft-spoken, easygoing deputy had more serious thoughts about her, hidden behind the casual flirting they had indulged in. Now that thought was confirmed when she read the disappointment in his face. "Casey . . . ," she started, then faltered, knowing that if she said what was on her mind, it would only make the situation worse. "Nothing," she answered, "there's no charge."

Eager to leave, he stood up. "I'm sorry I put everybody to so much trouble. I'd be glad to pay." When she shook her head, he immediately turned and started toward the door. Realizing that he was reacting badly, he turned to face her again. "I forgot to congratulate you. I'm sure Jared Ashton is a good man. My best to you both." He left then without giving her a chance to reply.

"Thank you," Charity said, barely above a whisper, after the door closed behind him. She stood there a moment, staring at the door, still wondering how her life would have been if Casey had proposed instead of Jared. Then she reminded herself that she had spent her young life cleaning and waiting tables, and that was enough. Casey Dixon was attractive in an untamed way, but she could not abide the idea of living like a squaw in a mountain shack somewhere. She turned then to find her father peering at her from behind the counter. He quickly averted his gaze and pretended to be drying a glass.

"What a goddamn fool," Casey muttered aloud as he stalked up the dusty street toward the courthouse, oblivious to people he passed along the way. *Damn nosey ol' bitch*, he said to himself, thinking of Ethel Ford and the fact that she had pushed him into expressing his feelings to Charity. He immediately regretted the thought, knowing that his compassionate landlady had his best interests at heart. *Ain't nobody to blame but me*, he silently admitted. *Of course she's gonna pick a lawyer over a saddle tramp. I need to get my head on straight and my mind back on what I do best.* With that, he headed straight for John Council's office, feeling a strong desire to get out of town.

The marshal looked up from his desk, surprised to see the young deputy so soon. "What's up, Casey? I thought you and Buck would be dead drunk by now."

"No, sir," Casey replied respectfully. "I've been doin' some thinkin' about Roy Blanton and his son, and I'd like to go back to the Choctaw Nation to check on a few places."

Council replaced his pen in the inkwell to give his full attention to the deputy. "Is that a fact?" he asked. "I thought you and Buck were pretty sure Blanton had gone back to Texas."

"Well, Buck is, but I ain't so sure. You know, I picked up Billy Blanton down near Broken Bow. And the folks down there told me Billy was raisin' hell around there for a week. I'm thinkin' the Blantons must have a hideout near there. Hell, we know they've got a place they always go to in Indian Territory, and most likely Billy was stayin' there. I figure it would be a good idea to find out if Roy went there to heal up instead of headin' back to Texas."

It was an interesting idea. Council gave it some consideration. After a few moments, he said, "You might be right. It couldn't hurt, but, hell, you and Buck just got back. Maybe I oughta send somebody else."

"I wasn't thinkin' about Buck goin' with me," Casey said. "I work just as well alone, and there ain't no reason to send two. We've come a long way on this case, and I'd like to finish it up. I don't need any time off. I'd rather be workin'. I've got a fair notion that Blanton has a place somewhere over in that country where the Mountain Fork River joins up with the Little River. I might be able to stumble across it." He didn't think it wise to tell Council that he intended to go into Texas Territory if he had to.

Council studied his deputy for a few moments, noting the intense look on his face. Casey Dixon was a good man, with a good head on his shoulders. If he had reason to believe he had a fair chance of running Roy Blanton to ground, then Council was inclined to okay it. "All right," he said, "go ahead. But, Casey, you watch yourself. A wounded Roy Blanton might be more dangerous than one that ain't."

"Yes, sir," Casey replied. "I'll be outta here by this afternoon, just as soon as I can draw some ammunition and supplies." His business accomplished, he wasted no time in exiting the U.S. Marshal's office.

He didn't bother dropping by the Deuce of Spades to say hello to Buck. He was afraid that Buck might decide to accompany him, and this was one time when he really needed to be alone. So he went directly to his room to pick up his rifle and saddlebags. He had hoped to avoid a confrontation with Ethel Ford, but he was not so fortunate.

She looked up expectantly when he walked back to his little room off the kitchen. "Well," she asked, "did you tell her?"

"More or less," he said, and attempted to brush past her.

She caught his arm. "And . . . what did she say?"

"She said she's gonna marry Jared Ashton in a couple of weeks, and asked me if I wanted to come to the weddin'," he replied stoically. "I said no."

Stunned momentarily, she didn't know what to say. "Oh, Casey, I'm so sorry. I know how you must feel."

He shrugged. "I'll get over it, but right now I've got to go. I'll be gone for a couple of weeks at least—gotta go back over in the Nations."

She released his arm and watched him as he went out the back door, heading for his room. *After this, learn to keep your big nose out of other folks' business*, she told herself.

Chapter II

On a hot, dry morning in early August, shortly after arriving home, Roy Blanton and his one remaining son rode slowly past the stores and saloons of Sulphur Springs, Texas. There was no fear of recognition for the two notorious outlaws because Roy always made it a point not to raid, rob, or kill close to home. Still, both men carefully scanned the weathered buildings they passed from long-established habits and the awareness that the Texas Rangers were still looking for them. In fact, this was only the second time either of the two had even been to town. Roy's wife, Cora, and his daughter would have made the trip all the way from White Oak Creek if there was a need to go that far for supplies. This was an errand, however, that only Roy could do.

Seeing a man leaning up against the front of the saloon, Roy pulled the big gray gelding he rode over close to the boardwalk and said, "I hear there's a doctor in this town."

"Sure is," the man replied. "Doc Davis. Keep on the way you're headin', go past the dry goods store 'bout a hundred yards. Little house on the right, settin' between two big oak trees." He walked over to the edge of the walk, when he noticed the bloody bandaging on Roy's left arm. "Looks like you got yourself a bad arm there."

"Much obliged," Roy said, offering no explanation, and rode on.

Left staring after the two strangers, the man went back inside the saloon. Walking up to the bar, he spoke to the bartender. "There was a couple of fellers out there lookin' for Doc Davis, and one of 'em looks like he mighta had a hand chopped off."

"That a fact?" the bartender and owner of the saloon replied. "Who was it?"

"Never seen 'em before." That was the end of the matter until later in the morning when Jim White walked into the saloon.

After tying the horses at the hitching post out front, Junior stepped up on the porch and knocked on the door. In a few minutes, a matronly woman came to the door. She paused to take a cursory look at the rough stranger at the door before peering around him to get a look at his companion. "Yes?" she asked.

"My pa's bad hurt—needs to see the doctor," Junior said.

She took a closer look at Roy, still seated in the saddle, and just then saw the bloody stump. "Good Heavens," she exclaimed, and held the screen door open. "Bring him on inside." She stood holding the door while the two men walked past her. Then she directed them to an examining room off the living room and left to fetch her husband.

"Good God, man," Dr. Davis uttered when he saw Roy's arm, "what happened to you?"

"Got my hand in the wrong place cuttin' some timber," Roy offered.

"Let's have a look," Davis said, and started unwrapping the bulky bandage. "Damn," he exclaimed when he had uncovered the stump. "Who did this?"

"There weren't no doctor there at the time," Roy responded.

Davis puzzled over Doc Garvey's pad on the injured limb for a long moment before asking, "What the hell is this?"

"Feller that put it on there said it was a piece of hog fat," Junior volunteered. "Said it was good for paddin'."

Davis shook his head, amazed. "It's good for infection and maybe blood poisoning. It's a good thing you didn't wait any longer before coming in. You might have lost your whole arm. I'm gonna have to take that mess off and clean that stump up some. We'll just have to see what happens after that. It might heal up all right, it might not, but I'll do what I can." He looked Roy in the eyes. "This is gonna be painful."

"It's been painful," Roy replied. "A little more won't hurt any worse."

"I'll give you something that'll help a little, but nothing's gonna take away all the pain. Get on the table over there and we'll get started." He walked to the door and called to his wife. "Doris, I'm gonna need some hot water in here."

While Dr. Davis was attempting to undo Doc Garvey's handiwork, Texas Ranger Jim White walked into the Sulphur Saloon and approached the bar. "Mornin'," Walker, the owner, greeted him. "I see you're still around this mornin'."

"Yep, I'm on my way back to Dallas soon as I wet my whistle," White replied.

Walker poured him a drink. "You were askin' about seein' any strangers around town. There was a couple of fellers came in lookin' for Dr. Davis this mornin'. Jack Thompson told them where Doc's house was, said one of 'em had a bad arm wound." Seeing that the ranger's interest was immediately aroused, Walker said, "Jack's still here, over by the table watchin' the card game."

Walker called, and Jack came over to the bar. "You talk to a couple of strangers this mornin'?" Jim White asked. When Jack replied that he had, White asked, "What did they look like?"

"They was a couple of rough-lookin' fellers is all I can tell you. One of 'em was a good bit older than the other'n. And the old one had one helluva bad arm—almost looked like there weren't no hand on the end of it."

Jack's report was enough to spark significant interest in the ranger. He took a paper from his pocket, unfolded it, and held it before Jack. "Did one of 'em look anything like this?"

Jack studied the artist's sketch for a moment, then replied, "Yeah, I think he did, the old one, a little bit, anyway."

"How long ago was that?" White asked. Jack told him that it was about an hour ago. It was likely that they were still at the doctor's house. It was definitely worth investigating. The ranger station in Dallas had been notified by the U.S. marshal in Fort Worth that the notorious outlaw Roy Blanton had been wounded in the arm in a shootout with two deputies. Two of his sons were killed and one son escaped with the old man. They were believed to be heading for Texas. *This might be my lucky day*, he thought. He thanked Jack and Walker, and hurried out the door.

"Well, it doesn't look as bad as I thought it would," Dr. Davis pronounced after removing the stitches that had held the hog fat pad in place. The puffy little holes left from the stitching looked more prone to infection than the cauterized stump. He sprayed the wounds as well as the bandages liberally with a solution of one-in-twenty carbolic acid to keep down the infection. "They'll probably heal in a few days. I'm gonna wrap the stump with a new bandage, and if you keep it pretty clean, I think it'll heal up proper. You need to come back and let me take a look at it in a week or so. It's still gonna pain you some, but it oughta get better day by day." He went over to a cupboard and got a bottle of laudanum from the shelf. "Here, you can take a swig of this whenever you need it. It'll help with the pain."

Roy swung his legs over the edge of the table and stood up. As he pulled his shirt on, he directed Junior to settle the bill. "Pay him whatever he wants," Roy said. "My arm feels better already." Although the doctor knew that was highly unlikely, the feeling that his arm was now receiving proper treatment was enough to make it so in Roy's mind. He felt ready now to head back to Indian Territory to settle his debt with the two deputies who had caused him this grief.

Particularly pleased to be paid for his services in cash instead of promises or produce, Dr. Davis escorted his patient to the door and wished him well. He failed to notice the stranger waiting beside the horses at the hitching rail.

"Mornin'," Jim White called out cordially when Roy and Junior paused on the porch steps, surprised by the ranger's sudden appearance, and noticing the badge on his shirt. When neither man returned the greeting, Jim continued. "This is a fine-lookin' horse you're ridin'—damn near white. You don't see many grays that look this white." It matched the description of the horse Roy Blanton was last seen riding. White stepped away from the gelding. "You fellers just passin' through town?"

Roy finally spoke. "Yeah, that's right, we're just passin' through." He stepped down from the bottom step and stood on the path.

"What happened to your hand?" White asked, moving over to directly face Roy, his hand resting casually on the butt of his pistol.

"I hurt it cuttin' timber," Roy said.

"Is that a fact? I bet it hurt like hell. Is this your son?" he asked, nodding toward Junior, still on the steps.

"Mister," Roy replied, "you ask a helluva lot of questions."

White smiled. "That's my job. You know, it's a funny thing, I got a sketch of an old son of a bitch named Roy Blanton last week. Reminds me of you. Long gray hair hangin' out from under a flat-crowned hat, big ol' bushy gray mustache . . . Damnedest thing, he rides a horse like this one here—got shot in the arm in a shoot-out—but him and one of his sons got away. Whaddaya say about that . . ."

The roar of Junior's .44 ripped the still morning air, cutting off the ranger's sentence. White's mistake was in taking his eye off Roy's son for a brief moment. His face registering complete shock from the slug that smashed his breastbone, he backed up a couple of steps and tried to pull his revolver. Junior fired again, this time splitting the ranger's forehead. White sat down on the ground, his eyes staring wide in shock. After a moment, he keeled over and lay helpless, the life draining from him in the blood seeping out on the dirt path.

The front door opened within moments of the second shot, and Dr. Davis stood in the doorway. A quick look at the body lying on his path, another at Junior, now turning to look at him, and the door was immediately slammed shut. Junior grinned, amused by the doctor's fright. "I don't know if he wants to see you in a couple of weeks or not like he said," he quipped.

"I wasn't aimin' to come back, anyway," his father said. "Let's git." One thing he knew for certain now

was there were soon going to be a helluva lot more
rangers in this part of Texas. It made up his mind to
leave for Oklahoma Territory a day or two sooner than
he had planned. He paused briefly to look down at the
ranger. "If you was aimin' at that badge, you sure as
hell missed it," he commented.

"I wasn't aimin' at his star," Junior claimed. "I was
aimin' for the center of his chest, right where I got
him." He was accustomed to his father's criticism. "I
aimed that second one right between his eyes, and I
got it right on the money, too."

"Yeah, I reckon," Roy conceded reluctantly, "but if
you'da missed, you coulda shot one of the horses."

Holding the horses back to a walk to avoid suspicion, they rode back along the main street, where several people had come out of the buildings, having
heard the gunshots. Passing the saloon, Roy recognized Jack Thompson as the man he had asked about
the doctor on their way in, so he pulled his horse over
close to the boardwalk as before. "Is there any law in
this town?" he asked.

"No full-time law," Jack answered, wondering if
there was any connection between the two strangers
and the shots just heard. "There's a ranger in town.
He just went up to Doc Davis' place. I thought he was
lookin' for you fellers." It fell out of his mouth before
he thought about what he was saying. He immediately
backed away, realizing that he may have said too
much.

Roy just grinned and said, "Yeah, we saw him. He's
still up there." He kicked his horse into a lope, and
Junior followed him out of town, looking back to grin
defiantly at Thompson.

"When you reckon you'll be back?" Cora Blanton
wanted to know. She didn't really care as long as he
left her a little money for coffee and flour and such. If

the truth be told, her life was a great deal more pleasant when the men were away, leaving her and Luella to take care of the place. She did kind of miss the younger boys. Junior was so much like the old man that it was like having two of the same person around, both ill-tempered.

"Hell, I don't know," Roy replied impatiently, "when I finish up with what I got to do. There's gonna be a little trouble stirred up over that ranger Junior shot in Sulphur Springs. I don't know if they'll be snoopin' around this far from there or not, but even if they do, this place ain't that easy to find."

"I know what to do if they show up here," Cora said. "Tell 'em I ain't never heard of anybody name of Blanton." There were many times when she wished it were true.

"I'll be goin', then," he said, and stepped up in the saddle, holding his stump up in the air while he mounted. "Let's go, Junior," he called. Then, while his son picked up the lead rope for the packhorse, Roy reached behind him and took out his severed hand. Carefully unwrapping the oilcloth, he frowned as he peered at the rotting appendage before wrapping it once again and returning it to his saddlebag. Without another word of parting for his wife and daughter, he started out along the creek bank with Junior and the packhorse close behind.

Chapter 12

"Goddamn this stuff!" Roy Blanton blurted angrily, and threw the empty laudanum bottle to smash against a rock. "It don't do nothin' to ease the pain, nohow."

Following silently along behind Roy, Junior steadied his horse when it was startled by the crashing bottle. He was beginning to worry about his father. The old man seemed to be getting more and more belligerent ever since they had crossed the Red River, causing Junior to watch him closely. When they camped at night, Roy would invariably withdraw to his bed and sit staring at the healing stump of his left arm. When he thought Junior wasn't watching, he would pull the grisly hand from his saddlebag and hold it against the stump as if willing it to reattach itself. It was an unnerving sight for Junior, causing him to wonder if the old man was beginning to lose his mind. Now making their way up through the Ouachita Mountains, they were within a few miles of their hideout. Maybe, Junior thought, his pa might be a little more at ease after they reached the cabin. Maybe the pain of the healing arm might lessen to some degree if he would take a little time to rest up before continuing.

"What the hell . . ?" Roy exclaimed when he started down the ridge that shielded the cabin and spotted smoke coming from the chimney. "By God, it looks like we got us some termites livin' in our house." Roy was never far from rage, and the prospect of drifters taking up quarters in the cabin he had built served to sufficiently fuel his anger. "Come on," he said to his son, and gave his horse a sharp kick.

"Leonard, we got company." William Bowden stood by the front door, staring at the two riders just reaching the bottom of the ridge and following the stream toward the cabin.

William picked up his rifle and went to the door to stand behind his brother. After studying the two strangers for a few moments, he turned to his wife, who was tending a rabbit roasting on a spit over the fireplace. "Bonnie, you stay back outta sight until we see who they are."

When the riders pulled to a stop at the edge of the tiny clearing around the house, the two brothers stepped outside the door to meet them. "Howdy," Leonard said, looking up into the grave faces of the strangers.

"Howdy, yourself," Roy returned, his narrowed eyes taking in the scene and making special note of the one standing close to the door with his hand hanging just inside the jamb. "We've been gone for a little spell. It was mighty kind of you boys to look after our cabin while we was away. I reckon you can clear out now that we're back."

Leonard glanced back at his brother, seeking confirmation of his own feelings on the matter. William slowly shook his head in reply. Confident that he and his brother were of the same opinion, he replied. "Well now, that's right interestin'," he said. "But we found this cabin abandoned, and there ain't been nobody come to claim it for over a month. So I reckon we look at it as bein' ours to claim."

Unable to hear the exchange between her brother-in-law and the strangers, Bonnie tiptoed up to the corner of the front window in time to hear Roy Blanton's response. "Well now, that is interestin'," Roy said, turning to Junior. "Ain't that interestin', son?" Junior nodded and grinned. Bonnie's gaze was captured by the old man's left arm and how odd his gestures seemed with no hand. "Well," Roy went on, "seein' as how we got back a little too late, you wouldn't mind if we watered our horses, would you?"

"Help yourself," William answered. "The water's free."

"Much obliged," Roy said, much to the amazement of his son. He stepped down from his horse. "How'd you fellers find this place? Ain't many folks know where this cabin is."

"I reckon we wouldn'ta found it if one of our horses hadn't got loose and run off when we was camped down near the river," Leonard replied.

"Yes, sir, she's hard to find, all right," Roy said, then glanced at Junior and said softly, "One in the door." Junior understood and without hesitation, pulled his pistol and shot William, standing in the door. A split second later, Leonard fell with a bullet in his chest from Roy's handgun.

Inside the cabin, Bonnie knelt at the window, horrified by the sight of her husband and brother-in-law shot down at point-blank range. Unable to move or think for a long moment while her conscious mind threatened to desert her, she remained frozen there while she witnessed the two men pumping two more bullets into the bodies. Only upon hearing the older man with the stump tell the younger one to see if there was anyone else in the cabin could she force herself to move. Terrified that she would be next to be executed, she scrambled away from the front window and ran to the kitchen. With no time to think about taking any-thing with her, she climbed out the window.

"Don't see no sign of anybody else," Junior called out from inside the cabin. "But supper's ready," he said when he saw the rabbit over the coals. "And if we'd waited a minute or two longer, it'da been burnt."

Roy walked in and started looking around. "I reckon there was just the two of 'em," he said. "There ain't but two horses out there." A few seconds later when he had gone into the other room, he wasn't so sure. "There's some women's clothes in here." He came storming out of the room, looking right and left for further evidence. Spotting the kitchen window, he said, "Go out back and look around. There mighta been a woman with 'em."

Junior stuck his head out the window and looked around. The cabin was built close up to the side of the ridge with thick forest starting within several yards of the back wall. If anyone was running up the slope, it would be impossible to see them. He looked down at the ground just below the window. It was wet, almost muddy where cooking water and dishwater had been dumped out the window. There were no footprints there and there should have been if someone had jumped out the window.

Taking hold of a sizable oak limb that brushed against the cabin roof, he climbed out the window, and paused to look back at the deep prints he had left in the wet ground. It seemed likely that anyone else would have done the same. Turning his attention to the ridge then, he moved into the trees, searching for some sign of flight, thinking that if it was a woman, she would most likely rush through the bushes and branches in a panic, leaving ample evidence of her passing. After making a wide sweep across the ridge, he finally had to conclude that, no matter the clothes, there had been no woman there. He returned to the cabin to tell his father.

Not satisfied that Junior had been thorough enough in his search, Roy went back over the area with him to see for himself. Like his son, he could find no evidence of anyone taking flight. "We can't have anybody knowin' about this place," he emphasized. "I don't know," he hesitated, scratching his chin. "There was a woman here at some time. I reckon she ain't around no more." The issue settled in his mind then, he said, "Go take the saddles off them horses while I see if them fellers left anythin' worth keepin'. We can drag them bodies off after we eat."

Shivering with fright, the petrified woman forced herself to release her hold halfway up the stout trunk of the oak tree next to the cabin's back wall, and carefully make her way down to the ground. Once her feet touched the ground, she made her way quickly and quietly up through the forest that covered the side of the ridge. The image of the sinister-looking monster grinning as he shot her husband was burnt into her memory. And the cold fear she had felt while clinging desperately to the tree trunk while he walked around below her, searching for her, would never leave her mind.

Back at the cabin, Roy and his son finished the rabbit Bonnie had been roasting. After telling Junior to get rid of the two bodies outside the front door, Roy picked up his saddlebags and went into the bedroom. He stood for a moment looking around the tiny room. Things were not much different than when he had left it. The one bed had been slept in, and the bedrolls were still stacked in the corner where his sons had left them. A few odds and ends of clothing that had belonged to the nesters were lying about where he had scattered them a short time before. He brought his gaze to focus on the bedrolls again, and he felt his blood run hot at the memory of the deaths of his sons. *Buck Avery and Casey Dixon*, he thought, and the image it brought to his mind made him scowl painfully. He opened his saddlebag and pulled out his rotting hand, oblivious to the pungent odor that immediately filled the room. He held the oilcloth under it to catch the putrid pieces of flesh and skin that were separating from the bones in an effort to save as much of his hand as he could. Before long, nothing would remain but the stark skeletal appendage. Still he could not part with it, knowing in his mind that he would need all his body parts when he came face-to-face with Satan. He held the ghastly hand up next to his stump. He could feel the hand, although it was not attached. He could feel the fingers move and the fist tighten, although there was no visual confirmation. He was convinced that, upon his death, the severed hand would return to his arm. *Before that day comes*, he swore silently, *I'll send Buck Avery and Casey Dixon to hell*. Then, hearing Junior approaching the cabin, he wrapped his hand again and returned it to his saddlebags.

"I swear," Junior remarked when he came back into the cabin, "them two fellers sure as hell didn't have nothin' on 'em worth a cent." Failing to see his father in the main room, he went into the bedroom. "They had a little tobacco on 'em and some papers for rollin', but that's about it."

As soon as he walked into the bedroom, his nostrils were assaulted by the sickly odor that pervaded the room. *He's had that damn hand out again*, he thought, but knew better than to comment on it. His father's ghastly habit was getting to the point where Junior was convinced that the old man was losing his grip on reality. To further shake Junior's confidence, since leaving White Oak Creek, his pa had started talking in his sleep almost every night, sometimes loud enough to wake Junior. And Junior would swear that it sounded like he was talking to his hand. He had never questioned his father's judgment, but he had to admit that now he was a bit more concerned that Roy might do something reckless that might get them both killed in his thirst for revenge. Thinking about it for a few moments, he told himself that surely his pa would be all right once he got used to having but one hand, even though, deep down, he was still not completely convinced.

He glanced up to realize that Roy had been staring at him as if reading his thoughts. He at once felt a frightful skip of his heart, and blurted the first thing he could think of. "Reckon we could use some coffee. I'll go make us some."

"We're goin' huntin' in the mornin'," Roy pronounced solemnly. "I need somethin' more than a damn rabbit to strengthen my blood. Then we'll see. I don't figure on layin' around here long."

"Whaddaya plannin' on doin', Pa?" Junior asked.

"Whaddaya mean, what am I plannin' to do? What I said I was aimin' to do. I'm gonna kill them two deputies, learn them and all the other lawmen that they're gonna pay for it when they come after Roy Blanton."

"How will we find 'em?" Junior was less than enthusiastic about his father's plan to retaliate.

"We'll find 'em," Roy replied emphatically. "If they're in this territory, we'll find 'em. By God, I'll ride into Fort Smith and shoot 'em down right under Judge Parker's nose if I have to. Don't nobody kill my boys and get away with it."

The proclamation did little to ease Junior's concern. It sounded like a suicide plan to him. He was craving revenge for his brothers' deaths, but not to the point of riding into the midst of no telling how many deputy marshals in Fort Smith. He felt sure that his father might feel differently after he had a chance to cool down a little, but he spoke no words of protest. Such was his fear of his father.

Thinking John Council's advice to take a week or two off a good suggestion, Buck decided he would take the time to visit his cabin on the Kiamichi River. It had been a while since he had been there, and it would give him a chance to do some work on the cabin. There were some things he needed and he was now five hundred dollars richer thanks to Roy Blanton's moment of generosity. The thought caused a frown to appear on his face as he realized the irony of it. He was fixed for the rest of his life with a fine house on the Kiamichi and half interest in the Deuce of Spades—and all thanks to his deal with the devil, in the form of Roy Blanton, the most notorious outlaw in the territory. Many times since then, his conscience had nagged him over his failure to resist temptation. And he had attempted to justify his crime by telling himself that the court owed it to him for all the outlaws he had captured or killed over his long years of service to the territory.

Now, with the return to the Nations of Roy Blanton, his one moment of weakness had come back to haunt him. As far as the five hundred he had just accepted, he figured he might as well have taken it. It was all just a part of one sin. One thing he was certain about, however, it would ruin him if he were found out. He had no family left. The only thing he had that mattered was his reputation as an honest lawman. And it had been touch-and-go for a while there with Casey Dixon's determination to capture Roy and the boys. It bothered him considerably that he couldn't play it straight with Casey, for he genuinely liked the young version of himself. Buck felt greatly relieved by the knowledge that Blanton had once again slipped out of the Nations.

Ready to leave Fort Smith, he decided to drop by
Council's office on the way out of town to have a cup
of coffee with his old friend. The marshal always had a
pot of coffee working on the little potbellied stove in
his office.

"I'm headin' out to my place on the river," Buck
replied in response to Council's greeting. "Do some
work on the place—God knows there's plenty to do,
maybe do a little fishin'."

The marshal grinned and shook his head. "Damn if
I don't envy you. If things keep up the way they've
been goin' around here, I might take off and join you."
They both chuckled at that, knowing that the marshal
seldom got the opportunity to leave his desk. Council
got serious for a moment. "You know, Buck, I'd be interested to know what you think of your young partner after ridin' with him. I know what I think about
him, but I ain't ever rode with him in the field."

"Well, John, me and you have known each other for
a long time, and you know I've always liked to work
alone. But if I've got to partner with somebody, I
couldn't find nobody better'n Casey Dixon. He ain't
got no bad habits that I could see, and he don't seem
to be afraid of anything." He paused to think for a
moment. "And he's quick to back up his partner. You
got yourself a damn good deputy there."

"I'm glad to hear you say that," Council said. "It
confirms my opinion of the man. He reminds me a lot
of you when you were just gettin' started in this business." He paused to finish the last gulp of coffee in his
cup. "He's not one to take it easy, even when he's told
to. I'll say that for him."

"Whaddaya mean?" Buck asked.

Council looked surprised. "I figured you knew.
Hell, he's on his way back to the Choctaw Nation—
said he's sure Roy Blanton has a hideout over near
Broken Bow somewhere."

His remark almost caused Buck to spill his coffee. "He what?" Buck blurted, struck by the thought of consequences that could arise for him if Casey managed to capture either Roy or Junior. Recovering before exhibiting the impact of the statement, he said, "He never said nothin' to me about goin' back over there without me. Hell, I told him Blanton's gone back to Texas."

"Maybe he's like you," Council said, "likes to go it alone." Then he chuckled and joked, "Maybe he figures you're so old you need a little rest."

"Maybe," Buck replied, doing his best to look amused while knowing he had a lot to lose if Roy Blanton had the chance to spill his guts. He immediately got to his feet. "I'd best get goin'. I've got a lot to do." He placed his cup on the table beside the stove.

"All right, Buck. Good luck with your fishin'," Council said.

Out on the street again, Buck paused to consider what Council had just told him. *That young panther*, he thought, thinking of Casey, *is going to keep on until he gets my ass in a crack for sure.* He had no choice in what he must do, thanks to Casey's bulldog determination. His saddlebags were already packed with supplies and ammunition, but his fishing trip to his cabin was going to have to wait. He stepped up in the saddle and headed toward Broken Bow with a worried mind.

The sorrel nickered a friendly greeting when Casey approached, carrying his saddle and blanket. He took a few moments to gently scratch the reddish brown gelding's face and neck. "You ready to get up in the hills again?" he asked softly. The last couple of days had seen a great deal of scouting up and down steep slopes, thick with forest, but the sorrel never complained. "We'll scout the other side of the Little River today. Maybe our luck will change." He threw the saddle on and tightened the cinch. Then, taking one last look to make sure his fire had gone out, he stepped up in the saddle and left the peaceful campsite beside the Mountain Fork River.

Striking no sign of anyone south of the Little, Casey spent that day following streams up into the hills, counting on blind luck to at least give him a trail to follow. It was to no avail. He found nothing more than a half-rotted shack, apparently abandoned years before. Just short of frustration, he feared he was only wasting time looking for a needle in a haystack. Consequently, he decided to ride into the little settlement of Broken Bow the next day on the chance that Roy or Junior had been seen in town.

Pete Drucker looked up from his forge when Casey walked the sorrel slowly by. Recognizing the deputy who had gone after Joseph Big Eagle's killer, Pete walked out in the street to hail him. "What brings you back to town, Deputy?"

Casey pulled the sorrel to a stop. "Howdy. Drucker, ain't it?" When Pete grinned and nodded, Casey said, "I'm lookin' for somebody. You seen any strangers in town lately?"

"Nope," Pete answered, then changed his mind. "Well, yeah, I reckon I have—a woman."

"A woman?" Casey replied, his response indicating no interest in the casual visitor to the town.

"Yeah," Pete insisted. "You mighta hit town at just the right time, 'cause there ain't no law here. She came into town on foot almost a week ago. Wasn't carryin' nothin' but the clothes on her back, tellin' a tale about somebody killin' her husband and his brother. I think she's half crazy; said she'd been wanderin' around in the woods for days." He shook his head in awe of his own account. "She looked it. Her clothes were all torn and she had scratches all over her face and arms."

"Where is she now?" Casey asked. "Is she still here?"

"She's still here. Mabel Marsh took her in. The poor woman didn't have no place to go, so Mabel and Wiley told her she could stay at their place until they could decide what to do. Wiley was talkin' about sendin' word to the Choctaw Lighthorse to see if they could send a policeman over to check her story out. You know, she might just be a little touched in the head, but she looks like she's been through a lot. Somethin' happened to her, and maybe her husband." He paused to judge the effect of his words on the deputy. "But now that you happened to show up, there won't be no need to send for the Injun police. You know Wiley, don't you? He runs the general store. He and Mabel live in some rooms in the back of the store."

"Yeah," Casey said, "I know Wiley." He remembered talking to him when he came in asking about Joseph Big Eagle. "I'll go over and talk to the woman. The man I'm lookin' for is an older man; might still be wearin' a bandage on his left arm. He's ridin' with a younger man, his son." He waited for Drucker's response.

"Naw, ain't seen nobody like that," the blacksmith said after scratching his head to trigger his memory. "Matter of fact, things have been pretty peaceful since you was here last time." He turned to go back to his forge. "You talk to that woman. She might be crazy, but she might know somethin' about them two you're lookin' for."

"Much obliged," Casey said, and nudged the sorrel.

After tying his horse at the rail, Casey stepped inside the general store. "Well, lookee here," Wiley Marsh exclaimed. "How you doin', Deputy? What you doin' back in Broken Bow?"

"Mr. Marsh," Casey acknowledged, and walked over to the counter.

"I reckon you musta took care of Billy Blanton, 'cause we didn't see hide nor hair of him since you went after him. We dug a right nice grave for that Injun policeman, right next to the graveyard." He smiled and waited for Casey's response.

"I appreciate it," Casey said. "I understand you and your wife took in a strange woman a few days ago."

"We sure did." He hesitated a moment before asking, "Are you lookin' for her?"

"No, not for her," Casey replied, "but I'd like to talk to her if she's well enough to talk. I sorta got the impression talkin' to the blacksmith that she might not be right in the head."

Wiley looked surprised. "No, she ain't that way at all. She was half starved and wore out. Poor thing, she watched her husband and brother-in-law get shot down and had to run for her life. She just needed to rest up and get some nourishing food inside her. She's got family in Oklahoma City, and as soon as she's up to it, she's gonna go there—with our help, of course. It's kinda strange how you showed up before we could send for a lawman to go after those fellers that shot her husband."

"I'd like to talk to her," Casey said. The thought crossed his mind that her husband's killer and the man he was after might be one and the same.

"I'll get her," Wiley said, and went directly to a door in the rear of the store. Holding it partially open, he called, "Mabel, bring Bonnie out here. There's a lawman here that wants to talk to her."

Mabel Marsh entered the store a few minutes later, followed by a smallish, slender woman of perhaps thirty years of age. It was difficult for Casey to be sure because of the many healing scratches and the hollow circles under her eyes. Her hair was neatly combed and she wore clean clothes, however, a fact that Casey attributed to Mabel Marsh's care.

"I didn't think you'd got word to the marshal already," Mabel said upon seeing Casey standing there.

"I didn't," Wiley replied. "He just showed up."

She turned to give Bonnie a gentle smile. "Come, girl, he's from the marshal's office in Fort Smith. He needs to talk to you." Bonnie stepped forward, her eyes averted so as not to meet the lawman's gaze, as if she were guilty of something.

"Ma'am," Casey said, "I understand you've been through a tough time. Mind tellin' me about it?"

He listened with interest while the shy and obviously frightened woman related her encounter with the men who killed her husband and his brother. There was little doubt in Casey's mind regarding her sanity when she described the two assailants. He was curious after hearing her description of the older of the two men. "The old man," he asked, "you say he was a one-armed man?"

"He wasn't one-armed," Bonnie replied softly. "He had two arms, but he didn't have a hand on one of 'em."

He felt the muscles in his arms tighten at that. "Which arm?" he asked.

"I don't know," she replied. "The left one, I guess. I was so scared. They killed my husband, just shot him down."

She looked as if about to go into tears, but she did not. "I'm sorry, ma'am. I know you've been through a lot," he said.

She looked up then to meet his gaze, a hint of fire in her eyes. "Are you gonna get the men that killed my husband?"

"Yes, ma'am," Casey replied, "I am." He studied her face for a moment, trying to decide if she was up to what he was about to propose. "That cabin you talked about, I've been lookin' for it for two days, and I ain't had much luck. Could you take me to it, or at least tell me how to find it?"

She didn't answer right away, uncertain herself. She had taken flight, blindly running for her life through thick forest and punishing brush. Her only thought had been to escape, not really aware in what direction she ran. At one point in her ordeal, she had discovered that she had circled back to the same stream. "I don't know if I can," she finally said. "I didn't know which way I was runnin'. I just happened to come out here in Broken Bow."

Disappointed, he started thinking about the chances of finding her trail and possibly following it back to the cabin, when she offered a better suggestion. "I think I might be able to find the cabin from the river— the way we found it the first time when me and my husband and Leonard left the place where the two rivers joined."

Eager to start out immediately, Casey nevertheless maintained his patience. "Are you up to it?" he asked. "I don't wanna cause you no trouble." He watched her expression closely before adding, "But I ain't had no luck findin' that cabin."

She didn't hesitate. "I'll go."

"Oh, Bonnie," Mabel exclaimed. "Are you sure you wanna do that? It sounds mighty dangerous to me. You got away with your life the first time. Are you sure you wanna take another chance?"

Casey looked at the storekeeper's wife, his expression apologetic. "Like I said, it's up to her. I don't mean to push her, but she could save me a lot of time if she knows how to find that cabin."

"I'll go," Bonnie repeated. "I want you to kill the son of a bitches that killed my husband."

"All right, then," Casey said, glancing again at Mabel, who looked more than a little surprised at the previously shy woman's sudden burst of rough language. "We'll start back first thing in the mornin', all right?" She nodded firmly.

Mabel Marsh shook her head in dismay. Then fixing her gaze on Casey again, she said, "You bring her back here safely, Deputy."

"I will," he replied, knowing that it would be his foremost priority.

After assuring Pete Drucker that he would be paid for his loss in the event of ill fortune, Casey borrowed a horse for Bonnie to ride. Early the next morning, he led the gentle dun up the street to the general store, where he found Bonnie waiting for him, ready to depart.

"You take care of her," Mabel admonished as she watched Bonnie mount.

"Yes ma'am," Casey replied.

Chapter 13

It was a new experience for Casey. He had never traveled with a woman before, and he was not sure whether he was setting too hard a pace or if he should stop to let her rest, or go to the bushes if she had to. He was afraid that she might be following along behind him, reluctant to tell him that she needed to stop. He soon learned that it was needless worry. Bonnie Bowden was a strong woman, accustomed to the sacrifices necessary to survive as the wife of the drifter that her husband had been. Roy Blanton's cabin had been her longest period spent under a roof in the past four years. Open camps in rugged places, lying low after her husband and his brother had stolen a cow, or somebody's chickens, riding hard lest the local law catch up with them was the life she knew during eight years of marriage. She had at first been fearful when Casey showed up at the store, wanting to question her. But that was only because he was the law. She had done nothing to be in trouble with the law, but fear of the law had been a constant companion during her entire marriage. Now that she was assured that Casey sought only to catch the men who had destroyed her family, the toughness that characterized her returned.

Much to her surprise, they came to the confluence of the two rivers after only a half day's ride. She had stumbled around in the forest for two days and nights, and she now realized that she must have wandered far and walked in circles more than once.

"Well," Casey said after pulling the sorrel to a stop on the riverbank, "here's where the Mountain Fork runs into the Little. I reckon you'll be takin' the lead from here."

She guided her horse up beside his and stopped. Looking up and down the river, she was not really sure where she was, and she began to have doubts that she could deliver on her claim to take Casey to the cabin. He watched her closely as she jerked her head right and left, obviously searching for something she recognized. He had a distinct feeling that it had been a wasted effort bringing her with him. "Are you sure this is the right spot on the river?" he asked.

"Yes, sir," she replied, and turned in the saddle to point back at the fork of the two rivers. "It was just this side of where those two join." She continued to scan the riverbank on the far side. "It don't look the same, though. It's been over a month ago, and I didn't have any reason to believe I was gonna have to remember any of this." Then another thought occurred to her. "We were on the other side of the river, and we crossed over to this side where a little sandbar stuck out like an island. It was shallow water there."

"All right," Casey replied patiently, "let's ride along the bank till we find that sandbar." He motioned for her to start. "You lead and I'll follow you."

Still a little uncertain, but determined to do her best, she rode slowly along the riverbank, back toward the way they had just come that morning. After a ride of approximately twenty minutes, she suddenly pointed toward a little spit of land that protruded from the north bank. "There it is!" she proclaimed proudly. "That's where we crossed over to this side." She urged her mount to quicken the pace and hurried to a shallow gully that extended down to the water. "See," she exclaimed. "Right here's where we rode up out of the river. Look down under the bank, right at the water. There's a stream comin' out under the ground, runnin' into the river." She pointed, and he could see that she was right.

Turning her horse to her left, she rode about fifty yards up into the cottonwoods and oaks to a small clearing where a strong stream worked its way down toward the river. "Yes, this is the place," she announced, confident now that she remembered correctly. "William said this is the same stream that's underground where it comes out at the river. Him and his brother decided we oughta cross back over and follow it on up in those hills." She pointed toward a tree-covered ridge to the south. "It'll lead you to the cabin."

"All right," Casey said, "I reckon I'd best take the lead now." His confidence was rising now that Bonnie seemed so sure of herself. It was ironic, he thought, that he had passed this particular point on the river at least three times during the past couple of days. He attributed his carelessness to the fact that the stream, when it reached the river, was actually underground, and he had missed it. He had spent time scouting any obvious streams that fed into the river, speculating that Blanton's cabin had to be built near water.

After half an hour of pushing through thick brush and tangled shrubs, following the meandering stream up into the hills, Casey had to wonder what possessed Bonnie's husband and his brother to continue the difficult trail. He was about to decide that Bonnie had been mistaken, when he caught his first glimpse of the cabin. *Damn*, he thought, amazed to see a fair-sized house built close against the hill behind it. He could imagine what a welcome and unexpected sight a sturdy, unoccupied structure had been to Bonnie and her husband. He dismounted and waited for Bonnie to catch up to him.

"We'll leave the horses here," he said. "I want you to stay with 'em while I slip up a little closer to see what's what. All right?" When she appeared to be a little uneasy, he gave her his pistol. "Take this. I don't think you'll have to use it, but hang on to it just in case." She accepted the weapon eagerly. He nodded and smiled to reassure her. Then, with rifle in hand, he started up the stream on foot, leaving her to hold the horses.

Working his way up through the trees and undergrowth, he arrived at a point a few yards shy of what appeared to be the main trail into the cabin. Picking a large oak tree for cover, he knelt to look over the situation. The house was set in a clearing that left it open in the front and on one side. The other side and the back were almost sitting in the trees. On the clearing side of the house a small corral had been built, large enough to hold maybe four or five horses. At the present time it was empty. One saddled horse was tied at the front porch. It was not the gray horse Roy Blanton rode. *Junior*, Casey thought, but where was the old man? It was cause enough to make him hesitate. He needed to know where both men were, and it was his intention to arrest both men. If he moved too soon on Junior, the old man might get away. Maybe there might be a chance to circle around to the rear of the cabin and get the jump on Junior, and possibly hold him until the old man showed up. *Right now*, he thought, *I can't think of anything better*.

Backing away from the tree, he made his way back down to Bonnie to advise her of his intentions. At first relieved to see him return, she became uneasy again when he told her what he was going to do. There ain't but one of 'em at the cabin. I think it's the son. I'm gonna try to get around behind and see if I can arrest him before he knows what's happening."

"Aren't you goin' to shoot him?" she asked. "The young one's the one that shot my husband. He deserves to be shot, just like he shot William."

He felt empathy for the young widow, but he had to explain that since he was a U.S. deputy marshal, it was always his job to allow a fugitive the opportunity to surrender. "They'll hang, anyway," he said.

"Then it don't make any sense to arrest them," she said bitterly, "if you're gonna end up killin' 'em, anyway."

He shook his head slowly, at a loss for a reasonable answer for her. "I'm sorry. It's the law, so I guess that's the way it'll have to be. You just sit tight down here in this ravine with the horses and you'll be all right," he said. "If things don't go the way I want 'em to, and somethin' happens to me, you get on that horse and ride to hell outta here."

She didn't reply. Instead, she did as he said, standing with the horses as she watched him until he disappeared into the trees. Though she stood quietly, her mind was not at all settled over the brief discussion she had just had with the deputy marshal. It made no sense to her. Roy Blanton and his son were representative of the vilest form of evil. To her, it seemed the same as dealing with rabid dogs; simply destroy them before they could do further harm. What good was served by capturing them and taking them back to Fort Smith to go to trial? As Casey had said, they would probably end up on the gallows, anyway. What measure of revenge would that grant her dead husband? The Blantons should be shot down like dogs, the same treatment they gave William and Leonard.

Thoughts of her late husband brought feelings of sorrow as well as guilt—guilt because she could not bring herself to grieve for him as much as she should. She told herself that she had loved William, even though he had carried her into a life of nomadic wandering. Raised in a house with four unruly brothers and a long-suffering mother, Bonnie could not resist the opportunity to escape when William Bowden asked her to marry him. She was only fifteen at the time, and he was ten years her senior. He filled her mind with hope when he told her of his plans to go west with his brother to start a cattle ranch.

Her mother and father advised her against the marriage, but she saw it as her only chance to leave behind a life of endless chores and cleaning up after her worthless brothers. Her dreams of romance and a new life were soon shattered when she realized that William had neither the means nor the brains to create a cattle empire. The years that followed proved to be nothing more than bouncing from one settlement to another, living off the land and the frequent petty thefts that sustained them. Through it all, she tried to be as good a wife as she could, believing her wedding vows to be sacred. In a way, she guessed that she loved William, but the guilt now felt was that she hadn't loved him enough. He was not a cruel husband. It was not his fault that he didn't possess the will and the talent to make a better life for them. And for that reason, he deserved to be avenged for his violent execution. She held Casey's pistol up and stared at it. She owed William that.

Making his way up the slope behind the cabin, Casey moved rapidly under the cover of the dense growth of oaks and pines. When he reached a point directly over the log structure, he descended the hill until he could see it plainly. As Bonnie had said, there was a single window in the back of the house, the very window she had escaped through. He continued his descent down through the woods, moving cautiously from tree to tree until reaching a large oak no more than twenty yards from the cabin wall. He paused there for a few minutes, watching the open window carefully. If his presence had been discovered, there was no indication from inside the house. Satisfied, he left the large oak and hurried to a position against the cabin wall beside the window.

With his back flattened against the log wall, he listened for any sound of movement inside. Nothing disturbed the quiet of the forest behind him other than the occasional song of a blue jay quarreling with his mate. Casey started to move when he was stopped by another sound, this one from within the cabin. Unable to identify it initially, he then realized it was snoring floating out the open window.

Sliding along the wall to the window, he slowly inched one eye beyond the frame. At first, he saw no one inside, and then his eye discovered the sleeping form of Junior Blanton, stretched out on his back on a bedroll. Risking his entire head then, Casey took a broader look around the inside of the cabin. There was no one else, only Junior, dead to the world; his pistol belt hung on a chair back near the door, his rifle propped against the wall beside it.

He glanced up at the substantial limb brushing the cabin roof. Another glance back at the sleeping body on the bedroll, and he decided the odds were in his favor to gain complete surprise. Without making a sound, he placed his rifle inside the window. Then he quickly reached up to grab the limb with both hands and pulled himself up and through the window, feet first. The sound of his feet landing upon the floor roused Junior from his slumber, but the notorious outlaw was not immediate in regaining his senses, giving

Casey plenty of time to recover his rifle and take a stance directly before his victim.

"Pa?" Junior muttered in the confusion of his sudden awakening.

"I ain't your pa," Casey said. "Get on your feet. You're under arrest." With his rifle leveled at Junior, he stepped back to give him room to get up.

Junior didn't move at once, still rubbing sleep from his eyes. Finally fully realizing what was going on, he spoke. "You're that damn marshal. How'd you get in here?"

"Get on your feet," Casey repeated. "We're gonna wait here for your pa. Where is he?"

"I don't know," Junior replied defiantly as he rolled over on his hands and knees, preparing to get up. "You know, you're about the dumbest lawman I've ever seen. You just walked into your funeral. There ain't no way you'll walk outta here alive."

"Is that a fact?" Casey replied. "Well, if I don't, you won't. Now, get up from there."

"I'm gittin'," Junior grumbled, moving slowly. Then he suddenly lunged up to attack the deputy.

Anticipating just such a move, Casey took a quick step to the side and slammed the side of Junior's head with the butt of his rifle, dropping the stunned outlaw to the floor. "I figured you'd make a dumb move like that. Now I'm gonna have to tie you to a chair while we wait for your pa. If you had behaved yourself, you wouldn't have that headache." He glanced around him, looking for a rope while Junior dutifully struggled to his feet. Seeing no rope, Casey prodded Junior in the back with the barrel of his rifle, and started him toward the door. "Now, Junior, I'm goin' to explain somethin' to you nice and slow so you'll understand what I'm sayin'. We're gonna walk out that door and get that rope off your saddle. We're gonna do it real easy so you don't get any ideas about tryin' to run and

make me waste a cartridge on your worthless ass.
Then we'll go back in the cabin and wait for your pa.
Is that clear enough for you to understand?"

"You're as good as dead," Junior grumbled, "comin'
here like this. You're just savin' Pa the trouble of
findin' you."

"Well, you never know, do you?" Casey said. "Now,
get that rope offa there."

Junior did as he was told, walking up to his horse
and untying the rawhide string that held a coil of rope.
When it was free, he suddenly spun around, threw it
at Casey's head, and took off running across the clearing toward the cover of the woods. Casey shook his
head in weary response. He did not want to shoot and
alert Roy if the old man was close by, but he could not
let Junior get away. Taking his time to make sure of his
target, he raised his rifle and sighted on the running
man's legs. The report of the shot startled him, for he
had not yet pulled the trigger. Junior went down with
a bullet in his chest. Casey glanced up then to see
Bonnie standing at the edge of the clearing, the pistol
still pointing chest high.

Surprised and bewildered, Casey could do nothing
for a long moment but stand there gawking at the
trembling woman as she lowered the weapon and fired
a second shot into the body already lying still. "Bonnie!" he finally managed. "Don't shoot! He's dead!"
He ran to meet her. She made no move to resist when
he took the gun from her hand, seemingly glad to surrender it. "What are you doin' here? Why did you
shoot?"

"He was gettin' away," she replied earnestly. "I
couldn't let him get away."

He started to tell her that he was not getting away,
that he was going to shoot him in the leg, but decided
it was no use telling her now. What's done is done, he
decided, but her vengeful action created a new set of

problems. "Come on," he said. "We'd best get inside. I don't know where Roy is, but if he's anywhere close, he's bound to have heard those shots." He hurried her toward the door. "Where are the horses?"

"I left them in the ravine," she said.

"All right," he said. "Go on inside. If the old man is anywhere about, it ain't gonna be safe out here in this clearing." While she hurried to the door, he grabbed Junior's body by his heels and dragged him out of sight in the edge of the woods. With any luck, Roy may not have been close enough to have heard the two shots Bonnie fired, and he might successfully set a trap for the old man. He had barely gotten rid of the corpse when he heard what sounded like the tormented howl of a banshee ringing out from the forest behind him. Startled, he stopped to listen, but only for an instant before he realized the origin of the mournful wail. Running flat out, he sprinted toward the cabin with rifle slugs kicking up dirt around his heels. Charging through the doorway as chunks of pine were blasted from the log wall, he slammed the door shut.

He was met by the terrified face of Bonnie Bowden. "He's found us!" she exclaimed, her eyes wide with fright.

"I reckon he has," Casey hastily replied, "and he's got us in a fix." He looked around the cabin they now found themselves trapped in. "Grab that rifle and gun belt by the door," he ordered. She jumped to do his bidding. "This ain't no good," he thought aloud. "He can keep us pinned up in here forever, or until he decides to burn us out." He thought it over for no more than a few seconds before deciding. "I'd rather be outside with him in the cabin." He motioned her toward the back window. "Come on, we're gettin' outta here."

On the other side of the clearing, a dozen yards or so back in the trees, Roy Blanton reloaded his rifle while emitting a constant moaning. As he fed each cartridge into the magazine, his moan increased in volume until reaching a high-pitched howl. Although loud and primordial, it could not drown out the screaming in his brain. He had arrived at the cabin in time to see his only remaining son—Junior, his eldest, the one he had the most hope for—dragged into the woods, dead. He had been almost blinded by the rage that filled his spine, firing wildly at the fleeing deputy in his fury. His family had been decimated one by one until all his sons were gone, and his thirst for revenge overpowered every other emotion or thought. Two men were responsible for his grief, Buck Avery and Casey Dixon, and Dixon was now holed up in the cabin that he and his sons had built. One thought was now dominant in his mind, to kill the two lawmen. He could not rest until it was done.

With emotions still too far out of control, he unconsciously fell back on his instincts, moving from one position to another—firing round after round at the cabin, blistering the window frames with lead—before moving on to other vantage points. Finally, when the barrel of his Henry rifle became too hot to rest on the stump of his left arm, he was forced to stop shooting. Still filled with rage, he stood defiantly at the edge of the clearing, hurling promises of death and destruction, not yet realizing that he was cursing an empty cabin. "An eye for an eye!" he yelled. "Your life for my boys!"

After a while, he became weary of his ranting and sat down on a tree stump, his eyes still fixed unblinking upon the cabin. Gradually, the fire that had heated his blood began to cool down to the point where rational thought once again entered. It suddenly struck him that there had not been one single shot of returned fire. *He ain't in there*, he thought. *He's gone out the back!* To test the notion, he stepped out from behind a tree and exposed his entire body. There were still no shots fired from the house.

Cursing the opportunity he had allowed for Casey's escape, he ran to the door and kicked it open, his rifle ready to spray the room with .44 slugs. There was no one there. They had gone out the back window. Dejected and spent, he sat down at the table to think about what had just happened. His mood lasted only for a moment, however, for as he thought about Junior's cold body lying in the edge of the trees, his anger rose again. *I've got to take care of my boy*, he told himself. *Then I'm gonna hunt that deputy down. He couldn't have gotten far.*

As a precaution, he grabbed his rifle again and scouted around the cabin to make sure he had, in fact, driven the lawman away. When there were no shots fired in his direction, and no sign that the deputy was close, he went back up the path to retrieve his horse. Then he hefted Junior's body up over the saddle and returned to the cabin to prepare his son for burial.

Almost two hundred yards from the cabin, Casey and Bonnie made their way over the ridge that formed one side of the ravine where their horses were tied. After going out the window, Casey had not sought to set an easy pace in consideration for the woman. He soon found that it was hardly necessary, for Bonnie stayed right behind him, stride for stride until reaching the ravine. There was no questioning the woman's stamina, but he now faced a different problem—what to do with her while he went back for Roy. When he voiced his dilemma, she immediately advised him that she was going with him. She insisted that she had demonstrated her ability, as well as her willingness, to handle a gun. "Anyway," she insisted, "I'd rather be in a gunfight than be left behind in these woods. The last time I was left in the woods by myself, I got lost for two days."

Casey took a moment to think it over. He didn't like

the idea of placing a woman in harm's way. On the other hand, however, two of them with rifles could snipe away at Blanton from two sides if they caught him in the cabin. "All right," he said, "but if he wants to surrender, we're gonna take him alive. You understand?"

"I understand," she replied, but without enthusiasm.

"Let's go, then," he said, climbing into the saddle. "I figure we'd circle up the slope until we cross that main trail into the cabin. That way, we'll come up on the cabin a little above it, like he did." He didn't wait for her reply. Giving the sorrel a gentle nudge with his heels, he was away. She followed right behind him.

Casey set the sorrel on the general line and the stout chestnut gelding made his way up through the trees without further direction. Spotting a narrow break in the leaves of the trees up ahead, Casey guessed they were approaching the path. A few yards more and he suddenly pulled his horse to an abrupt stop and held his hand up to warn Bonnie to do the same. He thought he had caught sight of something moving on the path above them. "Be still," he whispered as he stared at the opening in the trees. "A rider," he whispered again, and pulled his rifle from the saddle sling as he dismounted. "Hold the horses here," he instructed Bonnie.

Making his way quickly up through the frequent patches of rhododendron among the oaks, he hurried to cut the rider off. Angling across the ridge, he managed to gain the cover of a large tree trunk that afforded him a clear view of the path and the rider now approaching. With his rifle ready to fire, he prepared to challenge the rider. Hardly able to believe his eyes, he couldn't suppress the grin that crept across his face when he recognized the man. Stepping out from behind the tree when the rider was almost beside him, he spoke. "Buck, what the hell are you doin' here? Are you lost?"

Taken completely by surprise, Buck reined back so hard that he caused his horse to rear up on his hind legs. "Casey! Damn, boy, you scared the hell outta me." Settling his horse down, he looked around him as if expecting someone else to pop out of the woods. "How the hell did you find this place?"

"I had a guide," Casey answered. He turned his head back toward the slope and called out, "Bring 'em on up, Bonnie."

"Who the hell is that?" Buck asked when he saw the woman emerge from the trees, leading Casey's horse.

Casey explained the woman's presence and the circumstances that led her to cross his path. When she came up to them, he introduced her. "Buck, here is a deputy marshal. He's been doggin' Roy Blanton for more than a few years. Buck, this is Bonnie Bowden." Once the introductions were over, Casey had another question. "How come you're here, and how did you know how to find this trail?" Then he thought to ask, "Do you know where this path leads?"

"I was lookin' for you," Buck replied. "I was afraid you'd go get yourself killed tryin' to track Roy Blanton by yourself." He paused to grace Bonnie with a grin. "Course I didn't know you had took on a new partner. I just happened to stumble on this little trail up through the hills," he lied. "Where does it go?"

"Well," Casey replied, "if you'd kept goin', you'da found yourself on Roy Blanton's front porch."

"No," Buck reacted, pretending to be surprised. "I knew he had a hideout around these parts somewhere. I reckon it's a good thing I ran into you first." He studied Casey's eyes carefully, wondering if the young deputy had discovered more than he was telling. "Do you know if Roy and Junior are at the cabin? Have you seen 'em?"

"The old man is the only one left," Casey said. "Junior's dead." Then he explained how Junior had met his fate while trying to escape.

"And this lady shot him down," Buck repeated while giving Bonnie a look of surprise. Turning back to Casey, he asked, "Did you get a chance to talk to him before the lady shot him?"

"No. I was just fixin' to tie him up when he took off runnin'. I was goin' to shoot him in the leg to stop him, but he was headin' right for Bonnie, so she shot him. She thought he was gonna get away."

"So that just leaves one of the Blantons alive," Buck said, being careful not to show his relief, "ol' Roy, himself."

"That's right," Casey said. "He had Bonnie and me holed up in his cabin about an hour ago. We had to hop out the back window. We were fixin' to circle back when you came along, so you came at the right time. With three rifles, we can make it pretty hot for him if we catch him before he leaves the cabin—especially since we can cover that back window. I'm thinkin' that maybe we could take some of the fight outta him now that all his sons are gone."

"I doubt it," Buck responded. "He's more likely to be meaner'n ever. Ain't much chance of takin' Roy alive."

"I'd like to give him a chance to surrender," Casey insisted. "It don't seem right that, out of five of 'em, we can't bring one to face a judge."

"Oh, sure, we'll give him a chance to give up," Buck said, "but I don't think he'll take it."

Casey stepped up in the saddle. "Well, we can't stand around here talkin' about it. We don't know if he's still there. He might be fixin' to slip up on us while we're jawin' about what we're gonna do." He wheeled the sorrel and led off toward the clearing and the cabin.

Chapter 14

Junior Blanton had been a sizable man, and consequently a heavy load for a man two years shy of his sixtieth birthday. But Roy shouldered his son's corpse and carried it inside the cabin, almost stumbling when he stepped up on the tiny porch. Straining as he attempted to lay the body down gently, he managed to lower Junior onto the one bed in the room. Breathing heavily from the exertion, he stood over the bed for a few moments, gazing down at the cold, lifeless form, fighting the moan that threatened again from deep inside him. He thought of the two lawmen who had destroyed his family, and gritted his teeth, grimacing as he fought the bitter gall of his misery. *I gotta dig a grave*, he thought after a while, *give my boy a decent burial*.

Picking up a shovel, he went out to the side of the house opposite the corral and selected a spot for Junior's grave. With no hand on his left arm, he found it extremely difficult to handle the shovel in the hard ground. After managing to barely scrape away a small area of dirt, he encountered a maze of roots from the oaks next to the cabin. His frustration mounted as he found it impossible to dig using one hand, and he cursed the impotent stump. Finally, with nothing to show for his toil beyond a small patch of disturbed earth, he paused to lean on the shovel while he caught his breath. In the next instant, he jumped, startled, as a rifle slug snapped the handle of his shovel in two. With no time to determine from where the shot had come, he ran for the cabin door with two more shots striking the porch floor right behind his heels.

Fully as surprised as Blanton, Casey jerked his head around when he heard Buck's first shot. Buck fired twice more before Casey could question him. "I thought we were goin' to give him a chance to give up!"

"Damn, I forgot," Buck said. "I guess I just reacted without thinkin' about it when I saw him standin' there." Casey didn't comment further, and Buck wasn't sure his partner bought his excuse. Regardless of what Casey thought, Buck knew he could not permit Roy to talk. It would mean a prison sentence for him if Roy got the opportunity to tell anyone about the payoffs he accepted. "I'll give him a chance now." He cupped his hands in front of his mouth and yelled, "Roy Blanton! This is the law. We're givin' you a chance to surrender. Throw down your weapons and come outta there with your hands up!"

There was no answer right away, but after a few minutes had passed, they heard his answer. "Buck Avery," he yelled back, "is that you?"

"Yeah, it's me, Roy. Your killin' and robbin' days are over. Throw down your gun and walk out in the clearin'."

"The hell you say," Roy's response came back. "By God, I've bought and paid for your ass. You owe me, so why don't you just come in and get me."

The old man's answer puzzled Casey. "What's he talkin' about, Buck?"

"Damned if I know," Buck replied. "I think the old

fool has got his brains all scrambled up—drinkin' too much whiskey, I reckon."

"Blanton!" Casey called out then. "There ain't no use in any more killin'. Come on out with your hands up, and I give you my word you'll get a fair trial."

"Kiss my ass, you murderin' son of a bitch. I may be old, but I ain't took leave of my senses yet. You want me, you come and get me. We'll see who's still standin' when it's over." For punctuation, he sent a couple of rifle slugs whistling through the trees where they stood.

"We'd best move away from this spot," Buck advised. "He's already figurin' out where we are. We're gonna have to smoke him outta there." He gave Casey an understanding look. "You done the right thing, Casey, but Roy ain't gonna be took alive."

"I reckon you're right," Casey conceded. "I guess he's lost too many sons already to trust us now."

Feeling content that the whole affair was going to come to a satisfactory conclusion, Buck set to with a willing disposition. It could almost be described as lighthearted. "I expect we'd best split up and cover that cabin from three sides, since we got us three rifles." He grinned at Bonnie then. "That is, if you can shoot that rifle you're totin'. I ain't heard you say a word since I got here."

"Don't you worry none about me," Bonnie replied evenly. "I can use a rifle. I just hope I'm the one that gets him."

"She'll do," Buck said with a chuckle. Then he turned his attention to the task at hand. "There's windows on only three sides of the cabin. There ain't none on the side where the corral is, so we can cover all the windows. I figure if it gets too hot for him and he tries to break out, it'll most likely be the front or the back. So whaddaya say you cover the front, I'll cover the back, and we can let Bonnie cover the side with the window. That all right with you, Casey?"

Casey shrugged. "I guess so." He turned to Bonnie. "You got plenty of cartridges for that rifle?" She held up the cartridge belt she had taken along with Junior's rifle. "I guess we're ready then," Casey said.

Once all three were in place, the shooting began in earnest with the idea of ripping the cabin to pieces, concentrating on the windows, which offered the only positions from which Roy could return fire. After half an hour, during which the forest was alive with a sound like that of a military assault, it was obvious to Casey that the solid log sides would forever withstand the rifle fire, and the only hope was for Roy to get caught by crossfire through the windows. While he considered the futility of it, a random thought crossed his mind. *How did Buck know there was a window in the back of the cabin?* It puzzled him for a moment until he decided that Buck had probably assumed that when he told him he and Bonnie had fled the cabin before. He shrugged and reloaded.

Inside the cabin, Roy was hugging the floor to avoid the deadly bullets crossing from three sides. He tried to return fire, but found it impossible to shoot out of any window without exposing himself. He decided that it was too hot for him to remain. It was time to abandon the cabin. On his hands and knees, he crawled over to the bed where Junior's body lay. Grabbing the footboard, he dragged the bed away from the wall. Taking an extra ammunition belt, and a few basic essentials to survive in the woods, he said farewell to his son and prepared to leave.

Buck had purposely chosen to station himself at the rear of the cabin, where neither Casey nor the woman could see him. Like Casey, he soon concluded that they could fill the house with bullets until they ran out, with no positive results. Blanton was going to have to be smoked out, and they had no torches to light up—and nothing to make a decent torch with in the green bushes and trees. But he had something better. He had come prepared. While the shooting continued from the front and one side, he worked his way down through the dense forest to the back wall. With his back pressed flat against the wall, he reached inside his shirt and pulled out a stick of dynamite he had carried in his saddlebags.

Roy, *you know I'd like to give you the chance to give up*, he thought, *but you like to talk too much*. He lit the fuse and waited for it to burn halfway. When there were only a few inches left, he tossed it through the window beside him and ran for cover.

Startled, Casey almost stumbled backward when the explosion tore out one wall of the cabin, breaching the logs and sending pieces of the roof skyward. All firing stopped as Casey and Bonnie stared in disbelief at the smoking cabin. All was quiet in the clearing for a few frozen moments until the sound of Buck's voice carried from the rear of the cabin.

"Hot damn," he yelled. "I reckon that got his attention!"

With his rifle held ready just in case, Casey charged across the clearing and stormed in the door. He almost fired, but checked himself in time to avoid shooting Buck coming in the back window. The room was filled with thin gray smoke, but not enough to hamper vision. Casey and Buck looked at each other, astonished. Roy was not there. The body on the bed was clearly that of his son, Junior. "What the hell . . . ," Buck muttered, unable to understand.

A few moments later, Casey supplied the answer. Curious as to why the bed had been moved toward the middle of the room, he looked beyond it. Next to the wall, several boards had been removed from the floor, revealing a hole wide enough for a man to squeeze into. Peering cautiously into the hole, Casey announced, "Looks like a tunnel."

"Well, I'll be damned," Buck uttered. "The ol' son of a bitch had himself an escape tunnel." Then he glanced up to meet Casey's gaze. "I wonder how long he's been gone." Both men ran out of the cabin and rounded the corner to the side wall.

Searching frantically, they charged into the trees and brush. "Here it is!" Casey shouted. "Here's where he came out!" The opening was just barely inside the tree line. He stood up and looked around him in case he was about to be shot at. The forest was deadly silent with not even the sound of a bird in flight.

"Watch yourself," Buck warned. "That ol' fox might be drawin' a bead on one of us right now."

It was a thought that Casey had already considered. Then something else occurred to him. *Where was Bonnie?* This was the side of the house that she was covering. In the excitement of the dynamite blast and the discovery of the tunnel, neither he nor Buck had noticed that Bonnie had not come down from her position on the hillside. "Oh, God . . . ," he uttered, and immediately started up through the trees.

"What is it?" Buck asked.

"Bonnie," Casey answered, and continued up the slope. He did not call out for her, because he had a sinking feeling in his gut that she would not answer. Upon reaching a boulder about halfway up, he found what he had dreaded. It appeared that Blanton had taken her by surprise from the rear. Her throat was slit from ear to ear and she lay on a bed of oak leaves that were splotched with her blood. He knelt on one knee beside her and looked around him for signs of her killer. There was nothing to break the silence of the deep woods. The rifle and cartridge belt were gone. He was devastated. He felt responsible for her death. He should have never let her come along, should have left her at the river after she found the stream for him, or sent her on back to Broken Bow, anything to avoid this. He was still kneeling beside her when Buck came puffing up the hill behind him.

"Ah, now, that's a real shame," Buck said upon seeing the dead woman. "She was a spunky little lady, too." Feeling that was enough mourning for Bonnie, he said, "We've got a panther on the run, boy. We'll have to let her be for now. Roy's on foot, and he's gonna be lookin' for a horse." There was no need to say more. Casey sprang to his feet and both men went crashing recklessly through the underbrush in a wild effort to get back to where they had left the horses.

They were too late. All three horses were gone. "Damn him," Buck fumed. "He sure as hell skunked us. Now we're on foot and he's got the horses. Who'da thought the old fox woulda set himself up with a getaway tunnel? I never gave it a thought that he could get behind us and steal our damn horses."

It was difficult not to feel the fool after having the tables completely turned on them by the wily old outlaw. Casey might have seen a bit of humor in their predicament if the stakes were not so fatal, and their adversary were not the merciless killer that Roy Blanton was. Once again, the game had changed, and once again the hunter was the hunted, or maybe that was not the case at all. At this point, it was hard to say what Blanton would do. He still craved revenge, of that there could be little doubt, but would he escape while he had the chance? And plan his vengeance at another time? All these thoughts flashed through Casey's mind in a brief second, and in the midst of his consternation, one fact almost evaded him. "We're not really on foot," he blurted. "We've got his horses."

Buck lifted his head in surprise, irritated that it had not occurred to him as yet. "That's a fact," he said, and turned immediately to look toward the ruins of the cabin. There was no horse in the corral, but he remembered then that Blanton had not had time to put his horse away, and had left it saddled with the reins looped over a corner post next to Junior's. But now the animal was nowhere to be seen.

"It musta jerked loose when that stick of dynamite went off and scared it," Casey said. "It probably didn't run far. We'd better get down there and find it before he does."

Many scattered thoughts ran through the crazed mind of Roy Blanton as he circled down around the slope below his cabin. His sons were gone, his hideout discovered and destroyed. The passion to kill those who were responsible burnt in his veins, but foremost in his mind at this moment was the compulsion to retrieve his severed hand. He was not whole without this phantom appendage, and he could not tolerate the thought that it might fall into evil hands.

He had already escaped through the tunnel when he heard the blast that destroyed his cabin. In the safety of the trees, he turned to see his and Junior's horses break free of the post and gallop across the clearing and down the other side of the hill. He watched them for as long as he could see them through the trees before working his way up behind the woman on the ridge. Distracted by the explosion in his cabin, she was easy prey. He had no trouble in slipping up behind her and opening her windpipe with his skinning knife. He left her gurgling blood and gasping for air while he circled around to find their horses. Knowing he now had the upper hand in the game, he led the horses off in search of his own.

The forest was dense on this side of the ridge, but he caught sight of the gray gelding through the trees right where he suspected the horse might be. Halfway down the hill, a little pool was formed where a spring emerged from the ground in a cluster of rocks. The gray was standing beside Junior's dun, peacefully drinking from the pool. It lifted its head to respond to the greeting nicker from Casey's sorrel, and waited unafraid for the three horses to approach, recognizing its master astride Buck's horse.

Almost frantic in his haste to dismount, Blanton rushed to grab his horse's reins. Then he went immediately to his saddlebags to retrieve his bony hand. As he carefully unrolled the oilcloth, an acid stench wafted upward as he exposed the rotted appendage. Ignoring the grisly aroma, he pressed the hand, which was now little more than skeletal with a few shreds of skin and flesh attached, against the stark stump of his left arm. *He could still feel it!* Like a live flame, he could feel the burning sensation run through the fingers of the unattached hand. Unable to contain it, he felt the low moan begin down in his diaphragm and begin to work its way up until he roared out in anger. Renewing his vow for vengeance, he replaced the ghostly hand, climbed up on the gray, and led the captive horses away from the pool. The hunt was about to begin, but first he had to take the horses where they would not be found.

Having just reached the corral, and finding the two horses gone, both men stopped short when they heard the long, eerie howl of rage emanating from the forest below them. "Jesus!" Casey blurted.

"Roy," Buck said. "He's crazy as a tick. He beat us to those horses." They were still on foot.

Separating with about two dozen yards between them, they moved carefully down through the trees in the direction from which the sound had come. Convinced they were pitted against a crazy man, they were also aware that the man they hunted, crazy or not, was a cunning and devious tracker.

Reaching the pool in the rocks a few minutes ahead of Buck, Casey scouted the soft ground between them while he waited for the bulkier deputy to join him. "He was here," Casey said, pointing to the ground. "From the looks of these tracks, he had all the horses with him."

"We're in a helluva fix," Buck grunted, his face a mask of irritation, the result of his toes being jammed against the pointed toes of his boots as he made his way down the slope. "These boots sure as hell weren't made for walkin'," he complained. "I'm totin' too damn much lard to have to walk all over these hills."

"You won't be carryin' as much if we don't catch up with Blanton and our horses, 'cause we ain't got nothin' to eat," Casey commented. "Come on, this trail oughta be easy enough to follow." Wasting no more time to discuss it, he started out, following the obvious trail through the brush.

"Watch yourself," Buck reminded him, wincing as he took the first step after Casey.

The August afternoon was hot and humid, even this late in the day. Down near the bottom of the hill there was no hint of a breeze in the undisturbed leaves on the trees, and the air felt close and heavy. Casey looked back at Buck. The big man was breathing hard with great patches of sweat spreading under his arms. He paused to look up through the leaves at the sky. "That doesn't look too good," he remarked.

Buck followed his line of sight, peering up through the branches at the clouds building up over the hills. "Maybe it'll miss us," he said. "A little rain would feel pretty good right now, though."

Reaching the bottom of a narrow ravine, Casey followed the trail through bushes left with broken limbs by the four horses. About to climb up the other side of the ravine, he was forced to dive for cover when a rifle slug whined by his ear. He was almost on the ground before he heard the sound of the rifle that fired it. Several shots followed in rapid succession, and he rolled over behind a tree trunk and looked back to see if Buck was all right.

"Like I said," Buck called out, "watch yourself." He pointed toward a high point on the ridge that formed one side of the ravine. "He's up there, on that hog-back, in them pine trees."

Casey stared hard at the spot, hoping to pick Blanton out, but the sun was almost directly behind the little clump of pines, making it difficult to see. The old man was crafty enough to use the setting sun to his advantage. That thought spawned a second thought— the sun would soon be dropping behind the hills, leaving the dense forest in darkness.

Thinking the same thing, Buck crawled up beside Casey. "We're gonna have to back up and get up on top of that ridge. There ain't no way we're gonna go straight up this slope here without gettin' our asses shot off."

"I ain't sure we've got enough time to go back and circle around him before it gets dark," Casey replied. "We'll be stompin' around in these woods all night tryin' to find him—and that's if he's still there by the time we get there." He shook his head, puzzled. "Why doesn't he just take off and leave us to wander around in the bushes?"

"'Cause he wants us just as bad as we want him," Buck replied, "maybe more."

"Well, whaddaya wanna do?" Casey asked.

"Might as well pull back and see if we can work around behind him before dark," Buck replied. "Rather do that than set here while he takes target practice."

"Suits me," Casey said, and started sliding backward. When they reached a point where it was safe to stand up again, they backtracked as quickly as possible in a race with daylight as dingy gray clouds continued to drift over the hills.

A low rumble of thunder came to them from several

miles away as Casey led the way up a wooded slope that steepened gradually until it became necessary to slow the pace. He pressed on, climbing as fast as he could manage, grabbing small tree trunks and limbs to help him as he pushed up toward the crest. Behind him, he could hear the labored breathing of his older, heavier partner, and he knew Buck was having a hard time keeping up. Near the top of the ridge, he was stopped momentarily, startled by the sudden crack of lightning, followed almost immediately by the crash of thunder. He looked behind him at Buck.

"Damn!" Buck said. "That was right on top of us. We're fixin' to get our asses wet." His prediction was not long in fulfillment. The last rays of the setting sun peeked briefly beneath the solid blanket of storm clouds, then disappeared. In a matter of seconds they found themselves shrouded in darkness. Another sharp crack of lightning announced the start of rain. Large drops fell randomly to land with a rhythmic tapping on the oak leaves, followed by a gradual increase in frequency until a steady downpour set in. "Shit," Buck grumbled.

There was no need for further comment as both men tried to shield their weapons from the water already soaking their clothes while thinking of their rain slickers rolled up behind their saddles. Casey gave Buck a resigned shake of his head, then pushed on to the top of the ridge. Moving slowly while the rain pelted the brims of their hats, they made their way toward the hogback that Buck had pointed out from below. Because of the rain and the frequent rumbling of thunder, they were forced to move cautiously, stopping to listen every few yards when lightning flashed.

Finally reaching a point some thirty yards below the pine-covered knob, they stopped to look and listen. In a few minutes, another bolt of lightning flashed, illuminating the little stand of pines and telling them that Blanton was no longer there. Both men instinc-tively looked around them on all sides in case they had stumbled into a trap. "Hell, he's took off," Buck finally decided. With Casey still leading, they moved on up into the pines.

"Looks like he was lying right here when he was shootin' at us," Casey said, indicating a patch of dis-turbed pine needles. As he stared down at the ground, a tiny stream of water drained from the brim of his hat to fall on a metallic object lying on the pine straw. He picked up the empty cartridge to show Buck.

"Ol' Roy must still have plenty of bank money," Buck said. "He don't bother pickin' up his brass."

"He's probably usin' our cartridges," Casey said.

With the help of lightning flashes, they were able to determine in which direction Blanton had departed the knob. It appeared that he had gone down the other side of the ridge toward a shallow valley beyond. They started down through the trees as the frequency of the lightning flashes decreased and the center of the storm rolled past them. The rain, however, seemed only to increase in intensity. As the lightning moved away from them, the dank oak forest became darker and darker until their progress was slowed almost to a crawl, with them literally feeling their way from tree to tree. Behind him, Casey heard a sudden oath from Buck, followed by the sound of snapping bushes as the big man lost his footing and crashed to the ground. An instant later, the bright flash of a muzzle blast ripped the darkness, and he heard the crack of the ri-fle. Without having to think about it, he threw himself to the ground as two more muzzle flashes split the darkness. As fast as he could bring his rifle up, he fired two shots at the spot, then rolled over next to a tree trunk, expecting return fire. It came in seconds from a different location apart from the first. Seconds after, Buck fired off a couple of rounds at the spot.

"This ain't gettin' us nowhere," Buck said, crawling up close to Casey. "Our best bet is to try to work our way across this ridge above him. Maybe we can pin him down between us."

"All right," Casey said, "but we better not get too far apart or we'll be shootin' at each other." With that in mind, they started inching their way across the slope, doing their best to move silently. It would have been impossible had it not been raining steadily, masking the noise of their boots whipping through the undergrowth.

When they guessed they were over the general area where they had seen Blanton's last muzzle flash, they separated and prepared to descend the hill. "He might still be in that last spot, waitin' for us to come after him," Buck said. "One of us will have to draw his fire, and the other one be ready to shoot at his muzzle flash."

"It's as good a chance as we'll likely get," Casey said.

"I'll draw his fire," Buck said, "and you take the shot. You've got a better eye than me."

"All right," Casey replied, surprised that Buck would admit it.

"I'm gonna wait till I get about even with that tall clump of trees yonder." He pointed to the dark outline of treetops halfway down the slope. "You be ready with your rifle, 'cause you're gonna have to be quick."

"I'll be ready," Casey said, and immediately started down the hill, placing one foot carefully in front of the other to avoid tripping over a vine or root. When he got to a place approximately even with the tall trees, he situated himself so as to be able to swing his rifle around about one hundred eighty degrees. Then he waited, thinking it was like peering into a bottomless well, his eyes focused on the darkness. Across the slope, he heard a dead branch snap and guessed that it was Buck. He quickly pulled his rifle up to his shoulder, halfway expecting Blanton to fire at the sound. But the forest remained still, save for the steady curtain of rainfall. Judging from the sound of the broken limb, he figured Buck was just about in position. He held the rifle in place against his shoulder.

After what seemed a long interval, he couldn't help but jump when Buck suddenly fired. Almost immediately, the shot was answered from a rocky pocket about thirty yards below him. Casey reacted instantaneously, pumping four quick rounds in a tight circular pattern around the muzzle blasts. He wasn't sure, but he could almost swear he heard a dull grunt from his target. "I'm movin', Buck!" he yelled, and started scrambling down the slope.

"I hear you!" Buck yelled back, and followed suit.

The two deputies converged on the pocket, both men ready to open fire at the slightest movement among the rocks. Moving cautiously from tree to tree, they worked their way down until they could see that the pocket was deserted. Inside the cluster of rocks they knelt to examine the ground for confirmation that Blanton had been there. Catching sight of a small dark streak on one of the rocks, Buck rubbed across it with his finger, wiping part of it away. As it was too dark to see what it was, he held it up to his nose and sniffed it. "Blood," he said. "You got him."

It was a question now of how badly Blanton was hurt. There may have been a lot more blood around— it was too dark and rainy to tell. Whatever the severity of the wound, Blanton was able to run. And if he was able to run, he was also still dangerous. To add to their problems, Blanton knew these woods a lot better than either of the two chasing him.

Roy Blanton knelt at the side of the little branch that ran down the center of the shallow valley. Grunting with pain each time he touched the bullet hole, he tried to wash away some of the blood from his side. He wasn't sure how badly he was wounded. All he knew for sure was that it throbbed like all hell with each beat of his heart. *The lucky son of a bitch*, he thought, for it was just by pure accident that one of the shots thrown at him had hit him. The fact that he had been suckered into revealing his position behind those rocks only served to compound his bitterness. His concern now was that he couldn't seem to stop the bleeding.

When he had first been hit, he was determined to wait them out, hoping to ambush the two of them. But as the large stain on his shirt continued to spread, the more he worried that he might die before he settled with them. And the thought of Buck Avery standing over his bled-out corpse was bitter gall to swallow. As the pain increased, he knew he had to get away while he was still strong enough to ride. It was not over. *Hell, no*, he thought, *it's a helluva ways from being over*. It was a long ride to White Oak Creek in Texas, but that was the only haven available to him for medical attention. His side burning with each movement, he held his hand tightly against the wound and made his way as fast as he could toward the clump of willows where he had left the horses. He found them standing in the rain, their heads down, linked together by the lead rope he had hastily tied on when he escaped from the tunnel.

Grunting with the painful effort, he climbed up in the saddle and gave the gray a kick with his heels, turning the horse's head toward the stream. His intention was to follow it to the river, then head south to strike the Red River. In the rainy darkness, the descent down through the hills was not easy, especially leading four horses behind him. By the time he reached the

Little River, he was reeling in the saddle, gritting his teeth against the sharp stabbing pain in his side.

The early fingers of daylight found him on the south bank of the river, slumping in the saddle, straining to remain upright. Though reluctant to cut four good horses loose, he realized that they were too much trouble for him in his present condition. He led them as far as he thought he could manage before painfully dismounting and untying them from the lead rope. He got back in the saddle, and in an effort to scatter the other four horses, fired his pistol behind them and watched for a minute to make sure they galloped away. Satisfied they were scattering away from the river, he prodded the gray gelding to continue.

About an hour before sunup, the rain slackened to a slow drizzle, and stopped completely with the first light of day. Soaked to the skin, and dog tired from a fruitless search in a forest so dark it would have been possible to walk right by their quarry, the two deputies found themselves at a small stream that wandered through the center of a shallow valley.

"By God, we sure as hell stumbled on these," Buck sighed wearily, looking down at the hoofprints in the wet sand. They were not sure Blanton was not still stalking them until finding the tracks leading toward the river. "Looks to me like ol' Roy's hurt bad enough to run, all right."

"Where's he gonna run?" Casey replied. "If he's hurt that bad, he's gonna be lookin' for help."

"Crawl off someplace and die, I reckon," Buck speculated. As far as he knew, Roy and his four sons had made up the family. He didn't know about Roy's wife and daughter, or if he even had a place he called home.

"Well, he's sure as hell got away again," Casey

stated. "And this time he's got our horses and our possibles. We ain't even got a match to light a fire with." He looked at Buck and grunted. "You're sure a sorry-lookin' sight this mornin'."

Buck forced a chuckle. "You oughta see yourself. You look like you've just been pulled outta the river." They both shrugged simultaneously. There was little choice but to start walking. "Damn, my feet are already sore," he complained. "These wet socks ain't helpin' matters none."

There was brief speculation on whether or not they should climb back up through the woods to bury Bonnie, but conscience gave way to practicality. "We're already losing ground to Blanton," Buck suggested, "and the woman ain't got no family to worry about her, anyhow. I expect we'd better get started out of here. It's a long walk to Broken Bow." The thought caused Casey to feel a strong twinge of guilt. He had promised Mabel Marsh that he would bring Bonnie back safely, but what Buck said was true.

They followed the stream down to the river and started west along the bank, looking for a shallow place to cross over to the other side. When they finally got to a place that looked to be an easy ford, they started across, with Casey in the lead. He was almost to the middle of the river when he suddenly stopped short. "What's the matter?" Buck asked.

"Listen!" Casey said, and held up his hand to silence Buck. He turned around, scanning the bank they had just left, his ear turned to the wind. "There it is again!" he whispered to a puzzled Buck. Certain then that he recognized the sound, he started wading back toward shore as fast as he could manage in the hip-deep water. Buck, with no idea what had come over his partner, stood amazed, watching him pass. Then he followed him out of the river.

Up on the bank again, Casey scoured the tree line

until his eye finally caught sight of what he was looking for. "Come on, boy," he called out gently, and in
moments, the sorrel gelding padded slowly out of the
trees toward his master. "I swear, that's a beautiful
sight," Buck said with a chuckle as the horse walked
obediently up to greet Casey. "He musta broke loose."

A few hundred yards up the river, they found
Buck's horse grazing beside the water. The discovery
caused Buck to speculate. "Blanton must be hurt bad.
It ain't likely he'd let them horses go unless they was
too much for him to handle." The horse that Bonnie
had ridden had evidently wandered off alone. They
were no longer on foot, a situation for which they
were extremely grateful. The urgency to go after the
wounded outlaw remained, but the first priority upon
finding their horses was to make a fire and boil some
coffee.

Chapter 15

While drinking coffee and drying out a little, they talked over Roy Blanton's options considering the condition he was in. When they thought they were going to be on foot, their intention was to cross the river and walk to Broken Bow in hopes of acquiring horses there. Now, since they were on horseback again, they had to speculate upon Blanton's actions. If it was a doctor he was seeking, there was none in Broken Bow. If his intention was to heal on his own, he might be thinking of reaching Texas, hoping the deputy marshals would not pursue him past the Red River.

"For my money," Casey offered, "I'd bet on Texas. He's got some kind of hideout there—maybe even has family. Hell, those four hellions he raised must have had a mother. Maybe there's a home place somewhere on the other side of the Red."

"Well, if there is," Buck snorted, "the Texas Rangers ain't been able to find it." He thought about it for a few seconds, then added, "We ain't got much more to go on. The rain played hell with any tracks we mighta found—might as well head for the Red River. Maybe we'll strike his trail somewhere on this side." Though it was not spoken by either man, there was no intention to stop at the Texas border.

Ready to ride, they started west along the river, counting more on instinct and gut feelings than on an actual trail to follow. When they came to a cross trail that ran directly south, Buck suggested that, if he were wounded and eager to get to Texas as directly as possible, he'd take the south trail. Casey was in agreement, so they struck out along a wide valley on what appeared to be a well-worn wagon track.

It was midmorning when they crossed another trail that led to the west. Judging by the time it had taken since leaving the banks of the Little River, they agreed that it was most likely the trail to Idabel, over on the railroad. "Looks like we would have seen some tracks showin' up by now if we're really on Blanton's tail," Casey commented. The only fresh hoofprints since the rain were coming from Idabel, turning south toward the Red River.

Buck scratched his chin thoughtfully. "We might be chasin' the breeze out here." He glanced around him at the heavily wooded countryside. "You know, he just mighta been hurt so bad, he crawled off in the woods somewhere to die."

"I don't know," Casey replied. "I think if he thought he was dyin', he might not have run at all. He'd more than likely sat down and hoped we did find him, so he'd have a chance to take somebody with him."

"I reckon you're right," Buck reconsidered. "But we still ain't got a notion where the hell he is."

"Whaddaya say we keep on till we strike the Red. If we don't pick up his trail by then, well, I guess we'll have to think of somethin' else."

Buck shrugged. "Hell, might as well. I can't think of nothin' better."

* * *

Jim Blackhorse looked up from the scythe he was sharpening when he heard his wife calling him. "I'm in the barn," he called back. When she continued to call for him, he propped his scythe against a stall and walked outside. "I hear you, dammit. I said I was in the barn," he groused. "What is it?"

Seeing him then in the barn door, she ran toward him, obviously disturbed. "In the garden!" she gasped, her breath short from running. "I think there's a dead man on a horse!"

"Where?"

"In the garden!" she repeated. "I went to the garden to dig potatoes, and he was just settin' there, dead!"

Sufficiently concerned now, Jim dropped his file and ran toward the garden after his wife. Rounding the corner of the house, they stopped at the edge of the garden. As she had said, there was a big gray horse standing in the middle of his fall peas, munching on the leaves. In the saddle, a man sat slumped, his arms hanging limp at his sides, his chin upon his chest. He appeared to be an older man with long, dirty gray hair hanging below his hat brim.

"Lord have mercy," Jim uttered, hardly believing his eyes. His wife may be right; the man looked dead to him, too. He hurried down between the rows. "Easy, boy, easy," he repeated, hoping to keep the horse from bolting. The big gray gelding had no thoughts of running, and just continued eating the leaves.

"You need to get that horse outta my peas," Lilly said.

"Look at that," Jim said, pointing to the man's blood-soaked shirt. "Looks like he's been shot." He took the horse's reins and led him out of the garden. Glancing back at the dead man, he couldn't help but exclaim, "Damn!" when he noticed the left arm was missing a hand.

"You be careful, Jim!" Lilly warned.

Bobbing up and down with the horse's rhythm, the body listed to one side and began to lean over. Jim quickly reached up to steady him. Suddenly, the *corpse* came to life with the touch of Jim's hand on his arm. Startled, he jerked his arm away, and fumbled with his saddle sling in an effort to draw his rifle. His sudden return to life caused Jim and Lilly both to jump back in fright.

Catching his breath again, Jim tried to calm the stranger. "Mister, we don't mean you no harm. We're Christian people. It looks like you've been hurt bad. Let me take you in the house where you can lie down, and we'll try to help you."

His remarks caused his wife to frown. She was not sure she was comfortable with the sinister-looking stranger in her house. Who could say how a man like that could wind up in her garden? He was obviously the victim of a gunshot, but who was his assailant? Would they be showing up at her house next? Her frown, however, went unnoticed by her husband, who was bent upon doing the Christian thing.

Realizing that he was not in danger of being attacked, Blanton stared through blurry eyes at the man and woman gawking at him as he tried to figure out where he was. Moments before, he had been unconscious, a fact that he was just now able to comprehend. The last thing he remembered before Jim grabbed his arm was a feeling of desperation so dominant that he turned onto the road to Idabel, looking for a place to hide, knowing that he was too weak to defend himself. He had no idea how he ended up in this man's garden, but he knew that he needed help from someone, and as his rational mind returned, he figured he couldn't have found a better place to land. "Much obliged, friend," he managed to gasp before falling forward on the horse's neck, unconscious.

With his wife's reluctant help, Jim was able to carry the wounded man inside the house. "We can't put him on our bed," Lilly protested. "He's filthy. He'll ruin that spread."

"The man's hurt. We can't lay him on the floor," Jim replied curtly. "Now, swing his feet around that way so I can set his shoulders down."

Once Blanton was settled on the bed, Jim proceeded to take a closer examination of his patient. He took his hat off and hung it on the bedpost. "I expect he's as old as I am," he decided, "maybe a little older." The cruel eyes, now seemingly peaceful in sleep, did not appear so threatening beneath the heavy black eyebrows, giving the deadly predator an appearance more closely resembling that of a tired old man.

"Let's take a look at that wound," Jim said, and began unbuttoning Blanton's shirt. After some difficulty, he managed to remove the shirt and handed it to his wife. She took it with the same emotion she would have displayed had it been a dead skunk. Noticing her scrunched-up nose, he commented, "Might take a lotta boilin' in the wash pot to get all that blood out."

"I expect it would be best to wash it in cold water," she replied patiently. "Hot water will likely set the stain in."

Looking now at the blood-soaked underwear, he decided that he would have to cut it away, preferring that to stripping Blanton naked. Once he got down to bare skin, he was better able to evaluate the extent of the damage. "I ain't a doctor, but I'm pretty sure that's a gunshot wound." He looked at Lilly, hoping she might suggest the best way to treat the patient. He was answered with a blank stare. Finally he exhaled a deep breath and said, "Well, we'd best clean it up. You'd better heat up some water."

After the wound had been cleaned up the best the two of them could manage, Jim pressed a bandage to it to stop the bleeding. "Looks like he's lost an awful lot of blood. That's probably why he's so weak." He stood up over the bed then and declared, "That's all I know to do for him. He'll most likely need somethin' to eat to get his strength back when he wakes up—if he wakes up. I'll go put his horse in the barn."

It was well past suppertime when the patient regained consciousness. Roy opened his eyes slowly, listening to the noises around him, again wondering where he was. Feeling as if his side were on fire, he turned his head cautiously toward the sounds emanating from the kitchen. It came back to him then, and he remembered the circumstances. He started to get up, but quickly lay back down when he realized how weak he was.

Hearing the patient moving on the bed, Jim came from the kitchen. "Well, we was wonderin' if you was gonna come to or not. How you feelin'? I reckon you could use somethin' to eat. My wife's got some stew that we had for supper. It'll help you get your strength back."

Roy paused for a brief second while he studied his Samaritan, aware of the good fortune that brought him to this couple. "Friend," he said softly, "I'm much obliged for your kindness. I thought I was a goner when I was set upon by a gang of cutthroats and robbers on my way home to Texas." He cringed slightly when he tried to sit up more in the bed. "I reckon I ain't ready to ride again quite yet."

"Robbers," Jim uttered in response. "Where were they?" He was obviously worried to hear outlaws were close by.

Blanton tried to think fast to put his benefactor at ease. "A ways north of here on the road to Broken Bow," he replied. "They're long gone, but they left me in a sorry state. I guess the Lord was guidin' me when I bumped into you."

"He musta been watchin' out over you. There's some pretty mean boys hidin' out in the nations. We're kinda off the main trails here, so we don't see many visitors, and that's the way me and the old lady like it. I'd say you're lucky you got away with your life." He hesitated then, but decided to ask. "Looks like you've had your share of bad luck. How'd that happen?" he asked, nodding toward Blanton's left arm.

Blanton stared down at the grisly stump as if noticing it for the first time. "Cuttin' timber," he said. "My arm got in the way of an ax." Jim's question reminded him of his concern for the missing hand. "Where's my horse?"

"In the barn," Jim replied.

"My saddlebags . . . ?"

"Safe and sound, just like you left 'em."

Blanton breathed a sigh of relief. "Like I said, I 'preciate it."

"We're glad to do what we can for you," Jim said. "I just wish I knew more about takin' care of a gunshot wound." Remembering then, he introduced himself. "I'm Jim Blackhorse. That's my wife, Lilly, in the kitchen."

"Jordan, Roy Jordan," Blanton replied. He shifted his position, again grimacing with the pain it caused. "Did you get the bullet outta me?"

"Ah, no, sir, I didn't," Jim said. "Tell you the truth, I was afraid to go diggin' around in that wound. I didn't see no hole in your back, so I reckon it's still in there."

Roy frowned. He had hoped that Jim had taken the slug out of his side while he was asleep. He supposed that he would have a go at it himself, but not before he felt a little stronger. He knew a few men who were walking around with bullets still in them to no ill effects. "What about some of that stew you were talkin' about?"

Lilly was much more willing to tend to their patient after Jim told her that Blanton was an ordinary citizen who had suffered the misfortune of falling prey to a band of outlaws. "Poor feller," Jim said, "he was on his way home to Texas when he got jumped. I reckon they found out that he was harder to kill than they thought." All her misgivings disappeared when he complimented her on her cooking. They went to bed that night, content to sleep on blankets on the kitchen floor while Blanton occupied their bed.

Another day and a night passed before Blanton felt recovered enough to take up his mantle of vengeance again. The bullet had been too deep in his side to remove, so he decided it best to leave it where it was. The bleeding had stopped and along with it, most of the pain. As Jim had said, there were no visitors to the isolated farmhouse, so his recovery was without complications. His hosts had received him graciously, fully accepting his story about searching for coal deposits and his having a wife and daughter back in Texas. On his feet again, he strapped on his gun belt as if to leave. Jim and Lilly watched in fascinated interest as he flipped open the cylinder on his .44 and spun it with the stump of his left arm to make sure it was loaded. Clicking it shut again, he cocked the hammer back and pointed it at the puzzled face of Jim Blackhorse. There was no time for Lilly to react when Blanton pulled the trigger and the bullet smashed a hole in Jim's forehead. Eyes wide in confusion, the astonished woman never moved before the second shot sent her to join her husband.

Blanton calmly replaced the two cartridges with the man and his wife lying dead at his feet. He had nothing against the man and his wife who had come to his aid, but it had struck him that their little farm was a perfect hideout until he felt completely recovered. According to Jim and Lilly, there was no family close at hand to drop by unexpectedly, and no visitors as a rule. It was just what he needed. He might have spared the couple's lives a little longer to cook for him, but it would have been a nuisance to have to continue to play his part. He was free now to plunder the house, take what he needed, and rest up another day or two. He didn't like the turn of events that had cast him in the role of the pursued, and he kept reminding himself that he would once again become the hunter.

He went out to the barn to check on his horse, and make sure the big gray was fed. Then he turned him out in the corral with Jim Blackhorse's two mules. Before returning to the house to dispose of the two bodies, he got his hand from his saddlebag and took it with him, placing it on the kitchen table. Feeling a slight hunger pang, he went to the stove and returned to the table with a frying pan with the rest of the breakfast potatoes. Lilly Blackhorse had been about to clean the pan when she met her untimely death. He poured himself a cup of coffee, then rolled Jim's body away from the table with his foot to give himself room to pull back a chair.

Grimacing only slightly from the pain when he sat down in the chair, he stared at the ghostly hand in the middle of the table as he ate the potatoes. Concentrating on the grisly appendage never failed to provide a mental picture of the young deputy who was responsible. But his anger was no longer possessed by the insane rage that had boiled up inside him until he could not contain it. There was a calmness now when he thought about the coming hunt for the two lawmen— almost approaching joy in anticipation of the terrible vengeance that was to be his.

He took his time finishing his coffee before returning his attention to the two corpses on the floor. He considered leaving them where they lay, but reconsidered when he speculated that he might spend a couple of days in the house. So he dragged them one by one out the back door and left them on the edge of a cornfield. With the bodies out of the way, he turned to face Jim Blackhorse's dog. A pointer, bred to hunt birds, the dog nevertheless sensed the evil that had befallen its master, and bared its teeth in a warning growl.

"Git!" Roy commanded, but the dog stood its ground and threatened fiercely. Roy drew his .44 and dispatched the dog to join its master. He returned to the house then, wondering if there were any more nuisances to deal with before he could return his mind once again to the matter of Buck Avery and Casey Dixon.

After a full day's ride with nothing to tell them they were on the right trail, both deputies were nearing frustration. It was Buck who expressed his doubts about the wisdom of continuing on until reaching the Red. "What then?" he questioned when still a day's ride from the border. "I don't know what you think, but I think we're just fartin' in the wind. We ain't seen no sign of nobody following this trail. That ol' son of a bitch is layin' low somewhere, and probably laughin' at us runnin' around out here like a couple of dogs chasin' their tails."

"I couldn't have said it better," Casey replied. "I've been thinkin' that maybe he was wounded a lot worse than we think, and he had to go lookin' for help. What about Idabel? Is there a doctor there?"

"I don't know," Buck answered. "I ain't been to Idabel since the railroad laid tracks there. They didn't have one before that, when they used to call it Pernell. With the railroad, I wouldn't be surprised if they did now."

"I'm thinkin' Blanton mighta lost us a ways back when we passed that trail we figured led to Idabel. He mighta gone there lookin' for a doctor."

"Well, it ain't no more of a long shot than the one we're ridin' on now," Buck said. He gave it a moment's more consideration. "Matter of fact, it makes more sense. Whaddaya say we head west till we strike the railroad, then follow it on up to Idabel? If we run across his trail headin' toward the Red between here and the railroad, we can jump on it then."

"How the hell are we gonna know if it's Blanton if we do run up on a trail headin' south?" Casey asked.

Buck hesitated, feeling a little foolish. "Well now, that's a fair question. We wouldn't know whose tracks it was, would we? Hell, let's just go to Idabel and see if anybody's seen him."

"It ain't my fault the damn cow gets out," Tommy Snow grumbled to himself. "Sis is the one that always forgets to latch the gate. Pa oughta make her go look for the damn cow." His sister's defense was that it was difficult to make sure the latch caught when she was carrying a bucket of milk.

He gave the mule a kick with his heels. The mule trotted for a few yards, then settled back to a slow walk to further irritate Tommy. Ordinarily, he wouldn't mind searching for the stray milk cow, but he had just finished his chores and was planning to take a pole and some worms down to the creek. The troublesome cow was not in the usual places she favored when on one of her little vacations. The last time she got out, she found her way over to Jim Blackhorse's cornfield. Maybe, he thought, she remembered the way over there this time, so he headed the mule in that direction.

When he reached the lower end of the field, there was no cow in sight. He was about to turn around when he happened to look up to see a circle of buzzards that looked to be over the upper end, closer to the house. "Damn!" he uttered, thinking it might be the cow they were hovering over. *What if Mr. Black-horse shot it?* As soon as he thought it, he knew that was hardly the case. *More likely a dog, or maybe a raccoon or deer*, he figured. Still, he decided he'd better take a look in case it was his cow.

Riding up between the corn rows, he slid off the mule's back and walked the last few yards. Looking up, he saw that he was directly under the circle of scavenger birds, but he saw nothing that could be attracting their attention. He crossed over a couple of rows and almost stepped on Lilly Blackhorse's face. His heart leaped straight up into his throat, and he jumped backward so suddenly that he fell through the stalks. Scrambling over on his hands and knees, he crawled back to peek through the corn leaves to make sure he had seen what he thought he had.

Lilly stared up at him with eyes wide in shock. He almost gagged when he saw a line of ants making their way across her face toward an ugly hole in her forehead. Looking beyond her then, he saw Jim Black-horse, his body sprawled awkwardly where it had been dumped. Tracks in the soft soil testified that the two bodies had been dragged into the field. The horror of his discovery came to strike him like a hammer, and he quickly looked all around for fear that whoever had killed them might now be watching him.

For a few moments, Tommy's arms and legs did not seem to respond to his commands. He remained frozen there on his hands and knees for what seemed an eternity before his trembling limbs began to work again. Creeping slowly and cautiously, he backed away until he reached the row where he had left the mule. Offering a quick thanks to God that the mule was still there, he jumped to his feet and ran, afraid that at any second he might hear a gunshot. Once on the mule's back, he flailed desperately with his hands and feet to provoke the stubborn animal to run. It was incentive enough to cause the mule to trot all the way back home.

"Pa! Pa!" Tommy shouted as he charged into the barnyard.

Not waiting for an explanation, Wilson Snow yelled at his son. "Dammit, Tommy, I told you not to run that mule like that. The cow's already back in the barn. She was right there on the other side of the garden."

"Pa," Tommy blurted, nearly out of breath. "Murdered! Both of 'em, the Blackhorses! I saw 'em in the cornfield, both of 'em shot in the head!"

Stopped in his tracks then, Wilson turned to face his son. "What are you talkin' about?" he demanded. When Tommy breathlessly related all he had seen at the neighboring farm, his father was stunned for a moment. Realizing what he must do, he commanded, "Get back on that mule and get into town as fast as you can and get John Raintree." As soon as Tommy was off again, he ran to the house to fetch his shotgun. When she heard the news, Wilson's wife begged him not to go over there, but he said he had to go. Tommy might have been scared away before he knew they were really dead. They might need his help. With his wife behind him, arguing against his going, he ran to the barn and saddled his horse. Seconds later, he was galloping toward the Blackhorse farm.

As Wilson approached Blackhorse's cornfield, he reined back to have a look around before getting too close to the house. The flock of buzzards now making up the circle over the upper end of the field was testimony enough to confirm what Tommy had told him, that the Blackhorses were dead. *I oughta check to make sure*, he told himself, but his resolve was not as strong this close to the site of the murders. *Whoever done it might still be around*, he thought, and he began to question the wisdom in not waiting for John Raintree, the Choctaw policeman. Still undecided, he rode between two rows. Then, as Tommy had done, he dismounted and walked cautiously toward the top of the field. Before he got as close as his son had earlier, he was stopped short by a thrashing sound in the cornstalks near the end of the field. He yanked his shotgun up to his shoulder, thinking he might be under attack, but no one charged toward him. A glimpse through the corn leaves of a large black wing made him realize what the commotion was. The buzzards were already dining upon the bodies. It was enough for Wilson. "Let the police do their job," he muttered, turned, and retreated.

Chapter 16

The two deputies pulled their horses up to the railroad depot in the little community of Idabel and dismounted just before noon. Inside, they found the telegraph operator sitting at his desk, eating his dinner. "Can I help you fellers?" he asked, setting his plate aside.

"Yeah," Buck replied. "Is there a sheriff or Injun police or somethin' in this town?"

"There's John Raintree. He's Choctaw Lighthorse, but you missed him by about an hour." The operator took a long look at the two trail-weary riders and had a nervous thought. "You ain't thinkin' about a holdup, are you? 'Cause there ain't no money in the safe."

Buck looked at Casey and grunted. "I reckon we don't look like much more'n a couple of saddle tramps, do we?"

Casey smiled and displayed his badge. "We're deputy marshals, and we're tryin' to run down an outlaw that mighta passed this way."

Relieved, the operator said, "Like I said, you just missed John by maybe an hour. Wilson Snow's boy came stormin' in here lookin' for John. Said somebody killed Jim and Lilly Blackhorse. Said he saw 'em layin' in their cornfield, shot in the head."

There was no need to hear more. Casey and Buck exchanged quick, anxious glances. "How far is it?" Buck asked.

"Four miles, maybe five," the operator responded, seeing the urgency in the lawmen's faces.

"Where?" Buck demanded. "How do we find the place?"

The operator got up from his chair and led them outside. Pointing toward the north end of town, he said, "Just past the general store, there's a road on your right. Follow it till you come to a creek, about three and a half miles. Then you'll just have to look sharp after that for a wagon track leading off to the left. If I remember correctly, there's a big oak tree right there. I only been there once, or I'd tell you how far past the creek it is."

"Much obliged," Buck called back over his shoulder as he hurried after Casey, who was already stepping up in the saddle. Catching up with his partner, he commented, "Might not be our man, but it sure sounds like Roy." Casey nodded, thinking about his earlier speculation that Blanton might have given them the slip by turning off on the road to Idabel.

Wilson Snow waited by the big oak tree that stood beside the path to the Blackhorse farm, anxiously watching the road to Idabel for a sign of John Raintree. After what seemed like hours, he finally saw the Choctaw lawman approaching with Tommy following close behind. Wilson went out to meet them.

"Mr. Snow," Raintree solemnly greeted Wilson. He nodded toward the path by the oak tree. "Is that where Tommy said he saw the bodies?"

"I saw 'em, too," Wilson replied, even though he

did not actually see the bodies, only the appearance of a buzzards' feast. "Just follow that path. It leads right past the cornfield and up to the house."

"You say the bodies are in the field?" Raintree asked.

"Up near the house—just follow the buzzards."

"Anybody in the house? Or around the house?"

Wilson shook his head. "I didn't see nobody, but I didn't really go up to the house."

"All right," Raintree said. "I'll go see what I can find."

Wilson was reluctant to offer his help, but for the benefit of his son, he volunteered. "Want me to go with you?"

"I reckon not," Raintree said. Might be best if I scout around there by myself till I see what's what. How many horses did Blackhorse have?"

"As best I recall," Wilson replied, "he didn't have a ridin' horse, just two mules that he plowed with." Raintree nodded, turned his horse toward the path, and left father and son by the road.

Wilson had been correct when saying the bodies would be easy to find. Raintree left his horse by the path about a hundred yards short of the house and proceeded on foot. He intended to get a look at the situation before actually approaching the dwelling, so he took to the woods to the right of the path instead of going up through the cornfield. Reaching a point opposite the back corner of the house, he got a better look at the banquet of scavengers as they quarreled over the now-scant remains of Jim and Lilly Blackhorse. It was difficult to watch, for he knew Jim and his wife. Like he, they were Choctaw, and he had often seen them whenever they came to the general store in Idabel.

Forcing his attention away from the macabre scene, he moved to a new position opposite the small corral, where he discovered two mules and one big gray, almost solid white, horse. This told him that the killer was still there, and equally important, there was evidently only one person to deal with. Cocking his rifle, he moved cautiously out of the cover of the trees, and hustled across the narrow side yard to the side of the house. Then he slid along the wall to a window. Taking his hat off, so he would expose as small a target as possible, he peered in at the corner of the window. The room was a bedroom, and there was no one to be seen. Ducking down to pass under the window, he moved around the corner to a front window where he repeated the procedure. Peering cautiously with only one eye exposed at the corner of the window, he again saw no one, so he slowly exposed the other eye, hoping to see through the doorway into the other room. At first, he saw nothing. Then a black circle appeared before his face. He realized, too late, that the dark circle was the muzzle of a gun, for it exploded in his face in the next instant, and he crumpled to the ground beneath the window.

"Well, did you get a good eyeful?" Blanton mocked. "You was so all-fired anxious to peek in here." As a precaution, he stood just inside the window while he scanned the trees on the side of the clearing. "I saw you when you sneaked up through the woods," he said to the dead man. "Thinkin' you was gonna bushwhack Roy Blanton, was you? Well, you ain't the first Injun lawman that's made that mistake."

Although feeling some smugness in foiling the Choctaw policeman's attempt to surprise him, Roy now had to consider the possibility that there might be more lawmen coming. He might well have been caught off guard had he not been fortunate enough to have spotted the man running past the cornfield earlier. It had been pure happenstance that he had been out at the corral to check on his horse. He had to surmise that the lawman lying dead beneath the window and the man who had earlier fled from the field were not one and the same. How many others knew about the bodies in the cornfield? It was a question that irritated Blanton, for he thought he had found a place to hide out for a while. Now he couldn't afford to take a chance on his next visitors arriving as a posse. It was time to leave.

Buck and Casey found Wilson Snow and his son waiting under the shade of a giant oak tree beside the Idabel road. After identifying themselves as deputy marshals, they proceeded to question the two. "Are you the boy that came after the Choctaw lawman?" Buck asked. When Tommy said that he was, Buck asked him to relate what he had actually seen in the cornfield.

"He saw Jim and Lilly Blackhorse, all right," Wilson insisted. "I saw 'em, too, just like I told John Raintree. And he's been up there for the better part of an hour, I suspect." He looked at his son for confirmation. "About fifteen minutes ago we heard a gunshot."

"We better get goin'," Casey said. "How far is it to the house?"

"About a quarter mile," Wilson answered.

They set off at a gallop, following the narrow path that led through a dense section of woods before emerging to find a cornfield on one side of the path and forest on the other. Standing at the edge of the path, with the reins on the ground, they found John Raintree's horse. Thinking it a good idea to do as Raintree had, they dismounted and started out on foot, staying to the right of the path in the trees.

There was only an occasional squawk from the party of buzzards thrashing around in the cornfield, as the entire flock was now on the ground, their feast almost finished. The deputies paused only briefly to look across the path as they passed the upper end of the field, knowing it was far past the time to think about saving the dignity of the couple's death. They paused briefly upon reaching a point in the woods opposite the back corner of the house. There was no sign of activity outside the weathered board dwelling, and no sign of the Choctaw policeman. All was quiet except for a quarrelsome squawk now and then from the ravenous birds.

"Let's circle around to get a look at the front," Buck suggested. "It's quiet enough. That Injun, Raintree, was that his name? He might be inside and have the situation well in hand, but I don't trust ol' Roy. I expect it's the other way around."

That was precisely what Casey was thinking. "I'm afraid that shot those folks heard back there most likely came from Blanton's gun, and now he's probably long gone from here."

"Maybe," Buck allowed. "Let's see what's in the front of the house." He moved farther into the trees in order to gain a position where they could see around the front corner. When he stopped to wait for Casey to catch up, he pointed toward a front window and a crumpled figure lying below it. "I reckon Roundtree, or whatever his name was, found out it ain't too easy to sneak up on Roy Blanton."

Casey nodded and said, "I reckon." He could see the corner post of a corral on the opposite side of the house, so he said, "I'm gonna work around to the other side and check out the barn and corral to see if that big white horse he rides is in there." Buck nodded, content to wait until Casey completed his scout of Jim Blackhorse's place. It wasn't long before Casey returned. Finding Buck kneeling with a watchful eye upon the silent house, he said, "No sign of him or his horse in the barn or corral."

"He lit out," Buck said, hardly surprised. "We need

to take a look in that house to make sure before we go chasin' off after him."

"Reckon he tunneled out?" Casey joked.

Buck grunted in response. "I don't reckon he had to this time." He cocked his rifle. "Front or back?"

"I'll take the back door," Casey replied, and set off again through the woods.

Exercising proper caution, they approached the house from two sides, and as they expected, Blanton was gone. Buck found Casey standing by the kitchen table, looking down at a blood-stained smear on the floor. "Looks like he shot both of 'em down right here," he said. Then pointing to some additional streaks, he continued. "Dragged 'em out the back door."

Buck shook his head thoughtfully. "He sure leaves a trail of dead folks, don't he?" Then, looking up at Casey with a serious eye, he said, "A man like that needs to be shot, same as you'd shoot a mad dog. It's way past time to be thinkin' about arrestin' him and takin' him to trial." He paused then to study Casey's reaction to the statement.

Casey shrugged. "I guess we'll have to catch up with him first," he said. "He'll most likely make the decision for us."

"I'm just sayin' I ain't plannin' to waste no time talkin' when we catch up with the son of a bitch," Buck stated. He held his rifle up with one hand. "Judge, jury, and sentence, right here," he said.

Casey didn't reply, but Buck's execution talk struck him as a rather odd attitude for a man sworn to uphold the letter of the law. Thinking back over the weeks he had ridden with the easygoing legend, it stuck in his mind that circumstances had always dictated that Buck was forced to kill the members of the Blanton family who had at first been captured—Zeke, then Buster. Maybe things happened the way Buck said. Casey hadn't doubted it up until this moment. *If*

I didn't know better, he thought, *I'd think Buck wants to make sure none of the gang gets a chance to surrender.* The thought stayed with him only for a moment before he dismissed it as baseless.

A rather hasty search of the house yielded nothing beyond the fact that Blanton was not hiding there, and they were soon back outside looking for signs that might help identify tracks left by Blanton's horse. It was easy enough to distinguish the gray's tracks from the smaller hoofprints of Blackhorse's mules, and from the looks of it, Blanton had fled straight down the front path. "I'll go bring up the horses if you'll let those mules out so they can get to water and grass," Casey volunteered. "I expect we could put that Choctaw lawman in the ground, and maybe bury what's left of those poor folks in the cornfield," he said. "But it'll have to wait till after we catch up with Blanton."

"You're right about that," Buck said, peering up at the sky. "We ain't got more'n two hours before sundown. If Blanton's still nursin' that wound, we might be able to catch up with him before dark. If we don't, he's liable to give us the slip again."

With those thoughts in mind, Casey started back at a trot down the path beside the cornfield to retrieve the horses. Finding them grazing right where they left them, he climbed up on the sorrel and hurried back to the house to find Buck searching the pantry shelves for something in the way of supplies. "Looks like Blanton cleaned the place out of anything we could use," he said when Casey pulled the horses up at the porch. "This is all I could find." He held a small sack of coffee beans up for Casey to see as he stepped up in the saddle.

Casey swung the sorrel's head around and urged him forward on the narrow path leading away from the front of the house. Blanton had made no effort to hide his tracks, so there was no difficulty in following

his trail. Even so, Buck swung out wide of Casey, so
they could both keep an eye on the tracks running between them. In a half hour's time, they came to the
north-south road from the Little River, the same road
they had followed a few days before. Here they
stopped and dismounted, figuring it was going to take
a close look at the collection of tracks to determine if
Blanton went north or south. After a few minutes, Casey called out, "Hell, he went straight across." He
pointed to the obvious tracks on the eastern side of the
road.

Both men paused then to look in the direction indicated by Blanton's tracks. No longer following a path,
they led into a line of rolling hills, covered with hard-
wood trees. "He's lookin' to lose us in them hills,"
Buck said. He then looked up at the sky. "We ain't got
a helluva lot of daylight left."

As twilight filtered into the rapidly darkening forest, the tracks became harder to follow, causing them
to slow down to make sure they didn't miss the many
turns and changes in direction. "Damn if he ain't wanderin' all over the place," Buck exclaimed upon coming to another almost ninety-degree change of course.

"Maybe he's got a fever or somethin'," Casey said.
"Might still be sick from that wound."

"Could be," Buck allowed.

On the eastern side of a low hill they came to a
creek. Even in the fading light, they picked up the
hoofprints on the other side where Blanton left the
water and continued in an easterly direction. "He keeps
turning like this and pretty soon we ain't gonna be
able to tell which way we're headin'," Casey said.

Another twenty minutes found them crossing another creek. "He's doubled back!" Buck blurted, realizing it was not a different creek, but the same one they
had already crossed. "He ain't wanderin' around with
no damn fever. That old fox is leadin' us on a merry

chase. We'd best watch ourselves or we're liable to walk right into a trap."

No longer able to see the tracks in the darkness, they realized there was no choice but to wait until daylight to continue, aware as they were of the possibility that by that time, Blanton could be miles away. "I got a bad feelin' about this," Buck said. "He sure as hell give us the slip again, leavin' us out here in the woods in the middle of the night. He could be halfway to Texas by sunup, I reckon, but I got a feelin' he ain't runnin' no more. I think, by God, he's trackin' us now."

What Buck said was true enough, but there was really no choice for the two lawmen at this point. They couldn't track if they couldn't see, so they had no option but to sit tight and wait for the sun to come up. "Let's go down the creek a ways and see if we can find a better place to wait out the night," Casey suggested, "in case Blanton decides to backtrack, lookin' for us."

Riding up the middle of the creek, they went about one hundred yards before discovering a deep gully cut into the bank. "This oughta do," Buck decided, and guided his horse out of the creek. "We can tie the horses under them trees back yonder."

Thinking it best to keep a cold camp that night, they had to forgo coffee and a warm supper. "I reckon we could get a little shut-eye," Buck said, "as long as one of us stays awake while the other'n sleeps."

Casey would have been satisfied to sit up all night, figuring two sets of eyes were better than one, but he suspected the long day had been tiring upon the older deputy. Then he considered the fact that Roy Blanton was as old, or older, than Buck. He was probably tired, too—and he was wounded to boot. Most likely he was holed up somewhere in these dark woods, waiting just as they were. "Why not?" Casey replied. "I ain't sure I could go to sleep right away. Why don't you go ahead and grab a little sleep, and I'll wake you sometime before daylight."

"Suits me," Buck replied without hesitation, and made himself comfortable in the gully. In no time at all, he was breathing heavily in the deep sleep of the weary. Casey couldn't help but think that, as Buck himself had confessed, he was getting too old for the hunt. As for Casey, he had been truthful when he said he would not be able to go to sleep. Knowing the notorious outlaw was out there somewhere not far away was enough to keep him awake.

The dark hours ground by slowly but peacefully, with no sounds to disturb the night other than the noise of the crickets and the low grunts of the frogs on the creek bank. Off in the trees on the far side of the creek, an owl questioned the intruders upon his domain before flying away. Alert, Casey listened and watched the dark shapes of trees around him. About an hour past midnight he decided that all was going to remain quiet, so he chose to catnap a little himself. He woke Buck. "How 'bout it, partner?" he asked. "You think you're awake now?"

"Yep," Buck answered, and sat up. "I had me a good little nap. I'm rarin' to go." He stood up and stretched, then walked down by the creek bank to shake all the sleep from his brain. Satisfied that he was alert, he paused to relieve himself, then returned to the gully, ready to take over the watch.

Casey huddled up against the side of the gully, making himself as comfortable as the clay bank would allow. He closed his eyes, although he was still of a mind that it would be difficult to actually go to sleep. Sleep came, however, after twenty or thirty minutes.

Buck listened to Casey's light snoring for a few minutes before reaching over and prodding him on the shoulder a couple of times until Casey turned over on his side and the snoring ceased. *That's better*, Buck thought, and moved over toward the mouth of the gully to sit down again. He listened to the night sounds of the creek. All was peaceful. Thinking a smoke would be enjoyable right then, he got his pipe from his saddlebag and filled it from a pouch of rough-cut tobacco. *Ain't much left*, he thought, stirring the remains in the pouch with his finger. *That ain't gonna last till I get back to Fort Smith.* He tamped the tobacco down in his pipe and struck a match to light it.

It seemed instantaneous, but it was actually almost a minute after the small flash from the match when the peaceful night was ripped by the sudden crack of a rifle. Buck felt the ripple in the air caused by the bullet as it passed inches from his head. The first shot was followed by three more in rapid succession as Buck dived for cover in the gully, almost colliding with Casey, who was shaken out of a deep sleep. "Goddamn!" Buck blurted as they both scrambled for defensive positions in the narrow defile.

"Where is he?" Casey exclaimed.

"Damned if I know," Buck replied. "I didn't get a chance to see nothin'. We'll just have to keep a sharp eye and wait for him to shoot again."

"He damn sure knows where we are," Casey said. "How the hell could he see us?"

"I don't know. Maybe he's part owl. I wouldn't doubt the ol' son of a bitch." He had a pretty good idea how Blanton found them, but he preferred not to tell Casey. His pipe was lying on the ground somewhere near the mouth of the gully. As close as that first shot had passed by his face, it was a wonder the pipe hadn't been hit.

There was nothing they could do but wait and watch the darkness all around them for a muzzle flash. In less than a minute it came, preceded by the sizzling sound of a rifle slug and a solid thump when it struck the clay bank no more than two feet beside Buck.

"Gawddamn!" he cursed, and dived toward the back of the gully. "He's gettin' too damn close for comfort."

"There!" Casey exclaimed upon spotting the muzzle flash, and answered with two rounds from his Winchester, aimed at a dark clump of bushes fifty yards down the creek. Buck crawled up beside him and followed Casey's shots with two of his own. In half a minute's time, another shot came tearing across the top of the gully, this one from approximately twenty yards farther into the trees.

"He's on the move," Buck said. "The old bastard's got us pinned down." It was a helpless feeling. Blanton knew exactly where they were, and he could fire and move, hoping for a lucky shot, while they could only guess where his next shot was coming from.

After another move and a new series of shots on the gully, Casey said, "He seems to be movin' in a circle around to the right. We can't let him get between us and the horses." Judging from the distance between the last two muzzle blasts, Casey shifted his rifle to aim at a spot farther around to the right, hoping to be able to react quickly to the next shot. When Blanton's next shot came, however, it was from a position back to the left. Frustrated, Casey turned and fired anyway, knowing his shot was probably wasted.

No more than forty yards from the gully, Roy Blanton knelt by the creek, reloading his rifle. He had spent the greater part of the night on foot, searching upstream for the two lawmen who hunted him, only to find that they had gone downstream from the last crossing he had led them to. *No matter*, he thought, *I found them. And now, by God, I'll send the both of them to hell for killing my boys*. There was also another matter requiring vengeance. He would settle with Buck Avery. Avery was a double-crosser, and Roy would not abide a double-crosser. The big deputy had accepted money that was supposed to guarantee Blanton and his boys immunity from harassment.

As he inserted cartridges into the magazine of his rifle, he looked at the stump of his left arm steadying the barrel, and his anger boiled again in his veins. Hanging from his neck, a small flour bag from Lilly Blackhorse's pantry held the stark, bony trophy that was his hand. The bile inside him rose even more when he thought about the difficulty in tying the drawstrings, working with one hand and his teeth. "It's judgment day," he muttered, and rose to his feet.

Moving a little closer to the men in the gully, he took cover behind a sizable tree. Thinking to have the satisfaction of telling them their fate, he called out to taunt them. "How you doin' in that hole, Buck?" he called out. "Is it gettin' pretty hot in there? Ain't nobody been hit, have they?"

"You go to hell, Blanton," Buck responded. "If you've got any sense a'tall, you'll throw your rifle down and give yourself up. There ain't none of your gang left. You're gettin' too damn old to be runnin' around in the woods shootin' at people. Give up while you still got your life."

Blanton fired two more shots at the voice in the gully, then shouted, "There's your answer, you double-crossin' son of a bitch!" There was a short period of silence while he moved a few yards away. "I tell you what, Buck. I'll give you a chance to throw down your guns and come outta that hole. You can trust me. I ain't the one took the money and then double-crossed you." He moved again, moments before a shot rang out from the gully.

"What the hell's he talkin' about?" Casey asked.

"Hell, I don't know. He's crazy as a bedbug," Buck replied.

"This ain't no good," Casey said, "waitin' for him to plug one of us. I'm goin' out after him."

"You better watch yourself," Buck warned. "That old man's as much at home in the woods as a mountain lion. You'd best have eyes in the back of your head."

"Yeah? Well, I'm tired of waitin' around here doin' nothin'. I can crawl around in the woods as well as he can." He waited until the next shots came slamming into the side of the gully. While Buck fired back, Casey crawled out of the open end and slid down the bank to the water's edge. Pausing to listen and look around him, he then started to work his way along the creek, using the low bank for cover, as he moved toward the last place he had seen muzzle flashes. After a couple of dozen yards, he paused to listen, waiting for Blanton to shoot or taunt again. While waiting, he looked around him, realizing then that morning would soon be approaching. Already, the dark mass of forest was slowly beginning to take the shape of individual trees as the fragile light of predawn began to filter through the forest.

Suddenly, a rifle shot rang out behind him. Without either man knowing it, Casey had evidently moved silently past a position that Blanton had just reached near a laurel thicket. It struck him that one little slip or dislodged pebble could have ended his role in the game if Blanton had heard it. Casey immediately turned back to level his rifle at the thicket. Straining to make out a form in the confusion of branches, he could not determine man from bush. With no real target, he opened fire, spraying the thicket with four rounds. As soon as the fourth shot was fired, he quickly moved to a new spot where the bank rose to create a ten-foot hummock above the water.

Hurrying to go over the top of the hummock, he was suddenly slammed in the chest with a blow that staggered him, like a kick from a horse. The report of the rifle followed a split second later. Knocked off balance, he fell from the hummock, landing in the water, a faint image of a man with a rifle pointed at him, the last thing he remembered before losing consciousness.

Standing in the deep shadows beyond the thicket, Roy Blanton hurried to the creek bank to make sure the young deputy was finished. He arrived at the top of the hummock in time to get off one more shot before Casey's body drifted beyond a log extending into the water. He remained standing on the bank for a few moments more to see if the body was going to bob out from under the log again. When it appeared that it wasn't, a smug grin slowly spread across Blanton's face. *That leaves Mr. Buck Avery*, he thought.

Back in the gully, Buck was left to wonder about the exchange of gunfire, because it was obvious none of the six shots had been aimed in his direction. Knowing Casey must have encountered Blanton somewhere near the creek, he was undecided whether or not he should go in search of them, or stay put. It took but a moment to make the decision. He figured it was the best chance he would have to get out of the gully where he had been under siege all night long. Over the side he went, just as the first rays of the morning sun began to probe the deep woods, and shapes and forms started to take on definition.

Moving cautiously, taking only a few steps at a time before stopping to probe the awakening forest, he advanced toward the creek. His rifle ready, his finger on the trigger, he inched forward, listening for any sound that would cause him to react instantly. Suddenly, the warning came—a dead branch snapped behind him, and before he could turn to fire, he was halted by a steady voice. "Turn and you're dead," Roy Blanton warned.

Having no choice, Buck froze, knowing the only chance he had was if Blanton wished to indulge his vengeance by taunting him before his execution.

"Well, Roy, looks like you got the jump on me," he said.

"Looks that way, don't it?" Blanton replied with a chuckle. "The day'll never come when you can out-smart me. That young deputy you were ridin' with found that out a few minutes ago. Now, suppose you drop that rifle on the ground and turn around. I've been wantin' to have a little chat with you." Buck started to turn, but stopped when Blanton warned, "Drop the rifle first."

Buck slowly opened his hand and let the rifle drop to the ground before turning around to face his old adversary. "It's been a long time since me and you faced off like this," he said. "That time, I let you walk away."

"After I gave you fifteen thousand dollars," Blanton promptly replied. "Hell, Buck, you're a bigger crook than me. Then after you spent all the money, you come back and start ridin' my tail again. That makes you a low-down, double-dealin' son of a bitch."

"We had a deal," Buck protested, his hand casually hovering over the handle of his holstered pistol. "You wasn't supposed to come back in the nations with your robbin' and killin'. Hell, ain't Texas big enough for you?"

"You killed my sons, destroyed my family," Blanton came back, while watching Buck's hand closely, "and that trumps any deals we mighta had."

"Hell, Roy, we're both gettin' too damn old for this. That was a damn shame about your boys, but that was all Casey's doin's. You know these young hot-heads. Can't reason with 'em a'tall—just gun down ever'body. But me and you . . . why, we deserve a peaceful retirement. Why don't we just cut us a couple of poles and go fishin' somewhere?"

"Like I said, Buck, the day ain't ever come when you could outsmart me. Now, if you hurry, you can catch up with your partner before he gets to the gates of hell."

It was close. There was not much more than a fraction of a second between Blanton's rifle and Buck's pistol. To the man crawling painfully up the riverbank behind Buck, the sound of the two weapons sounded almost like one loud report. Both men staggered, but only Buck, mortally wounded, sank to the ground, having had the disadvantage of being forced to draw his pistol.

With a .44 slug lodged in his hip, Blanton winced with the pain, but forced himself to limp over to finish the job on the big deputy. While Buck stared helplessly up at his executioner, Blanton pointed the rifle at his face. "This is for Junior and Buster, and Zeke and Billy," he growled, "and for this." He held his left arm up to show the stump. A moment later, he dropped the rifle before he could pull the trigger as a bullet in his shoulder from Casey's .44 spun him around. Just then discovering the wounded deputy crawling up from the water, preparing to shoot again, Blanton had no choice but to dive into the creek to escape a certain death.

Since Blanton had dropped his rifle and was wearing no sidearm, his only chance was to swim for it. Although in severe pain from two bullet wounds, he forced himself to thrash the water in an attempt to get away. When bullets from Casey's pistol started to pop the water around him, he dived under the surface. Holding his breath in the dark water, he tried to make it to the dead tree that had shielded Casey earlier. His lungs about to explode, he finally felt the branches of the tree under the water, and then bumped into the solid trunk. With just enough air left to swim under the trunk, he struggled to put it between himself and Casey's pistol. As he started toward the surface, however, the flour sack containing his severed hand snagged on a branch and held fast. In a panic to free himself from the ghostly hand, he tugged violently at the stubborn drawstring, but the effort only increased his need for air. Unable to hold his breath any longer, he gave in to a low moan of frustrated rage deep in his gut that finally bubbled up to form a silent roar, and his lungs filled with the dark creek water.

With one hand pressing the wound in his chest, Casey made his way painfully along the creek bank, watching for some sign of Blanton's body resurfacing. There was nothing for a long while until, finally, the branch holding Roy's hand released its victim and the notorious outlaw bobbed slowly to the surface. There was no doubt that Blanton was dead. That confirmed, Casey made his way back to Buck.

The old deputy marshal's eyes flickered open when Casey knelt beside him. Fading fast, he struggled for breath, fighting to keep from choking on the blood filling his lungs. "Blanton?" he rasped painfully.

"Dead," Casey replied. Then, desperate to do something to help him, he said, "Let's see if we can help you sit up."

"No," Buck protested, "let me be." He closed his eyes for a few seconds. When he opened them again, he said, "I thought *you* was dead."

"Not yet," Casey said, trying to smile at the dying man.

"I done some things I ain't proud of," Buck strained to say, uncertain how much of the conversation between Blanton and himself Casey might have heard.

While pulling himself up from the creek, uncertain if his gun would even fire, Casey had heard enough to know what Buck referred to. He could not say that he was totally surprised or shocked to hear it. There had been many clues even in the first weeks they had ridden together. He had just never considered that a lawman of Buck's reputation could have taken a bribe from the likes of Roy Blanton. Kneeling here now, watching the final minutes of the territory's most respected deputy marshal, he could see no purpose in sullying that respect. "Hell, Buck," he said softly, "we've all done things we ain't proud of. But you cleared the territory of the Blanton gang. That's somethin' you can be proud of."

"Yeah, I reckon we turned out to be a pretty good team," Buck said, laboring with every word. "I don't think I ever partnered with any man as good as you."

Casey could not help but be concerned by the tone of finality in Buck's voice. He tried to encourage the big lawman to hang on. "Don't be talkin' about things you're gonna regret sayin' after I get you back to Fort Smith," he said in as cheerful a voice as he could fashion. "I'll bandage that wound and we'll rest up for a bit before we start back."

Growing weaker by the second, Buck forced a smile. "I'm done, partner. I ain't leavin' this valley." When Casey started to protest, he raised his hand to stop him. "I ain't feelin' too good. Let me talk while I still can." He was interrupted by a sudden spell of coughing, and he brought up blood with each cough. Casey thought he was already in the process of dying, but Buck fought for time. He had something he was determined to say. "Promise me you'll do somethin' for me. I ain't got no family. The closest thing I've ever had to family is Frenchie Petit. When you get back to Fort Smith, go see Frenchie. Frenchie's an honest man. Tell him I said to tell you how to find my cabin on the Kiamichi."

"You've got to quit that kinda talk," Casey interrupted. "We'll go back to Frenchie's together."

"Dammit, will you let me talk?" Buck strained. "The cabin's yours now, that and anythin' you dig up under the back cornerstone." Seemingly exhausted by

his effort to speak, he lay back and closed his eyes. A
trace of a smile crept across the big lawman's face.
"You're a good man, partner," were his last words.

"So are you, partner," Casey muttered, knowing
Buck could no longer hear him. He sat there for a
while, almost forgetting the hole just below his shoulder until the throbbing returned to remind him that he
was alive. The realization of that was enough to alert
him that he still had obstacles to overcome himself. He
was wounded, and he wasn't sure how bad. But he
was breathing, and he wasn't spitting up any blood.
The sun popped up over the hill behind him, sending
light through the dense forest and giving birth to a
bright new morning. He sat there for a long while,
trying to make sense of everything that had just happened. There was guilt on his conscience also. He had
promised Mabel Marsh that he would take care of
Bonnie, and that bothered his mind.

After a while, he decided there wasn't much he
could have done differently to prevent the woman's
death. It was time now to take care of Buck. "I got a
hole in my chest, and it's a long ride to Fort Smith," he
announced, "but I'll damn sure get there."

As usual, Casey Dixon accomplished what he had
set out to do. He made it back to Fort Smith, and
brought Buck Avery's body with him, determined to
see that the late deputy marshal got the burial he deserved. His report to John Council stressed the faithful
performance of duty on the part of Buck Avery. Council was properly grieved by the loss of his oldest deputy and thanked Casey for returning the body. He
insisted that the young deputy should take some time
to recuperate from the wound that was already showing signs of healing, even though the bullet was still
inside. "This time, I'll take you up on it," Casey responded.

Remembering his promise to Buck, his next stop was at the Deuce of Spades to give Frenchie Petit the news of Buck's death. He found the gray-haired little Frenchman seated at a back table, working on his ledgers. When he was told the news, he didn't say anything for a long moment. Then he just shook his head in disbelief. "Buck dead—I didn't think the day would come, but I reckon it had to, just like for every-body else." He continued to stare at the ledger before him on the table, his mind obviously elsewhere. "Buck and me, we go a long way back," he mused. Then he raised his head and cocked an eye at Casey. "Did he say to tell me anything?"

"Nope," Casey replied, "just said to have you tell me how to find his cabin on the Kiamichi. He said he wanted me to have it."

Frenchie paused again, studying the young man seated across the table from him. Finally he called out, "Charlotte! Bring us in some coffee." Turning back to Casey, he said, "We got some things to talk about . . . partner."

While Casey puzzled over that, Frenchie sat back and waited for Charlotte to bring in the coffee. When she went back to the kitchen, he began. "When you two were in town a week or so ago, Buck went to see that young lawyer, Ashton, and had him draw up his will. Buck damn sure musta liked you, because he left everything he owned to you—not only that cabin of his, but half ownership of the Deuce of Spades." Frenchie paused again, reading the astonishment in Casey's eyes. "He thought a lot of you, son. I don't think he wanted you to wind up down-and-out with-out a pot to piss in, like most lawmen."

Almost staggered by the news of his sudden wealth, and still somewhat in a state of shock, Casey Dixon walked out of the Deuce of Spades. He stood for a moment on the sidewalk, studying a map that Frenchie had drawn roughly, showing him how to find the cabin. *And whatever's buried under the back cornerstone*, he thought.

After a moment he climbed in the saddle and turned the sorrel toward the south end of the street. As he approached the door of the Cook's Corner, a couple walked out. He could not avoid the sudden sting in his heart, even though his expression did not expose it. He nodded politely.

"Oh, Casey," Charity McDonald Ashton exclaimed. "I heard about Buck Avery. We're so sorry."

"Yeah, I'm gonna miss him. I heard you two got married. Congratulations." He nodded to Jared Ashton. "I'll be by to see you in a week or so." He tipped his hat then and nudged the sorrel.

Charity stood watching for a moment as he rode away. Then she turned to her husband. "What is he coming to see you for?"

"I imagine to get copies of Avery's will. It's amazing, but that old deputy marshal owned half of the Deuce of Spades, plus some other property, and he left it all to Dixon."

Well, shit . . . , she thought.